What We Know Now

M. J. Parisian

Dedication

For my mom.
The best parts of me are because of you...

Part One

"Every ending is also a beginning.
We just don't know it at the time."

Mitch Albom,
*The Five People
You Meet in Heaven*

Chapter One

Every morning when I run, there is a moment when I know exactly how my day is going to unfold. Today, when that moment hit, I had the distinct feeling I should go back to bed. It's not that I'm psychic, but the signs were unmistakable.

One: My mom called, waking me from a dead sleep, to tell me that she's worried about me. "I have a funny feeling," were the exact words she used. My mom is a lot of things, including a best-selling self-help author, but "visionary to my life" certainly isn't on the list.

Two: My husband, Andrew, left before I woke up and didn't make any coffee. He always made coffee. If there was a reason he needed to be at school so early, he failed to tell me. He only left a sticky note on the kitchen table. *I had to leave early. XO, Andrew*.

Three: My boss texted me for a 9:00 meeting this morning. Given I work the evening news shift at WKND, this was a giant monkey wrench in my day.

A smarter person would've made a pot of coffee and relaxed with the news, but training for a marathon "exceeds the limit of what is considered normal"

(Andrew's words, not mine). He didn't understand my need for five-year plans or training schedules. Andrew's motto was always *"let's roll with it."*

Either way, I want to go back to bed.

Of all my issues, it's my mom that is weighing me down. I don't have that she's-my-mom-and-my-best-friend kind of relationship with her. It's more like we tolerate each other and go our separate ways. For her to call me as early as she did felt ominous.

By my third mile, I realized I couldn't outrun her words and looped back home. The last thing I needed this morning was to worry about being late for a meeting.

I loved my job as the evening news producer for an NBC affiliate, WKND. It was fast-paced and demanding, but left me feeling exhilarated every night. Even on the slow news evenings.

As I walked into work, my manager, Tim, was standing at the receptionist's desk, chatting with Sherry, our office manager. Their conversation came to a halt when they spotted me and Sherry's eyes darted back to her computer.

Tim looked at his watch. "Thanks for making it in so early, Grace," he said. "Let's head back to my office... an issue has come up that we have to deal with."

He glanced at Sherry before turning, and she tried to smile, but it didn't reach her eyes.

I'm getting fired.

My mind raced to the story about the political scandal involving two senators last week. I held off on it for a day to verify sources, but every other news station went with it. Our ratings tanked, and Tim ripped me a new one.

But fired?

Tim was not only my boss, but my friend. He was the one person at the station who had my back from day one, even when I made countless mistakes in the beginning. He taught me what anchors wanted in copy, what producers wanted in a piece, and how to put it all together.

My heart started racing. Tim's face was pasty and he was sweating through his shirt. An empty hollowness settled into my gut.

"Have a seat," he said, walking behind his desk. "Look, something has come up, and there is just no easy way to say this."

"I know what you're going to say," I interrupted him. "But can I please get a second chance?"

His brow furrowed. "Second chance? What are you talking about?"

"I know last week's rating drop was all my fault, but please don't fire me. Give me another chance."

He wiped the sweat from his brow. "Gracie, I'm not going to fire you. But something has come up, and I wanted to give you a heads-up on a story we're running tonight."

I released a breath I had been holding and leaned

back in my chair.

"Okay, shoot. I'm in the mood for something big," I said.

He shifted in his seat and stared at his desk calendar. "Well, we have several sources for a story at Patterson High School."

"What is it?" My nerves turned into curiosity. Andrew taught at Patterson, and not only was this going to be a good story, but I was getting a first dibs on the gossip. He loved that.

"Ah, Jesus, Gracie," he sighed. "There are, uh, several young girls accusing one of the teachers of sexual misconduct."

"I knew it! It's Peter Markson isn't it?" My heart was racing again, but in a good way. I needed to get over there and look into this.

"No, Gracie." He paused, running a hand through his dark hair. "Actually, Andrew has been named as the offender." For the first time since I walked in the building this morning, his eyes locked on mine.

"Wait." I didn't understand. "Andrew is accusing girls?"

He closed his eyes and sighed. "Grace, the girls are accusing him. One girl claimed they've had an affair for the past year and she's pregnant. That's how this story broke."

My stomach lurched. "Please tell me this is a joke," I whispered.

He walked around his desk and sat next to me. "I

wish it were, but it's going to be the lead story on every news channel tonight and will most likely be picked up nationally by Friday. From what I've heard, this is going to be another Letourneau. I can't believe I have to be the one to tell you this."

The room began to spin. A chill ran through me. Everyone I knew would hear this story by tonight.

"What the fuck," I whispered, dazed. "What the hell am I supposed to do?"

"Why don't you take a day – a week even – to figure out what is going on," he said. "This is still just information from the students. No one has heard Andrew's side of the story yet."

"Have you tried to contact him at all?"

"I found out yesterday afternoon, and have left three voicemails and sent two texts," he said, standing. "He's not responding."

I thought about last night. I tried to remember if he was different, but nothing seemed out of the ordinary when I came home. He was watching TV, *The Late Show*, his hand propped up behind his head as usual. I asked how his day was, he said "uneventful," and quickly rolled over when I got into bed. I just figured he'd had a long day and needed some sleep.

Was this why he left so early?

"What the hell!" I shouted this time. I stood and started to pace. "I'll get to the bottom of this," I said, pulling out my phone.

I dialed his number and listened. The unanswered

rings echoed through my head. I stared at my phone, the picture of Andrew and me in Jamaica stared back at me. I hadn't changed the background in three years.

Do I go over to the school? Why would these girls say this about him?

"What is going to happen to him?" I asked, wishing he had answered his damn phone. What was the truth?

He shook his head. "From what I know, the police will act quickly and bring him in for questioning. Most likely today." He sat behind his desk again, loosening his tie.

"If they find sufficient evidence against him, they will charge him with sexual misconduct, and he will have to wait for a bail hearing."

I stared out the window, following a cloud coasting by. In the last five minutes, my life had been forever changed. Shattered.

His phone beeped. "Uh, Gracie, the police just walked him out of school. Handcuffed." Another beep. "Every news station is there covering this." He set his phone down. "What can I do to help you?"

I ran my hands through my hair. How the hell does he think he can help me through this?

"I gotta get out of here," I said. I wiped my eyes, realizing my hands were covered in runaway mascara. "I'm not sure when I'll be back, but I'll keep you posted." I stopped on my way out the door. "Will I have a job when I return?"

"This job is yours until you say you're moving on," he replied without hesitating. "I hope to see you soon."

Walking out, the sunshine blinded me. Not knowing where to go or what to do, I did the only thing I could think of: I called my mom.

Chapter Two

Despite the fact that I rarely visit my mom anymore, I still love the drive up north. It's as if there's an invisible shield near Cadillac and once you cross it, everything seems calmer. Today was no different.

My mind replayed our jail visit like a newsreel clip.

Sitting at the table with him, handcuffs rattling against the metal table.

The admission of guilt in his downcast eyes.

The tears leaving tracks on his face before they silently hit the table. And with every replay, I found another reason to blame myself. When did this start? How could I be married to someone with a penchant for young girls and never suspect anything?

Of course it was true, just as Tim had suspected. However Andrew denied the baby was his. His head dropped to his hands when I informed him I was leaving town.

"But I *need* you," he begged. "The jurors will be more sympathetic if you're standing by my side." He reached for me across the table, brown eyes pleading with mine. I jerked away so quickly that the guard glanced over at us.

It was surreal to see someone so strikingly handsome, sitting there so beaten. His eyes never left me as I walked to the door. *Stop. Don't leave me.* I saw fear in those eyes, but I wasn't sure if it was his or a reflection of my own.

"Please don't shut me out," he begged, but we both knew I would. There are some things you can't forgive.

When I arrived home from the jail, news trucks from all over Michigan lined our quiet neighborhood street. Tim was right. This story would go national quickly.

I refused to stay and be a feature in this media frenzy. Bitterness burned in my stomach, but I knew what I had to do. I called Tim, thanked him for everything, and gave him my verbal resignation, effective immediately.

He wished me luck.

Framed pictures of Andrew and me scattered our small Cape Cod, and I picked them up, one at a time, looking for any evidence. All I saw were smiles from past vacations. Graduation day at Michigan State. Sailing in Jamaica. One of us on our wedding day with him holding a red umbrella over us as we left the church on that rainy day in June. It's the little things in a marriage that make the memories special, and now they're all tainted.

Every lie Andrew told this past year confirmed that these images were not our reality. Our reality involved secrets, lies, and teenage girls. Still holding the wedding picture, I threw it violently against the brick fireplace. It shattered into pieces, like our lives.

As I had stood in our living room, staring at the shattered glass, I wondered what he would miss. Was there anything about our life together that he would regret losing?

⸺

For early April, the weather was one of those perfect spring days that all Michiganders love: clear blue skies, brilliant sunshine, and puffy clouds. Days like this remind us why we tolerate the grey, bleak winters that seem to last forever. In Michigan there are two seasons: winter and construction. Thankfully most of the back roads on the way to Frankfort were construction-free.

As the miles passed, I found myself thinking less of Andrew and instead started analyzing the stress and conflicts my mom and I shared over the years. To say we don't see eye to eye is an understatement. Before my dad died, he would try to buffer the tension between us, but it rarely worked. She always complained about my headstrong and stubborn attitude, and I would disagree with her simply because it felt right. It never mattered what she believed in or wrote about. I dismissed it as unsubstantial.

When Andrew and I became engaged, she quietly voiced her opinion about him and begged me to rethink getting married. "There's something off about him," she told me more than once. Those words pushed me to marry him sooner, to spite her. Every family gathering became tense, and eventually we stopped visiting. It seemed we were only able to tolerate each other with long-distance phone calls.

My brother Gordy was like my mother: kind, generous to a fault, and predictable. Over the years, he became the perfect mediator between my mother and I, and I hadn't talked to him yet, but knew Mom filled him in with the details.

It was a mistake to watch the news last night. Part of me wanted to see how the story broke without me running the show, and the other part wanted to see how big the story was. Sure enough, it headlined all four local networks, and WKND didn't hold back for my sake at all. I watched in horror as they showed him walking out of Patterson, head hanging low. They had footage of me entering our driveway, sunglasses on with no expression. They interviewed Jerry Tanner, Principal of Patterson High School, and several other teachers who expressed utter disbelief that something like this was going on.

Just past Cadillac, I stopped for gas and coffee. I

had left early this morning, needing to beat the media. As I walked in to pay, Andrew was smiling at me from the front page of the local paper. They used his teacher photo from the yearbook last year, the classic, aging high school football star. Feeling jittery, I skipped the coffee and paid for the gas in cash.

I prayed no one in East Lansing would make the connection that I was the daughter of the Julia Dunham. Other than Andrew, the only other person who knew was my first college roommate, and I haven't talked to her in years. At work, I withheld the information to avoid being asked to have my mom do an interview.

With an hour left in my drive, doubt crept into the pit of my stomach. Should I have stayed to see how it all played out? Was he truly guilty? Did these girls seduce him somehow?

Uncertainty hit me in waves, as one question loomed bigger than all others: how had I not seen this happening?

I snapped the radio off with a jab and let the silence fill the car for the remainder of the drive. The tightness in my chest became unbearable as I passed under the iconic lighthouse sign, welcoming me back into a town I had abandoned long ago. Would I find answers here?

As our classic beach home came into view, I thought it ironic the Queen of Self-Help's daughter had found herself in such a predicament. I shook my head at the irrational thought that my problems could be solved here, of all places.

I simply had nowhere else to go.

Chapter Three

Baskets of red geraniums and white petunias hung on my mom's porch. Her cat Rumi stared at me from the front window as I pulled into the driveway. He was a snow-white Persian with a face that looked like he had run into one too many walls. Cute was not his thing.

Unlocking the front door, the scent of chocolate greeted me. My stomach growled.

"Hello?" No answer. "Mom… are you home?"

I dropped my bags in a heap by the front door and walked toward the kitchen. Every view from the back of the house overlooked the beach and Lake Michigan in its navy-blue glory. There was a note on the granite counter, sitting by a plate of chocolate chip cookies.

Gracie, I have a class to teach until noon.

Be back soon… make yourself at home!

Love, Mom

I blew out a breath of air I had been holding since I walked in. I grabbed two cookies and a Diet Coke out of the fridge and planted myself in the breakfast nook. The kitchen had always been my favorite room in the house, and she had expanded it to include a sitting room to the left of the dining area. The clock showed that it was 11:45.

I watched a guy on the beach playing fetch with a black Lab in the water. He looked back at the house a couple times. There was something so familiar about him. The dog was relentless with the game. If he didn't throw the Frisbee quick enough, he'd get a bark from his furry friend. I envied the simplicity of their moment. I sipped my soda and tried to forget my husband was sitting in jail right now, two hundred miles away, with an alleged underage and pregnant girlfriend.

My phone buzzed inside my purse. My heart raced as I scrolled through all the notifications from emails, texts, Twitter, and Facebook.

I had sixteen missed calls, forty-two text messages, one hundred and five Facebook notifications. To add insult to injury, Andrew was trending as #MIbadteacher. I turned my phone off without looking at any of them.

The bathroom just off the kitchen was as tiny as I remembered. I splashed cold water on my face and looked in the mirror. I didn't recognize the woman looking back at me. My hair hung limp and dreary, and dark circles shaded under my eyes, making me look far older than twenty-eight. My mom would want to make me over when she saw me.

The garage door came to life, and my heart raced.

From our conversation yesterday, I couldn't tell what she was thinking. Would she say that she told me so?

I steeled myself for the worst from her.

Rumi padded over towards the garage door in the kitchen, and sat down, waiting. Just inside the walkway, my mom had an ornately framed chalkboard with a quote written on it: *"What would you do if you knew you could not fail?"* I had never seen this quote before… *what would I do*?

I couldn't waste time thinking about it, as my mother, Julia Dunham herself, came walking through the door with an armful of groceries.

"Here let me help you," I said, taking the bags from her.

"Darling, I'm so relieved you're here," she said, her voice thick with emotion. We set the bags down on the island in the center of the kitchen and she gathered me into her arms. She wrapped her arms wrapped so tightly around my waist, my breath caught in my throat and came out in a whoosh.

I sobbed as she held me close, releasing all the pain I had held inside to get here. In that moment, all I wanted was someone to take care of me and tell that everything would be okay. I have always been the one in control of everything – the news, my moods, a situation – and this unfamiliar feeling of helplessness overwhelmed my senses.

I felt a shift had already taken place.

My mom pulled me away and held my shoulders. "I

know it seems like this is the end, but we will get you through this." She pulled me in again, and then released me with one final squeeze.

"It's been a while since you were here, and I really didn't know what you would want to eat, so I picked up a little of everything," she said, piling lemons in a bowl. "You're so thin. You're not on one of those crazy vegan diets, are you?"

"No, Mom, I couldn't diet if my life depended on it. I just run when I can, and watch what I eat."

"You run?" She raised her eyebrows. "What are you running from?"

I sighed and helped her put the groceries away. We made small talk about the beautiful weather, the crappy economy, and how Jeri, her assistant, had recently lost her husband. We talked about everything that had no significance in my life, the safe subjects, to avoid the giant elephant in the room.

"Why don't you go on the patio, and I'll bring some sandwiches out," she said.

The familiar resistance to my mother seeped into my thoughts. *Why can't she just let me be?* I opened the sliding French doors to the patio. The air was crisp, but the sun felt warm on my skin. The lake was surprisingly calm for this time of day, and I couldn't wait to feel the sand between my toes. No matter what my history was with my mom, I was relieved to be home.

My mom came out with a tray of sandwiches,

grapes, and tall glasses of lemonade. She remembered my favorite, turkey and cucumber. I tried to savor every bite and forget my reason for being there.

"So, what do you think is going to happen now?"

I stopped chewing, my old instincts kicking in.

"I thought we'd go for a long walk, come back, and get black-out drunk," I said. "After that, I might be open to some of your infamous motherly wisdom."

She continued to nibble on her grapes and smirked, looking out at the lake. "Look, I know you're going through something horrible – life-changing even – but you don't need to be nasty to me. I'm on your side. I always have been."

"I'm not trying to be *nasty* to you. I simply don't have a fucking clue as to what is going to happen now," I pushed my plate away. "My husband is in jail, I am currently unemployed, and you can't wait to fix me. How is my life affecting you?"

"For starters, you are sitting here cursing at me. That affects me," she said. "I was just trying to open the conversation, not fix you."

"Mom, don't," I said. "Don't take my words as a punishment to you. I curse. A lot. It isn't about you."

She sighed and took a sip of lemonade. We sat and ate in silence, minutes feeling like hours. I wondered if I would be better off back in Lansing.

"Okay," she said. "I'm going to clean up and get your things to your room." She stood and stacked everything back on the tray. "Why don't you take a slow walk to the lighthouse and breathe in some fresh air. Come back when you feel a little better."

Covering my face with my hands, I listened to the door slide open, then close. *Why was I pushing away the only person I could trust right now*? I rarely felt regret when my mother was involved, but I knew I overreacted and wished I could take back my blunt comments.

I stood and stretched. My neck ached from the tension I carried, like a heavy backpack slung over my shoulders. I kicked my shoes off by the gate and walked across the sidewalk to the sand. The path was lined with several benches, each scattered with people enjoying a rare sunny day. I avoided eye contact with everyone, wondering how long that would last in my new world.

I found myself drawn to an old rotted log sitting in the sand. My mom used to tell me the sound of waves would soothe me as a baby, and it remains true today.

An older woman with two small children walked by, her jeans rolled above her ankles and her hands stuffed into the pocket of her sweatshirt. She glanced my way, and I looked down.

"Gracie Lou?" My heart fluttered. Only one person ever called me that, and her voice reminded me of hot chocolate on winter days and backyard picnics.

Ellen Babcock was my friend Linny's mom, and my second mom through my teenage years. I stood and threw my arms around her neck. She pulled away, tears in her eyes.

"Well, I can't believe it," she said. "What on earth are you doing home, Gracie?"

"I needed to get away for a bit," I lied.

She raised her eyebrows. "Are you okay? I can't wait to tell Linny I ran into you. You know she finally opened that bakery she's always talked about. Bab's Bakery!"

When we were younger, Linny made these chocolate chip cookies that could have put Toll House out of business. I hadn't talked to her in years, but followed her life on Facebook.

"I saw something about that online." I eyed the little girl. "Are these her kids?" Both had the beautiful red hair and freckles, the Babcock trademark.

"Yes, this is Charlotte and Trevor," she said proudly, holding up one hand and then the other. Charlotte, the older one, gave me a small smile, but Trevor studied the lake. "So how long are you in town? I'm sure Linn will want to see you before you head back down."

"I'm kind of here indefinitely…" I said, trailing off. Her smiled faded, and she glanced at my left hand. "My work has put me on an assignment up here, and I don't know how long it'll take."

"Oh, good." She patted my hand. "You'll have to stop to see Linny at the bakery. I think you'll love what she's done with the old bank. Completely gutted and remodeled the place. It's like an old-fashioned soda shop now."

Linny's husband, Barry, was a partner in one of the oldest law firms in town. If anyone could afford a complete remodel, it was Linn.

"I'll have to get in there tomorrow then," I reassured her. Trevor yanked on her arm, pulling her towards the water.

"I'm going to let you go," she said, relenting. "I'll let Linny know to give you a call later, okay?"

"Sounds good, Mrs. Babcock," I said, heading back towards the house. "You have fun with those beautiful grandkids."

She smiled and waved. The kids continued to pull her towards the water.

I brushed the sand off my feet before going through the back door. I heard the floor creak upstairs.

My clothes were stacked on the dresser. "You didn't have to unpack my things, Mom," I said, leaning on the door jamb. The last thing I wanted was a lecture on the state of my wardrobe, having packed only jeans, shorts, and T-shirts. My mother had a reputation to uphold, and dressed accordingly.

I didn't.

"I just wanted to get you settled, dear." She stood with her hands on her hips and blew her wispy bangs out of her eyes, a habit I've hated since I was twelve. I pulled out my hair elastic and ran my hands through my hair, collapsing in the rocking chair. My room hadn't changed since I moved out ten years ago, although black and white photos in weathered wood frames hung on the walls had been added.

"I've taken a couple photography classes over the years, and thought I'd display some of my work in here," she explained, modestly. "I hope you don't mind."

"They're lovely, Mom." And they were. Beautiful shades and lighting, hitting just the right amount of texture. "You'll have to show me some tricks while I'm here."

She sat on the bed, crossed-legged like a teenage girl. "What would you like to do tonight? We can go out to dinner or just stay in. I bought more groceries than I have in a long time, so I'm ready for whatever you need."

I can't remember the last time I ever stopped to think about what I needed.

My life with Andrew had become a routine of work, school, and running. I didn't notice anything missing or different. My eyes closed, and I saw the young girls from the news last night. How and when did they meet? Did he say he was going to tutor them, help them with school work? Get them through the next test?

My breath was shallow and a sharp pain pierced my heart.

"Gracie, don't." My mom stared at me, shaking her head. "You can't keep playing it over in your mind."

I doubled over, the tears flowing. She sat at my feet,

resting her arms on my legs. "It's okay, Gracie. Everything's going to be okay."

I cried for those young girls.

I cried for the kids we were never going to have.

I cried for the shattered lives of everyone involved.

I cried for myself.

Chapter Four

Daylight was fading when I woke up, the lake breeze blowing in felt cool and damp. I stretched and felt the weight of Rumi curled up at my feet. He looked at me with disdain.

From the stairway, I could hear Nora Jones crooning softly. Mom was wrapped in a blanket on the patio with a glass of wine sitting beside her. Grabbing a wine glass from the cupboard, I joined her outside.

She smiled and tipped her head towards me when she heard the door click. It wasn't forced or fake.

"Well, hello, Sleeping Beauty," she said, sliding the bottle of merlot across the table.

"Why did you let me sleep so long?" Closing my eyes, I savored the sound of the waves rolling in.

"Something told me you needed it," she said. "Besides, I never wake a sleeping child."

"I'm hardly a child anymore, Mom." I raised an eyebrow and poured a glass of wine.

"You'll always be my child," she said quietly. "And if sleeping brings you any kind of peace right now, then sleep you will get."

"I guess I needed it." The merlot smelled fruitier than I expected, tasting slightly of cherries.

Chardonnay was my drink of choice, but this wasn't bad.

"What are you thinking for dinner? Want to go out for a bite, or maybe I can just whip up something here?"

"I don't want to be any trouble while I'm here," I said. "I can find something to eat."

"Well, I have to eat as well," she said. "So, let's go out tonight. Tomorrow, we can plan some dinners and make sure we have all the groceries." She drained her glass and set it on the table. "I'm going to change, and we can head out then."

"Sounds like a plan." My stomach growled. Cooking was the last thing on my mind.

Dinner was at Lakeside Landing, which boasted an upstairs deck area for seasonal dining. All the tables were occupied, so we opted to sit at the bar and share a couple appetizers with our drinks.

The bartender was also the owner of the restaurant, Jimmy Darnell, aka my high school crush. I shot my mom a sideways glance, knowing her intentions were clear.

"Well, if it isn't Gracie Dunham and my favorite customer," he said, smiling. He wore a black Lakeside T-shirt and a Red Sox hat on backwards. Feeling exposed, I forced a smile. Jimmy hadn't changed a bit, except he looked even better now than he did ten years ago.

She ordered a glass of pinot noir this time,

chardonnay for me, and she winked.

"Why would you bring me here knowing *he'd* be here?" I whispered. It was no secret how I felt about Jimmy in high school.

She continued to smile as he poured the wine. Two other couples sat at the bar. "I'm sure you eat like a bird now, but the fried portobello mushrooms are to die for here," she said, avoiding my question.

"Since when did you eat anything fried?"

"Since I had these mushrooms," she said, closing her menu. "Seriously, they're the best thing here."

"I think all I can manage is a salad tonight," I said.

Jimmy brought the drinks back and set a bowl of snack mix in front of us. "So, ladies, what'll it be tonight? Just the drinks or ordering dinner?" My cheeks burned.

"We'll share an order of the mushrooms, and she wants a salad."

He cocked an eyebrow. "Any salad in particular or want me to surprise you?" Flirting was his gift. I would've given anything for this interaction back in high school. Now, I wanted to crawl under the bar.

"I'll have the side salad, hold the cheese, with ranch dressing, please." How is it possible I forgot how blue his eyes were?

He took the menus from us. "Sounds good." He sauntered to the kitchen at the end of the bar.

Baseball was on both TVs behind the bar, the Tigers leading the White Sox four to two at the bottom of the sixth. My first Tigers game was also one of our first dates. Andrew called me early on a Saturday morning and said not to make plans for the day. Every time I see the Tigers on TV I'm reminded of the day I fell in love with him and baseball.

"You haven't heard a word I've said," my mom said, eyebrows raised.

"I was just watching the game." I took a sip of wine. I snatched a cheese cracker from the mix in front of us. "What were you asking me?"

"I was just saying that Jeri was going to try and meet us out tonight for a drink. She's already had dinner, but wanted to come out and see you. She's doing surprisingly well since Victor passed."

Jeri, my mom's assistant, has been part of our family for as long as I can remember. She's been at all the big moments of my life, and I knew that I could trust her with my recent turn of events.

"God, I can't remember the last time I saw her," I said. "I think it's been three years."

"It has," she confirmed. "At Peter's graduation open house. You and Andrew came up for the weekend."

"That's right, I remember the tent collapsed."

"Yes, and Peter hired a DJ who kept playing rap songs with swear words. Jeri was mortified for months. Made him apologize in all his thank you notes."

Jimmy came over to wipe down the bar in front of us.

"So Jimmy," she said, "how's your mom doing?"

He frowned and his shoulders drooped and inch. "She's doing okay, Mrs. D. Not sure she'll ever adjust to living alone in that house though."

"I hadn't heard, Jimmy." His dad was the original owner of Lakeside. "I'm so sorry."

"Thank you," Jimmy said. "It was a while ago. Charlie seems to be having a harder time than anyone, though." Charlie was his older brother and best friends with Gordy growing up.

"I'm sorry to hear that. I know how hard it is," I said truthfully. Losing a parent sucked, especially when you're close to them.

He shook his head and looked up to check the score. "You look good Gracie," he said. "What brings you to town? Is your husband here?"

"Nope, he stayed home for this trip," I said, keeping my voice as light as possible. The truth would come out within the next couple days, but I wanted to hide for at least one more night. "He couldn't get work off, and I needed a vacation from mine." I struggled to explain myself under his steady gaze.

His hair was a little longer than I remembered, and it was curling at his neckline. I tried to remember why I was here.

"You still with the news station?"

"I am," I said. "I've built up some vacation days, and thought I'd come see Mom for a while."

Jesus, Gracie, stop talking!

A waitress brought out a large plate of deep fried mushrooms, golden and crispy.

"I'll let you enjoy these for a bit before I bring your salad out," he said, walking towards the end of the bar.

"Why didn't you tell me his dad died?" The woman seated beside my mom shot us a look.

"Shhh, keep it down," she snapped. "It's not like I've talked to you lately, and when we do, it's usually about your work and Gordy's kids."

The mushroom was almost as big as the plate, and the first bite was unlike anything I had ever tasted. The crispy breading evened out the woodsy taste of the mushroom and exploded in my mouth with the spicy ranch dressing.

"That look on your face said it all," she said, smiling. "They're incredible, aren't they?"

"Is there cheese in them? What is that other flavor?"

"He won't tell me. I think he marinates the mushrooms before he breads them, but he'll neither confirm nor deny." She took another large bite and smiled. "Honestly, I couldn't care less, as long as he keeps them on the menu."

I nodded in agreement.

Jimmy refilled my glass. "You're either having a moment, or you're enjoying them."

I blushed again and his smile grew wider.

"These are amazing," I said, focusing on the plate.

"Ready for your salad?" He leaned on the bar with

both elbows.

I reverted to my sixteen-year-old self, wanting to be noticed but too nervous to talk.

"Actually, if you haven't made it yet, let's forget it. These are better than I imagined."

He winked. "No problem." I watched him walk back to the kitchen. The guy from the beach was sitting at the end of the bar, reading the paper.

"Mom, who is that sitting at the end of the bar?" I asked.

"Honey, that's Charlie Darnell. Jimmy's *brother*? Gordy's best friend all through high school."

"Holy crap, I didn't even recognize him." The last time I saw him was probably thirteen years ago at their graduation.

"Yeah, he had moved back a few months ago after their dad died. Runs the bar with Jimmy now, but he never really seems happy."

"Huh, I saw him on the beach earlier with a dog. I didn't realize it was him."

"He brings that dog to the beach every day. He always stops by if he sees me outside."

The White Sox were closing the gap with two men on base and no outs. I was focused on the TV and felt a hand on each shoulder. Jeri's smile was like a warm blanket on a cold night, and I reached around to give her a tight hug. She held me close whispering that everything was going to be okay. For the third time today, I cried.

"Sugar, how are you?" She twirled her hand in the air, signaling Jimmy to get her a drink. He jumped at the order.

"I'm actually pretty numb," I answered. "I keep crying, so I know it really happened."

She took a long drink of her gin and tonic and winced. "That fucker. If he ever gets out of jail, I'm cutting his balls off."

My mom laughed. "Oh boy, here she goes."

I'll never know how the two of them have been friends for so long. They are as polar opposite as two people can be, yet they seem to bring out the best in each other. I have longed for a friendship like theirs.

She took the barstool next to mine and reached across to grab the snack mix. Jeri has looked the same since I was a little girl. Short pixie haircut, and beautiful deep-set brown eyes that missed nothing. No one read a situation like Jeri did. She was never without her bright pink lipstick. Bright lips and wide smile were the Jeri trademark. Only she could pull it off and make it look completely normal.

"So," she said between bites, "what are we going to do? What's the plan?"

"I haven't a clue," I admitted, sipping my wine. "How are you doing, though? I'm sorry about Vic."

"Oh, I'm doing okay. Thankfully, your mom keeps me busy." She waved Jimmy over. "Honey, we're going to need some of those fruity little shots you like to shake for the youngsters. And make them pronto."

He smiled and winked, grabbing the cocktail shaker and keeping one eye on the game.

"So the best thing you can do is keep moving forward. Don't look back and try to figure out what you did, or what he did. Well, we *know* what he did," she said. "You? You are better than him, and this is going to be the best thing for you. You'll see."

"Here we go ladies," Jimmy said, setting down four shot glasses. "What are we toasting to?" His eyes locked on mine.

My mom reached for my hand under the bar and squeezed.

Jeri fixed her eyes on my mom's. "To new beginnings?"

"I think that's about right," my mom agreed. "To new beginnings."

We clinked our glasses, including Jimmy, and drank the pink mixture in one gulp.

"Whew, what the hell was that?" Jeri wiped her mouth.

"That's a Pink Pussycat, Jeri," he said, stacking the shot glasses. "What do you think?"

"No comment." She smirked, taking a mushroom from our plate. "Hey Jimmy, she needs a refill."

He eyed me and raised his eyebrows. "You're gonna feel this in the morning," he said, nodding to the wine glass.

"I already do," I said, but didn't stop him.

Before the night was over, I had two more shots, and the Tigers hung on for the win. Charlie waved from his end of the bar, but never came over to say hi.

Arm in arm, I left with Jeri and my mom, ready for this day to be over. I didn't know what tomorrow would bring, but getting through today felt monumental.

Chapter Five

The aroma of coffee woke me up the next morning, and briefly, I forgot where I was. The moment passed quickly, feeling the piercing headache behind my eyes. My stomach clenched as images of Andrew sitting across from me in jail rose to the surface of my memory. *Please, don't shut me out…*

I tiptoed downstairs where my mom was in the kitchen reading on her iPad and watching *The Today Show*. Matt Lauer was grilling a political spokesperson. She quickly flipped the TV off when she heard the floor creak.

"Good morning." She grabbed a yellow coffee mug out of the cupboard, filled it with coffee, and ordered me to sit.

"Do you need cream or sugar? I can't remember."

"No, black is fine," I said. "But I need Motrin more than coffee right now. My head is pounding."

She smiled, and slid a bottle over to me. "I had one myself this morning. It's been a while since I've had anything other than wine."

"I blame Jeri for this," I muttered, relishing my first sip of coffee. Why couldn't I make coffee like this at home?

"Gracie," she said. "I hate to be the bearer of bad

news, especially when you're not feeling well, but you have to know something."

"It's national?"

She nodded, lips pressed into a line. "It broke this morning on all three major networks, as well as the twenty-four-hour news channels."

"Do they mention me at all?"

"They only mentioned that they haven't gotten any comments from you. They've shown the house a few times, one clip of you driving up, but other than that, nothing. It's all about him and the girls."

"I need to see what's going on back home." I reached for the remote, but she pushed it out of my reach.

"I don't think that's a good idea." She set some buttered toast down in front of me. "This will help with the headache."

"Mom, I don't *want* toast. What I want is to see how they're handling the story."

"You asked for it, but I can't watch it anymore." She jabbed the power button, refilled her coffee, and went to sit on the patio.

Grabbing the remote, I flipped from station to station, desperate to see Andrew. To see proof that my life was imploding on a national stage.

My stomach dropped when I saw my house on TV. Clips of Patterson High School, the Ingham County Jail, and even WKND splashed across the screen. The pounding in my head became unbearable and the voices became muffled. I broke into a cold sweat and ran for the bathroom to throw up. I had wanted to do that since I found out, but I didn't feel relieved. I felt empty. And alone. In forty-eight hours, everything I had worked for had vanished, and my new reality involved me sitting on the floor in my mother's bathroom.

Cleaning up the best I could without a toothbrush, I went back to the kitchen and dumped my coffee. Gulping down more Motrin with water, I turned the TV off and searched for my phone.

My mom poked her head in the door, her phone to her ear. "Jeri wants to know if you want to meet her for coffee while I'm in class today."

I couldn't think of anything better than to spend a morning with Jeri. "Yeah, sure."

"Okay, I'm going to let you two figure out the details," she said to Jeri before handing me her phone.

"Hey, Jeri, I should come over there and smack you for this hangover."

"Ha, I'd like to see you catch me," she scoffed. "Besides, you needed to blow off a little steam."

"Have you seen the news this morning?"

"I have, and others have been through worse," she said. Her lack of pity was refreshing.

"Understood," I said. "But I doubt I'll be the best company today."

"Also understood, but I guarantee your mood will lighten with some sweets from Bab's. I think she puts crack in her cupcakes, they're so addictive."

Linny would love that compliment. "Okay, name the time. I just threw up my coffee, but I think the Motrin will start to kick in a bit."

"Excellent news. I'll pick you up in an hour," she said. "Your mom has class until noon, so we can take our time, maybe browse the bookstore too."

"Now you're speaking my language," I said. "Okay, I'll see you soon."

"Bye, sugar."

Picking up my own phone, I scrolled through the notifications again.

I ventured into email first. The majority of them were from co-workers, including Tim, who had sent at least ten. Without reading them, I deleted the emails, then disabled my email address. I needed a clean slate, and I didn't want to answer any questions about Andrew. He would be tried in the press, and people would form their own judgements. They wouldn't need mine. Nothing killed a story faster than "*no comment*" from someone involved.

Next, I went through the texts and voicemails, doing the same thing. I wanted to use my phone without being reminded of Andrew and all his lies.

Lastly, I went onto my mom's laptop and fired up my Facebook account. I had three hundred and forty two notifications and thirty eight friend requests. I went to my account settings and deactivated my account. If I was going to get through this, I couldn't fuel anyone's gossip. I had to face it head on without hesitation or question.

My mom's home phone rang and I looked at the caller ID, seeing it was a Lansing area code. It wasn't my work number, so I just let it ring and go to voicemail. *Please don't let the vultures find me here.* I broke ties with my infamous mother long ago by never using my maiden name for anything.

I left my phone charging and headed upstairs. The high pitch of my mom's hairdryer could be heard from the stairs, so I showered quickly before she left.

Wrapped in a towel, I poked my head into my mom's room. She was picking through her jewelry to see what would go with her classic white blouse and dark wash jeans. My mom had a knack for making any outfit look like a million bucks, a trait I never acquired.

She glanced my way. "Good shower?"

"Perfection," I said, clutching the towel tighter. "Aveda is my favorite."

She smiled. "Aroma therapy is good for the soul, and you can thank Jeri for that. She thought you might need it."

"Have fun at class," I said. "I'll be at Linny's bakery with Jeri if you get out early."

She raised her eyebrows and nodded. "I may just do that. Thank you for the invite."

Back in my room, I cracked the window. Rays of sunlight streaked the floor through the shades, and the wind rustled through the leaves of the maple tree outside my window. Opening the blinds, I took a deep breath of lake air and watched a woman and her dog running along the packed sand with nice even strides. I had signed up for a marathon in Lansing this September, and had started training for it in March. I didn't know much, but I knew the training schedule would help me get through this mess. I couldn't wait to run on the beach later.

Jeri had a habit of being early for everything, so I dressed quickly and let my hair air dry.

My mom was already gone when I got downstairs, and the muscles in my shoulders eased a bit. It had only been a day, but the underlying tension was putting me on edge. Part of me wanted her to say she told me so, and that she always knew better. Get the words out in the open that she never approved and this was my own undoing.

I turned the TV on again and switched it to MSNBC this time. My heart raced seeing a photo of Andrew from Patterson in the left corner of the screen with "Suspected Serial Statutory Rapist" under the picture. Next they ran footage of him being led out of the school by the ELPD with his suit coat over his head. They showed the courthouse, and mentioned his arraignment would be today at 11:00 a.m. My stomach turned. *Should I be there with him?*

"Turn that off," Jeri said quietly. Startled, I dropped the remote.

"Jeez, don't you knock?"

She dangled her keys from her finger. "Your mom and I agreed a long time ago that I could let myself in so I wouldn't interrupt her if she was writing," she explained. "Why would you be watching that?"

"It's like a train wreck. I know I shouldn't be watching, but I can't stop."

"Darlin', that train wreck is *your life*," she said.

"I know," I said. Her eyes narrowed. "I wanted to see if there were any developments."

"Why don't you leave the developments to us. We will tell you what you need to know."

"Can we just go?" The walls were caving in on me, and I needed some air. I unplugged my phone, happy to see there were no calls or texts since I erased them all.

"My car's out front. You might want a hat, because with this beautiful weather, the top is down."

"Ugh. I didn't bring any hats with me," I whined. I loved the idea of convertibles, just not riding in them.

"Your mother has a few in the closet by the garage. Grab one of those."

Grudgingly, I grabbed one that had a heart on it and said "Life is Good."

She bit her lip, "Well, isn't that… sweet?"

"She seems to be out of the ones with 'Life Sucks' across it."

She laughed. "Good to know you can still crack a joke at a time like this. Whoever said time heals all wounds was full of shit."

It felt good to smile.

Chapter Six

As we pulled up to Bab's, I smiled at the immediate charm radiating from the storefront. Large showcase windows with "Bab's Bakery" lettering were shaded by yellow-and-white striped awnings. Wrought iron benches sat in front of each window with flower pots resting beside them. Mrs. Babcock was right. This was everything Linny ever wanted.

"Shall we?" Jeri prompted, breaking my thoughts.

"Is it as cute on the inside?"

"Even more so," she said. "It's hard to believe this used to be the old bank. C'mon, Linny is going to bust seeing you."

I grabbed her wrist. "Do you think anyone here knows?"

"Sure, I bet some people already know. It was all over the news this morning. However, I'm not sure how many people will connect you to him, unless they know you personally." She wiped a tear that had started to trickle down my cheek. "Let's get you some sugar and caffeine. You're as pale as Casper right now."

I wiped my eyes, glad I didn't bother with makeup this morning. I followed her into the shop, a bell above the door ringing our arrival. A few customers sitting at tables briefly looked up, but then went about their own business. A young girl with a blond ponytail stood behind the counter waiting with a smile.

"Welcome to Bab's Bakery," she said, smiling. "What can I get you?" She wore white jeans and a pastel pink shirt with "Bab's Bakery" on the front pocket. Between the pastel colors and Jack Johnson playing overhead, I may never leave this place.

"We will both have the house blend, but I think we need a second to figure out what we want to eat," Jeri said to the young girl.

"Sounds good, I'll get those coffees," she replied.

The swing door behind the counter opened, and a woman with classic Babcock red hair and a tray of muffins swung through.

"Gracie?" Linny said, smiling brightly. "My mom said you were in town for the week, but I didn't think you'd actually get in here." She slid the tray in the display case in front of us, and walked around the counter. She wasn't shy about letting anyone know how much they meant to her. "Bring it in, girlfriend."

"This place is amazing, Linn," I said into her shoulder. "I am so proud of you for finally doing this."

She held me at the shoulders, eying me from head to toe. "Gracie, you look incredible! Do you eat at all?"

"Please," I said. "I still eat like a horse, but now I like to run."

"Damn, it agrees with you." She pulled away, noticing Jeri. "Oh, hey Jeri. How are you?"

"I'm well, thank you," she said. "I knew that Gracie had to see your place, so I thought we'd have breakfast here."

Her eyes lit up. "Well let's get you something to eat then!" She walked back around the counter. "What sounds good? Muffin, cinnamon roll, or I think we might even have a few mini quiches left in the kitchen."

"I was trying to narrow it down between the Blueberry Crumble Muffin or the Sin Roll, but I can't decide," I said.

"Oh hell, let's go with the Sin Roll," she decided, taking it out of the display case and sliding it on a plate. "I'll warm it up too. How about you, Jeri? What's it gonna be?"

Jeri, who had been smiling since we walked in the door, looked in the case. "Three Little Birds or the Lemony Snickets?" she asked.

"Mmmm, let's go with the Snickets with your coffee," Linny said. "Those are my favorite cookies in the world." Looking at this display case, that said a lot.

"Why did you name those cookies Three Little Birds?" I asked, pointing.

She smiled. "It's after the Marley song. I wanted to

call them Every Little Thing's Gonna Be Alright Cookies, but we decided that name was too long." She grabbed our plates, and walked over to a table with us. "So I sell them in threes, and they're my little birds. Those with a glass of milk could solve the world's problems," she added.

"Maybe you should've gotten those," Jeri said out of the side of her mouth.

Linny gasped. "Oh my God, Gracie. I saw it on the news this morning, and didn't put two and two together until now."

A dull ache crept up my neck, and I sighed.

"Yes," I said. "My husband is currently in jail awaiting arraignment this morning." I no longer felt like eating.

She sat there, staring at me, mouth gaping.

"Breathe Linn," I said, patting her hand. "I'm here trying to stay away from the reporters, so please keep this as much to yourself as you can."

"Of course," she quickly replied. "I just can't believe it. What are you going to do?"

I shook my head. "I have no clue. I'm still just trying to get through an hour without crying, but that's not working out so well."

"If you don't mind my saying so, I think you're handling this remarkably well," Jeri said. "Most women would be in the fetal position bawling their eyes out."

"I would for sure," Linny nodded. "Are you staying

at your mom's indefinitely then?"

"Yeah. I'm sorry I lied to your mom. I just wasn't ready to talk about it yet."

"Don't even think about it. And I won't say anything to anyone, either," she said, standing. "I'm going to get back in the kitchen and let you two be. Will you leave me your cell number before you go?"

"Absolutely, I'd love to see you again," I said, squeezing her hand.

She walked away and I met Jeri's eyes. "Can't say that I'm hungry now. I might just save this for my mom."

"Nonsense, you have to eat," she said. "You're skin and bones, and a little sugar will do you some good right about now."

I cut a slice, surprised it was still warm. The name didn't do it justice. It was sinful and gooey and melted in my mouth with the cream cheese frosting. I would never be able to make something like this. I shook my head.

"It's not good?" Jeri asked, eyebrows furrowed.

"No… just the opposite. It's too good. I want to cry again because it's so good."

"I think there will be lot of things that will move you to tears in your future," she said. "Tell me Gracie, do you believe in fate or divine intervention?"

"What do you mean? I'm not much into my mom's philosophy of everything happening for a reason, if that's what you are asking."

She nodded slowly, nibbling on her cookie. Her eyes narrowed on mine and a chill went down my spine.

"Do you think this is something I brought on myself, like karma?" If my mom wouldn't talk about it, maybe Jeri would.

"Oh no," she said quickly. "That's not what I meant. I just wondered if there is something bigger than us, telling us you need to be here now."

"Jeri, you've lost me," I said, pushing my plate away. The hairs on the back of my neck tingled. "What's going on?"

"Something has come up, and well… I'm just glad you're home right now," she said.

"You're starting to scare me. What's going on?"

She wiped her mouth with a napkin and set it on the table. "Honey, I have breast cancer. I found out last Friday, and haven't been able to tell your mom yet."

My eyes welled up, and she shot me a look. "Gracie, I swear to God, if you start crying again I'll walk out and you'll be stuck here."

I sighed, my thoughts scattered. "What stage?"

"I'm stage three, and yes, it's treatable," she said. "It's going to be ugly, and painful, but I'll beat this."

"And here I've been going on about my jackass husband, feeling sorry for myself," I said. "I'm so sorry, Jeri."

"Oh sugar, the way I see it, we're *both* fighting for our lives for the next year. The pain and suffering is going to be different, but we both have a battle."

"Is there anything can I do?"

"Well, that's why I'm here with you. I need help telling your mom because she is going to flip." She pushed her third cookie over to me. "Here, eat this. It's heavenly with the coffee."

The lemon cookie, topped with a lemon glaze, exploded in my mouth.

"Whatever you need," I said. "I can help you tell her if you want."

"Yes, I'd like to do that today, if possible. She'll want to fix everything right away, but we need to remind her that healing, for both of us, is going to be a process."

I ran my hands through my hair. "Jeri, I don't even care about myself right now. I just want to make sure you're getting the treatment you need."

"But you *have* to worry about yourself. Your life is going to be a shit-show once everyone finds out your mom is the Queen of Pop Psychology. God help us all then."

"This will die down, like all stories. Next week the president will do something stupid, and I'll be off the hook."

"I think you're underestimating the public's need for this kind of gossip. You're going to need some armor, and need to keep your mom and friends close to you. People you can trust and lean on."

I chewed my lip as she sipped her coffee. The blond ponytail came over to refill our mugs for us.

"Gracie, there's another thing I'm going to ask you, and I'm not sure how you're going to react," she said, leaning back in her chair, arms crossed.

"I'll do whatever you need."

She smiled. "I need you to help your mom while I'm going through treatments. I'll work as long as I can, but my doctor said he'd like me to take it easy once the chemo treatments begin."

"Help out, as in be her *assistant*?" I asked. "Jeri, you know my mom and I don't see eye to eye on her work. There has to be someone who would kill to be her right hand."

"Well, of course, there are many people in town that would love this position. They're the same people who'd like to see me keel over so they wouldn't have to worry about me coming back," she said. "But the thing is, I think you're here for a reason. The timing is uncanny, and I have learned over the years not to believe in coincidences. In my heart, I think you're here to help me and your mother through this. Not the other way around."

"Jeri, I can't get through a shower without crying," I said. "I'm not even fit to take care of Rumi right now."

"Well, Rumi is a pain in the ass, and isn't worthy of your help." *Did anyone like Rumi other than my mom?*

"I still think you're over-simplifying this issue. My mother isn't going to want my help either," I said.

"Of course she will. It might just take a few beats for you both to see what needs to be done."

"A few *beats*? Jeri, we will go through this lifetime not knowing what needs to be done," I said, resisting. "I think she's going to have a bigger problem with this idea than I am."

"Look, you were excellent at a high-pressure job back in Lansing. This is nothing compared to that. You'll arrange book tours and signings, reserve classrooms, take registrations for her weekend retreats, and of course help with the retreats themselves. It's a piece of cake compared to what you've been doing," she said. "I think you'll even enjoy it once you get the hang of it."

"It's not the work I'm worried about. I think you're underestimating our conflicts over the years," I said. "I'm not saying no, Jeri. You have to fly this by mom before we decide anything."

"You'll do it if she agrees?"

"There is only one person in this world that I'd do this for, and it's you," I conceded. "If it means that much to you, of course I'll do this."

"I guess that means we'll have to tell your mother now."

"I can't imagine how she's going to react. You two are so connected… it's like you're sisters."

A lopsided smile played on her lips. "We have been from the beginning. We have always brought out the best in each other just by being ourselves."

"I don't think I've ever felt that way with anyone. Not even Andrew."

She looked at her watch. "Should we head back to HQ and wait for her to come home? I'd like to get this over with, and I'd like you there too, if you don't mind."

"I don't mind," I said, feeling oddly at peace with the decision. It felt good to have something other than Andrew to think about.

We said our goodbyes to Linny and headed back home. I pulled my hair into a ponytail instead of using the hat and let the sunshine wash over me. I knew I was hiding from the truth, but perhaps letting others in was the best way to go. I wasn't ready to announce it to the world, but I was a little less afraid of how others would react.

—

We arrived home, each grabbed a bottle of water, and sat on the patio. My stomach was in knots. Having to deal with my issues was enough to stop my mom in her tracks. This would derail her.

Jeri pulled out her planner, and we went over schedules and appointments for the next month, trying to figure out how much longer she would be able to work. Not coming back wasn't an option for anyone involved. I didn't want to do this the rest of my life, and she needed something to live for.

The back door slid open and my mom walked through, carrying an iced tea. "Can I get you anything?" she asked us.

I eyed Jeri, and we shook our heads. She sat down in the shade, sliding her sunglasses to pull her hair back.

"So, what are we discussing?" She took a sip and looked at both of us expectantly.

"We have a bit of a dilemma, but Gracie and I have worked this morning to try and figure it out."

"Oh, Lord, don't tell me another Barnes and Noble is closing?" The famous booksellers had always been my mother's favorite for book signings.

Jeri's shoulders slumped. "Oh honey, I wish it were that trivial."

My mom's face froze in a half-smile. "Has something happened this morning?" She looked at me, searching for an answer. "Are you okay?"

"Mom, I'm fine," I said. "Nothing new happened, but I'm sure his arraignment is all over TV by now."

She checked the time. It was 12:15 and I checked my own phone to see if I had any messages. I didn't.

She turned her attention to Jeri. "Spill it. I know you too well, and you've been acting funny since Saturday."

Jeri took a deep breath and blew it out slowly. "Truth is, last Friday I found out that I have stage three breast cancer, and I meet with an oncologist tomorrow to figure out how to proceed." She paused, eyes locked on my mom's. "Gracie and I have been talking this morning, and I asked her if she would take over my duties for the time being, and she's agreed."

All three of us sat there for what felt like an eternity. My mom slapped the table and started to laugh.

"Oh, this is good," she chuckled, wiping her eyes. "You've even made my makeup run. Is this supposed to make me see that your situation isn't really that bad?"

Jeri stared at her hands, waiting for her to calm down.

"Wait," she said, stopping and looking at us. "You're kidding, *right?*"

I closed my eyes, and rested my head in my hands.

"Oh for God's sake, this is true? You're really… *sick?*" She looked at Jeri, pleading with her eyes. Jeri nodded slowly, her eyes welling up with tears.

"I'm sorry I didn't tell you sooner," Jeri whispered. "I wanted the weekend to process it. Then this happened with Gracie, and I just thought I should wait to tell you."

"What in the hell is going on in this world?" Her chair scraped the tile as she bolted up. My mom stormed off towards the beach.

"Let me go, sugar," she said. "I need to help her through this one." She ran to catch up to my mom.

I watch Jeri chase after my mom, looping her arm around her waist to pull her close as they walked. My mom, the proverbial optimist, had been given another crisis to deal with, and her words, *"that which doesn't break us, only makes us stronger,"* echoed in my head.

I hoped she was right.

Curiosity got the best of me and I walked inside to check out the news on the arraignment. I saw Andrew in his navy-blue suit and the grey silk tie I had given him for Christmas last year. He had bags under his eyes like he hadn't slept. His parents sat in the first row behind him, holding hands, with a deer-in-the-headlights expression on their faces. What must they be going through? While I was never close to his dad, his mom, one of the kindest people I knew, would've done anything for us. For her Andrew. My heart broke for her.

My phone rang, the caller ID saying it was Tim from work. I picked up on the third ring.

"Gracie?" He sounded breathless and rattled. "Are you okay?"

"Yes, I'm fine," I said. "What's going on with Andrew?"

"Have you heard about the arraignment?"

"I turned it on, but I haven't heard anything yet."

"Well, he pleaded innocent, which we all knew he would, but the DA is clearly making a statement with this case. You know he's up for re-election this year, right?"

"Yes, but what does that have to do with Andrew's case?"

"Gracie, this case is *national*. Also, it seems that a new student pops up with each passing day, and they are charging him with three counts of criminal sexual conduct, first degree. The judge denied him bond, so he has to stay in jail until the trial starts."

"Oh my God, his parents must be freaking out," I said. I watched my mom and Jeri walking towards the lighthouse as he continued.

"That's an understatement. Mrs. Foster was wailing in the courtroom."

"What have you heard?" I asked Tim. "Are these girls telling the truth?"

In the news business, we lived by the theory that when one person steps forward, it's their word against the accused. Guilt was eminent when more than one person stepped forward.

He didn't respond right away. "Gracie... wherever you are, stay there. The press hasn't found you, and I know that's a matter of time, but right now, just stay put. Let him figure this out."

"So you think he's guilty."

"With every fiber of my being," he said. "If I were one of the parents, I'd take my chances on bringing a shotgun in the courtroom."

I sat down on the kitchen floor and leaned against the cupboard door.

"Oh, shit Gracie," he sighed. "I'm sorry. I'm having a hard time keeping this story in perspective."

"It's all right, Tim," I said. "It doesn't even feel real to me. I just can't believe this had been going on and I never noticed a thing."

"Well, the good news is he's stuck in jail for the time being, so you're safe. You are out of town, right?"

I smiled. "Yes, Tim, I'm out of town. But people already know about it here too."

"Well, hunker down, honey. It's just getting started," he said. "I can't even imagine what this place is going to be like in July when the trial starts."

"Three months? That's all he gets to prepare?"

"I'm telling you, the prosecutor is going for the jugular with Andrew," he said.

I shook my head at the absurdity of it all. "Tim, I have to get going. Will you keep me posted… even if it's just a text?"

"Of course I will," he assured me. "Just stay out of town."

I thought of Jeri and my mom, knowing I'd be here even if my life was normal. "That's actually a promise I don't mind keeping."

"Good. I'll let you go. Take care of yourself, G."

He disconnected, not waiting for goodbye.

Rumi found me sitting on the floor and trotted over. He purred and rubbed up against my leg, circling from one side to the other. I heard footsteps and the back door slid open. Both my mom and Jeri walked in and looked down at me. Jeri had a sad smile on her face, and my mom looked like she had aged ten years in ten minutes.

"Everything okay?" I asked.

My mom rolled her eyes and walked through the kitchen and up the stairs. "What's going on?" I asked Jeri.

"Your mother is a tough old bird. She'll take an afternoon to sort this out in her head, then come down and have a glass of wine. She'll be ready to talk then."

I stood and wrapped Jeri in a hug. "I am so sorry you are going through this. I promise I'll do whatever I can to help both of you."

She smiled, "Sugar, you are more your mother's daughter than either of you will ever realize." She loaded her bag. "I'm going to be home this afternoon. Let me know if your mom isn't herself tonight. Otherwise, I'll be here at the normal time tomorrow."

"Is there anything you want me to do for you?" I didn't want her to go, but knew they both needed some space.

Her hand was icy cold as she reached for mine. "I think we are all going to need our strength for the next few months. Go upstairs and take a nap, read a book, or go for a walk. Do something that will get you out of your head for a few hours."

"I think I'll take you up on that nap," I said. "I'm so tired and want to forget everything."

"Good," she approved. "I'll see you tomorrow. Call me if you need anything before then."

"Promise," I said, walking her to the front door. "You do the same." We hugged, and she left.

The only other thing I remember is the sound of waves as I fell asleep on my bed. For a brief moment, I had the strangest feeling of calm wash over me, like everything was going to be okay. Then, everything went black.

Chapter Seven

I rubbed my eyes and stretched, noticing the sun settling in the water. Not wanting to sink further into this hole, I grabbed my favorite running pants and a long-sleeved T-shirt. I changed quickly and found my headphones, anxious for a run.

James Taylor was singing downstairs. When my mom is in healing mode she uses cooking and music as her favorite therapy. Everyone survives somehow.

I sat on the bottom stair and laced up my running shoes, listening to *Sweet Baby James*. Gordy and I probably know every James Taylor song by heart, as this was all she would listen to the year after my dad died. I associate his music with a pain and melancholy that I'll never be able to explain to anyone. Only Gordy would understand.

"Hey there," I said, walking into the kitchen. It smelled like the small Italian restaurant Andrew and I used to go to when we were dating. "It smells delicious, Mom. What's for dinner?"

"Oh, just pasta with homemade marinara," she said, wiping her hands on a dish cloth. "Did you have a good nap?"

I smiled, feeling like a child again. "I did, but I'm starting to think that napping the days away isn't going to help anyone anymore." I sat on the barstool and munched on a red grape from a bunch drying on a napkin. "I thought a run would help clear my head before dinner. Do I have time?"

"Of course, this is just simmering." She went back to stirring the pot. "You take your time, and I'll start the water when you get back, so you're not rushed. It's going to be a beautiful sunset for this time of year."

"Perfect, thanks," I said. I walked towards the door and stopped. "You okay, Mom? I can't imagine what you're going through."

"Of course you do," she said, simply. "Jeri is part of your life too, and you have a newsworthy husband to boot."

I blinked, offended. "Well, I'll be back in a little bit." I slid the door shut without waiting for a reply. In order for me to stay here, I would have to moderate my reactions.

The air was chilly but felt so freeing compared to the warm kitchen. I took a deep breath, and let myself out the back gate. The beach was empty, and after walking about forty feet, I turned on some music and let my legs carry me away. The stiffness I felt earlier melted away as my muscles loosened up. The last time I ran, my life was still normal. As my feet pounded the hard sand, I knew this was hell, but I'd rather face the truth than be in the dark.

The sun was sinking quickly, so I turned to head

back. The music pushed me the rest of the way until the lighthouse was close and I could see the glow of the kitchen light on at home. I heard a dog bark from higher on the beach and stopped in my tracks. I pulled off my headphones so I could tell where it was coming from, and saw Charlie Darnell sitting on the same log from yesterday. He had his dog by the collar, keeping her from charging me.

"Hey Charlie," I yelled, standing still.

He smiled and waved me over to join him. "Hey Gracie," he said. "I'm going to let her go, but she won't hurt you. She just wants you to pet her."

The dog tore away from Charlie and sat down in front of me, ears on high alert. I let her smell my hand first, and then bent to give her kisses on the snout. "What's her name?"

"Sadie," he said. "Just start walking over here, she'll follow." And she did. He stood to hug me, holding me longer than I expected. The Charlie I remember from my teenage years didn't have broad shoulders or strength. I felt safe in this hug.

We sat down on the log together, and Sadie sat in front of me, one sandy paw on my pants.

"It's been a while. How long you in town?" Charlie asked. *Did he know about Andrew*?

"Indefinitely, for now," I said. "We just found out today that Jeri has cancer, and I'm going to help my mom while she goes through treatments."

His face dropped. "Oh man, that's horrible," he

66

said, shaking his head. "Cancer sucks."

"I just heard about your dad last night. I'm so sorry. He was a good man, Charlie," I said, still petting Sadie. "I remember him in the restaurant, smiling behind the bar. He always gave me change for the jukebox."

He nodded. "Thanks. It still catches me off guard sometimes." He picked up a stick beside him and threw it towards the water. Sadie looked at him and blinked, but stayed where she was. "Apparently I don't give her enough love."

"Clearly," I said. "This dog is deprived."

"Has she started chemo yet?"

"Not yet. I think she is going in this week to see what the next steps are. It's going to be rough, but she'll be fine."

"So…" he hesitated. "Do you want to talk about it?" I stopped petting Sadie and met his eyes. He shrugged. "Gordy called me yesterday."

My heart sped up and I focused on Sadie. "What's to say? My life is a train wreck, and it's just a matter of time before everyone here knows it."

"Correction, *his* life is a train wreck. Don't think that for one second that anyone is going to think any differently of you."

His eyes were piercing. I couldn't hide from them, so I looked away instead. "It's just difficult knowing that someone I loved, someone I built a life with, could do these horrendous things. I didn't have a clue, and I'm embarrassed this is my life."

"Gracie, you're being a little hard on yourself, don't you think?" He stood up and reached for my hand. "Let's walk, I'm freezing sitting here."

Sadie ran towards the water and grabbed her stick, and brought it back to me. I threw it down the beach in front of us, and we both watched her take off.

"I think I'm trying to get used to the fact that my life as I knew it is over, and there is nothing I can do to bring it back."

"I couldn't believe it when Gordy called me yesterday. How are you dealing with it?" he asked.

Sadie was walking along with us now, her tongue hanging out the side of her mouth as she panted.

"I've been napping a lot," I said, smiling. "And this was the first time I've run this week, so that will help. Plus, now I have my mom and Jeri to worry about. That distraction alone will keep my train wreck in perspective."

He walked along with me, hands in his pockets. I couldn't get over how much he had changed in ten years. His presence broke through the walls I had built in the last two days.

"I'm impressed. I'd want to kill him if it were me. You're being logical about all this." His voice was quiet and calm. Like the waves, it soothed me.

"Logical isn't exactly the word I'd use at this point," I said. "I feel like a coward running away from my life, quite literally," I motioned to the path I just came from. "I just want to stay here until it all goes away and pray the press doesn't find me. I can see the headlines now: '*The Queen of Self-Help Can't Even Help Her Own Daughter.*'"

He stopped walking and turned to face me. "Gracie, you have to focus on what you can control, and the media isn't on that list."

I turned away, looking out at the lighthouse reflecting on the water in the twilight. This view has been such a solace for me… and now, hopeless.

His sigh broke my thought. "I wish I could stay, but I've gotta get to the restaurant," he said. "It's karaoke tonight, and there's always a crowd."

"Thank you for letting me talk," I said. "I haven't spoken about it since I found out."

"You might want to call Gordy sometime. He's really worried about you," he said, stepping forward and wrapping me in another hug, his body heat radiating through the dampness of my shirt.

"I will tomorrow," I promised. "Does Jimmy know?" I needed to know.

His eyes dropped to Sadie. "Not that I'm aware of. He didn't say anything about it last night."

"Good," I said, nodding.

"You should stop by tonight," he said walking away from me. "First drink's on the house."

"I'll think about it but make no promises," I said. "Besides, I can't sing." He smiled and gave me a wave before turning around, walking towards the sidewalk.

Looking out at the lake, I slowed my breath down with the waves. My shirt was freezing now, and I shivered. On my way back to the house, I glanced at my phone, relieved there were no alerts.

No news was officially good news.

Chapter Eight

My mom was filling up a pot with water when I walked in.

"Did you have a nice visit with Charlie?" she asked, smiling.

"Actually, it was," I admitted, not giving her any more information than that. "He wants us to come to karaoke tonight."

She put the pot on the burner, and pulled out a cookie sheet for the garlic bread. "Why don't you pour us a glass of wine," she said. I turned the TV on as I searched for the corkscrew. I hadn't heard anything all day, but I had to see what the reporters were saying.

My mother glared at the TV and tried to grab the remote. I've been taller than her since the seventh grade, so holding it over my head kept it out of her reach.

"Why you think you need to drag yourself through his *scandal* is something I'll never understand." Her anger took me by surprise.

I slammed the remote down. "Because he was my life up until a couple days ago," I snapped. "It's a little difficult for me to pretend nothing happened."

"I'm not asking you to do that." Her voice was

quiet, calm, but simmering with anger. "I just want you to look forward as opposed to letting him rule your life from a jail cell two hundred miles away. Who the hell cares what happens to him anyway?"

"Why don't you just say it Mom? You know you want to."

"Say what, Grace? What on earth are you could you possibly expect me to say?"

"That you told me so! That I never should've married him in the first place! That you're always right, and I don't have a clue about my own life!" I was screaming at my mom, but I knew this was really about me. It was all true what I just said, and the shame was eating away at my soul.

I shook my head and walked to the sitting room at the end of the kitchen. My mom continued to rattle around the kitchen. I heard her open the wine, and the *glug, glug, glug* as she poured a glass. She quietly set the white wine on the coffee table in front of me.

"Do you honestly believe that's what I want to say to you?" Tears were running down her cheeks. "No matter how I have ever felt about Andrew, I would *never* want you hurting like this. *Ever.*"

Even when my dad passed, I don't remember my mom crying. She was stoic, strong, a pillar of grace.

"I know Mom. I do," I sighed. "A part of me blames myself for all this. I should've seen something was going on. Better yet, I never should've married him, like you warned me."

Her back straightened and she wiped her tears. "Listen to me. You are not at fault for anything he has done. And as for how I felt about him, he was never good enough for you. I knew it back then, and we all know it now. This is not 'I told you so.' This is 'I'm sorry I didn't try harder.' My instincts are rarely wrong, but I doubted myself because we always seemed to clash."

The oven beeped and she got up to put the bread in.

Beside the glass of wine was a brochure for my mom's class, "Eight Steps to a Better Life!" Curious, I picked it up and opened up each flap, wondering if my life could improve in eight steps. On the inside it had pictures of her teaching, sitting with a cup of tea, and one of her standing on the beach outside our home. The copy explained the pricing, schedules, and general overview of the course. One of the flaps had testimonials of satisfied customers, and I was surprised that I didn't recognize any of the names.

I noticed she had changed the music to John Mayer, and I took a sip of wine, slowly unwinding. I turned to look in the kitchen, "Mom... I'm sorry. I said some horrible things."

She looked up from the cutting board where she was chopping cucumber for a salad. "Thank you," she said. "I am too, truth be told."

We never apologized in the past. We would throw harsh words at each other and never think twice. At least I never did.

"So, does this really work?" I asked, waving her brochure for her to see.

She smiled, still focused on chopping. "Well, I'd say about seventy-five percent of those who take my class find their lives are better by the end of the course." She paused to pop a small piece of cucumber in her mouth. "The other twenty-five percent find they didn't really want to change to begin with."

"Do you ever get tired of trying to fix people though?" I wasn't trying to be difficult, I just wanted to know what she did.

"Gracie, I don't assume that I'm fixing anyone. Ever." She stirred the pasta boiling on the stove, then checked the bread in the oven. "The people who attend my classes and retreats fix themselves. I'm merely giving them the tools to do so."

I sipped my wine letting that thought settle over me. If I was going to work with her, I had to understand what she did and why she was so incredibly popular.

"Should I be taking the class?" She stopped in her tracks. "I mean, if I'm going to be helping you, I should know a little about this, shouldn't I?"

A small smile crossed her face, a real smile, not the professional one I see all the time, and briefly, I saw someone other than my mother. Someone softer.

"I can give you all the material, and it might help to

sit in the back and observe a few classes," she said. She pulled the bread out of the oven and began cutting it with a serrated knife, eyebrows creased. "Actually, I think that's a great idea if you came to a couple classes. The next one meets on Tuesday if you want to join."

I walked over to set the table, getting the plates and silverware. The napkins were already folded on the table, having been washed recently. She brought the bread and salad, setting them on the table. My stomach growled as she placed the pasta bowl in the middle of the table with a container of parmesan cheese.

Conversation through dinner was hit or miss. I chose my words carefully, keeping it as light as possible. When Jeri called to meet her at Lakeside, we both jumped at the offer.

After cleaning up and changing, we were out the door within twenty minutes and on our way.

"You know it wouldn't kill you to put a little makeup on, Gracie," she said, keeping her eyes on the road. "Winter took all your color away, and you're positively washed out."

"What does it matter what I look like right now? It's not like I'm trying to impress anyone."

"Who said anything about anyone else? Makeup is for yourself and always should be."

"Like you really believe that," I snapped. "Makeup is about other people being comfortable with your looks and little to do with helping yourself feel better."

"I'm sorry you feel that way." She chewed the inside of her lip.

I folded my arms across my chest and slumped down in the seat.

She shook her head and sighed.

Two steps forward and three steps back. This was our dance.

Lakeside's parking lot was full, and I stopped my mom before we got out. "Are you sure about this? It looks awfully busy."

"Yes, Gracie, this is a bar. The general idea is to get as many people in there as possible."

"I'm just not sure if I'm up for a crowd. Isn't there any other place we could go?"

"I saw Jeri's car parked up front," she said. "She needs us right now."

We walked in quickly since the spring air had turned chilly in the past hour. Lakeside was warm inside, close to stifling. A thin blonde with too much makeup and too little clothing was on stage trying to sing Adele.

Jeri was sitting at the far end of the bar watching, ice water sitting beside her. Charlie sat on one side of her and Jimmy stood behind the bar near both of them, scanning the bar for customers in need of a fresh drink. He had a light blue Lakeside T-shirt on with jeans, and he looked even better than he did the other night. I shook my head and tried to focus my thoughts on something else. I could feel his eyes on me, and even my mom looked back at me with raised eyebrows.

Jeri's face brightened when she finally saw us. Charlie smiled and nodded, but went back to the crossword puzzle in front of him. Jimmy took his towel from his hip pocket and wiped down the bar near Jeri, then slung it back over his shoulder.

"Well, well, this is a nice surprise," he said. Charlie looked up at him and visibly sighed. "What can I get you to drink tonight?"

"I'll have a merlot, please," my mom said, sitting down.

"Hmm, I'll just have a Diet Coke to start with," I said. Jimmy blinked.

"All right, okay," I said. "Surprise me."

"Atta girl," he said, grabbing a short tumbler. "You know you can't come here on karaoke night and not drink anything."

"Lesson learned," I said, raising my hands in mock surrender. "Is it always this busy for karaoke?"

He rolled his eyes and nodded. "Yes," he said. "Love the business, hate the singing, but you'll learn to shut it out quickly."

Charlie was watching us. Jeri whispered something to him, and he smiled and shook his head.

"So, Gracie, are you and your mom going to be able to work together?" Jeri asked, smiling.

My mom raised her eyebrows and smirked.

"I think we will have to compromise a bit, but we'll be able to keep the dream alive until you come back," I said.

My mom raised her glass to toast me. "Here's to old friends with new agendas," she declared, winking at me.

"Hey, I resent that," Jeri said, winking. "I didn't get sick to try and mend your relationship."

She joined in our toast and I winced at my first sip. Two parts vodka, one part cranberry juice. I turned to face the stage, watching a man pushing fifty singing "Takin' Care of Business."

I sat back and took another sip of my drink when two hands covered my eyes from behind.

"Guess who?" I'd know Linny's voice anywhere.

I turned and hugged her, happy to see her tonight. Her hair was pulled back with some loose bangs in front, showing off her deep-set brown eyes.

"What are you doing here?" I pulled up a barstool next to me.

"Barry is home with the kids, and Jeri thought you guys might be here tonight," she said. "You looked so sad earlier, and I wanted to come out and see you."

I smiled at her kindness and hugged her

again. "Thank you, it means a lot."

She spotted Jimmy at the other end of the bar waiting on two twenty-somethings flirting shamelessly with him. His mouth twitched when he saw Linny.

"Well, well, well, if it isn't Grace-Linn back together again," he said. "What can I get you Linn – the usual?"

"Indeed," she said. "Make it a good one, too, Jimmy." He pulled out the silver shaker under the bar and went to work. "He hasn't changed a bit, has he?" She smiled wickedly.

"Stop it right there," I protested. "There will be no shenanigans tonight or in the near future with Jimmy Darnell."

She continued to smile and watched him work. He set her drink, a martini, on the bar. "Ohhh, these are the best," she said, taking a sip. "Try this, Dunham. You will never drink anything else again."

My mouth puckered with the first taste.

"*Yellow Starbursts?*"

"Yes! He invented it just for me last year." Jimmy slid another martini in front of me.

"I figured you'd want one after you tasted hers," he said, taking my other drink away. "I should've made this earlier when you asked me to surprise you."

"I'm so happy you're home," Linny said. "I don't care if it's temporary, I'm just glad to be around you again. It feels like time hasn't passed us by."

I had that same feeling as well. I couldn't remember when Linny and I went our separate ways, or why, but it felt right sitting next to her now. Like nothing had changed at all.

I had friends back in Lansing, but I hadn't been really close to anyone since college. Even then, once Andrew and I started dating, I became the girl who ditched all her friends for a boyfriend. Eventually, it became easier to be Facebook friends instead of real friends.

"Tell me, Linn," I said between sips, "how are things with Barry and the kids? You seem to have the perfect life."

Her smile faded. "Looks can be deceiving from the outside," she said. "We're all good, but lately it just feels like something might be missing."

"I think that's normal when you have kids and you're both working a lot," I offered. "I can't get over everything you've accomplished in ten years."

"Hey, none of this," she said, wagging her finger in front of me. "There is no pity party tonight, or I'll have to have our bartender make something stronger for you."

I laughed, "If he makes this any stronger I'll be singing up there by the end of the night."

"You heard the girl," she snapped at Jimmy. "We need something stronger."

Jimmy cocked an eyebrow. *Could all men do that or was it just the Darnell brothers?*

"These are plenty strong, and if I didn't know any better, I'd say you two were trying to get me drunk."

"Jeri might have mentioned that you're needing to release some steam, whatever that means," she said, grinning. "I know some other ways you could release steam."

Jimmy was at the other end of the bar with the flirty girls ordering shots. In their low-cut shirts. And very skinny jeans.

I looked down at my own outfit, wishing I had taken a little time to at least put some mascara on now. I hated when my mom was right.

"So, tell me about your life before all this blew up," she said. "Were you *happy*?"

"We *seemed* happy," I sighed. "At least, *I* was happy with my life, but obviously he wasn't. I honestly don't know how any of this is my life now."

"What are you going to do?" she asked. "I mean, obviously the marriage is over, but will you go back to Lansing or stay here?"

"I'm staying here for the time being," I said. "Jeri is having some health issues and wants me to take over her job until she is able to come back. I will probably be here until the end of summer, at least."

Her face brightened into a huge smile. "I know it sucks, but the selfish side of me is so excited. I just want my friend back." She raised her glass to toast. "To friendship and fresh starts."

I clinked her glass and took another sip. I looked up

and Jimmy was watching us, chewing his lip. I held his gaze then looked away, heart fluttering. I wanted to stare into those eyes and hide, simultaneously.

The drink was going down quickly, and I felt fuzzy. "Can I get some water?" I asked Jimmy.

He served us tall tumblers of ice water, each with a lemon slice.

"Did you see that?" I asked Linny.

"What? That smokin' gaze he's been giving you?" she said. "It's about time you noticed."

"No, he just looked at me with pity, like he knows something," I said. "Did you say anything to him?"

"What, between ordering drinks and making toasts?"

I sighed and took a long drink of water.

"Look, Gracie, he's gonna find out sooner or later. Why don't you be the one to tell him? Take control of the situation before it destroys everything around you."

If my mom had said those words I'd have laughed at her, but somehow coming from Linn it felt true.

"I'll think about it," I said, draining the ice water.

"Oh, this I gotta see," Linny said, turning around in her barstool to see the skinny jeans take the stage.

I glanced at Charlie and he rolled his eyes. My mom and Jeri were watching the girls and snickering about something, and I couldn't help but wonder what I'd be doing with Andrew if none of this happened.

What would we be doing? I shook my head.

"Penny for your thoughts," Jimmy said, leaning on his elbows in front of me.

I looked at him and then at Linn, who shrugged her shoulders.

"I'm here because my husband cheated on me with teenage girls," I blurted out. "His students. He slept with his students, and one of them is saying she's pregnant now. That's why I'm here. I can't go back home."

A muscle in his jaw twitched. "Is there anything I can do?" He reached over and squeezed my hand.

I shook my head. "I hadn't said the words out loud yet and was tired of pretending."

Mom, Jeri, and Charlie were watching me. Linn was right. There was power in owning the truth, no matter how ugly it was.

We sat and watched for a while longer, sipping our drinks, and I felt relaxed for the first time in a week. My mom and Jeri decided to leave, asking Linny to make sure I got home safely. Charlie was quick to agree as well. I hugged Jeri and told her I'd wanted to meet with her tomorrow and get a calendar going for Mom.

Once they were gone, Charlie moved over by us and relived many of our high school memories. Being three years younger than Gordy, I missed out on the trouble those two seemed to find. At one point, the bar was so busy Charlie went back help keep up with the drink orders.

I looked at my watch and couldn't believe it was past midnight already. Linny was teetering on her barstool, swaying to the music.

"Hey Linny," I said. "How are we getting home?"

"I have no idea," she giggled. "Maybe one of your Prince Charmings can take us."

I shot her a look. "I'm done with men," I said. "I didn't choose so wisely on the last one, and I am never going through this again."

"But that doesn't mean you can't have a little fun." She leaned towards me to spy Jimmy and Charlie at the other end of the bar. "Oh, yes. I think you could have a lotta fun with him."

I followed her view. "Strictly out of curiosity, which one would you have *fun* with?"

"Oh no, you first. I'm married, so technically I shouldn't even answer that question."

"Please, you're married, not dead. And you already admitted to thinking one of them was cute enough to have fun with. Which one?"

She bit her lip and looked down the bar again. Charlie noticed and walked towards us.

"Ladies, do you need anything?"

Linny giggled.

"What's up with her?" he asked.

I took a sip of my drink and shook my head. "I think she's had enough," I said.

"I think you've both had enough." His eyes were studying me. "Do you want something to eat? Snack mix?"

"Yes!" Linny startled us. "Snack mix! I want snack mix."

He shook his head, smiling, and pulled out a bowl from under the bar.

"Can I get a Diet Coke?" I asked. "Water just isn't cutting it anymore."

He eyed Linny picking out the cheese crackers and grinned. "I think I'll make that two."

"I may have had too much to drink, but I can still hear," she said, munching.

"You stay put, Linn. I'm going to the bathroom," I said, sliding off the barstool. My legs were wobbly from the run.

The noise from the bar faded away as the door shut. I looked at my reflection, noticing the redness in my face, and the crease in my forehead. *Did I always look this uptight*? Washing my hands, I let the water run cold and splashed my face. The coolness calmed my skin at once. Opening the door, I ran into Jimmy.

"What are you doing?" He blocked the doorway, his arms folded.

"I wanted to see if you're okay," he said. "I promised your mom I would make sure you didn't drink too much."

I rolled my eyes. "And what would be wrong with me drinking too much? I think I'm entitled."

He held his hands up, "I know, I know. Like I said, I just wanted to make sure you were okay."

I sighed. "I'm sorry." I leaned against the wall by the door. "I didn't mean to snap at you."

"No apologies," he said gently. "Honestly, I'm a little impressed with how well you're handling it."

"Everyone keeps saying that, but I feel like such a coward."

"When I saw it on the news this morning I couldn't believe it was your Andrew."

I smirked. "My Andrew wasn't just mine." He was close enough for me to smell his aftershave, and my stomach did a flip-flop. He tucked a strand of hair behind my ear, and a shock went through me. His eyes darted to mine. *He felt it too.*

"I'd better get back to the bar," he stammered. "Charlie is going to wonder what I'm doing back here."

Linny's face brightened when she saw us walking back towards the bar. "Atta girl," she whispered when I sat down.

"He was just checking to make sure I was okay."

She was still clutching the snack mix, which lacked any cheese crackers. "I might have sent him back there to check on you," she slurred.

"Why would you do that, Linn?" I shook my head, annoyed. "How are we going to get you home?" I asked her.

"Correction. How are we going to get both of you home?" I hadn't noticed Charlie standing behind us.

We both looked at him and Linny hiccupped.

"Could you take us home? Except my car will be here, and Barry will kill me…"

He shook his head, rubbing his five o'clock shadow. "Wait here for a sec," he said, walking towards Jimmy.

"Remind me next time that you can't hold your alcohol any better than you did in high school." She looked at me and laughed, and I couldn't help but laugh with her.

She hiccupped again, and continued to giggle. "I haven't had this much fun in a long time."

I nodded, pulling her into a side hug. "For the record, I'm glad I'm here too. This is where I need to be right now."

Charlie walked back. "Okay, ladies. I'm going to take you both home, and Linn, we will get your car home to you safe and sound. What you tell or don't tell Barry is up to you."

"Oh thank you, thank you, thank you," she said.

He looked at me and winked. "So, we can go anytime you're ready."

We both grabbed our bags and waited for him to get his keys. Jimmy came around the bar and wrapped me in a hug, my senses on overload. "You're trembling," he whispered.

I nodded into his shoulder, and he pulled me away. "I'm here every morning by ten, so call me if you need anything."

I smiled up at him. "Thanks," I said, and pulled

away before he said anything else. "I'll see you soon."

He squeezed my hand and walked back behind the bar as Charlie came around. "Ready, ladies?"

Linny saluted him. "Aye aye, captain."

"How did the two of you drink the same amount and she's like this?"

I shrugged. "Beats me. Must have been the carb-loading I did before."

"Well, let's go so I can get back and help close," he said.

As we walked out the door I turned to wave to Jimmy, who was watching us. He waved, and I turned to follow Charlie.

—

Charlie's truck only had the bench seat, so the three of us piled in close. When I opened the door, Linn pushed me in so I had to sit next to him.

Linny lived close to Lakeside in a huge Victorian house overlooking Lake Michigan. Many of the homes in this area have been in the same families since they were first built. Every generation or so would remodel them with no expenses spared, and Linny's home didn't look much different.

"Oh Linn, I'll need to see this in the daylight," I said, admiring at her house in the moonlight.

She squeezed my hand. "I'll hold you to that."

She opened the door and tumbled out. "I left my keys with Jimmy at the bar. I really appreciate you guys getting my car home."

Charlie nodded. "No problem, Linn. Get some sleep."

She shut the door and I scooted over to the passenger seat as he pulled out of her driveway.

He glanced over my way. "You okay? It looked like you were able to relax a little tonight," he said.

I sighed and looked over at him. My breath caught noticing how handsome he looked, the dashboard lights glowing.

"I know everyone is really worried about me, but I am so tired of people asking me how I am. I would love for someone to tell me I looked like hell or say something completely inappropriate."

He nodded. "Fair enough," he said. "Would you rather I told you that even though I can tell you didn't take two minutes to get ready tonight, there were about four guys that would rather be driving you home?"

My head fell back to the headrest. "I said inappropriate, not *inaccurate*. Although you are spot on about my prep time. Maybe even a little generous."

He chuckled. "I'm not inaccurate. Guys were watching you, my brother included."

"Well I don't *want* anyone to watch me. I just want

to hang with my friends and family, under the radar."

"Under the radar is only going to last for so long," he warned. "Pretty soon, they're going to be looking at you, wondering if you're the wife of the teacher sleeping with his students."

"I know," I said quietly. "I'm going to need thicker skin by then."

We drove down the main drag through town, and I wished my house was farther away. I didn't want this ride to end.

"Can I ask you something personal?"

"Shoot," he said, glancing over at me.

"What happened to your marriage? Why did you get divorced?"

We turned onto Carlington, a few blocks away.

"That is going to be a conversation for another time," he said. "Not because I don't want to tell you, but I really need to get back and help with closing."

"Sure, next time," I said. "Stop by if you bring Sadie out to the beach tomorrow. I'll just be home, trying to figure out the next few months."

He pulled into the driveway and switched his headlights off. Needing air, I opened the door quickly.

"Thank you for everything," I said, sliding out of his truck. "I really appreciate your ignorance of my baggage."

"Your baggage doesn't scare me," he said. "Your ability to drink your friend under the table is a bit concerning, though."

"It's one of my many talents." I joked. "See you soon."

As I walked up the front door I saw Rumi sitting in the window, waiting for me. I locked up and tip-toed upstairs, Rumi following me.

I brushed my teeth, threw on an old T-shirt, and crawled into bed. I cracked the window open, letting the waves calm my thoughts. The blanket was pulled tight under my chin, and I settled deeper into my bed. It was then, hidden in the darkness, that I missed Andrew. His smile. The twinkle in his eye when he told a funny story. His voice.

I sighed and rolled over, thinking about my dad instead. When I was little and couldn't sleep, he would tell me to count my blessings from the day. *What were the good things in your day, sweetie?* A tear trickled onto the pillow, but I was determined to find the blessings.

Seeing Linny again.

Helping Jeri.

Charlie and Jimmy.

Apologizing to my mom.

The sound of waves.

Chapter Nine

I woke up to my phone ringing loudly. It was Linny.

"How are you feeling this morning?" I answered.

"Ugh, like hell," she groaned. "But I'm more interested in you. Did you get home okay last night?"

"Did you think I wouldn't? Or were you asking me something else?"

She giggled, and I heard pans clanging in the background.

"Are you at work already?"

"Duh, I make breakfast for half the town," she scoffed. "I'm here by five-thirty every morning."

The clock read 8:20, and I cringed. "How long are you there today?"

"I stay until the lunch crowd clears out. Most days I come back later before closing."

"I'll stop by for lunch in a bit," I said. "I want to see what's going on here first, but I'll let you know."

"Sounds good. I gotta go, anyways. I'll see you later," she said, before disconnecting.

Downstairs, the coffee smelled intoxicating, a note propped up with a mug by the coffee pot.

Sorry to leave without saying goodbye! Her appointment is at 9:15, and we'll be home after that.

I poured my coffee and curled up on the couch.

Looking outside, the sunshine lit the lake to a brilliant navy blue this morning, the lighthouse standing proud.

It was unnatural for me to wake up and not go about business as usual. I missed the hustle and bustle of getting a story just right, and the chaos in the newsroom right before airtime. And I envied their opportunity with Andrew's story. This was a big one, and why we do what we do. Stories like Andrew's came along once every year, if you're lucky.

My mom's book sat on the coffee table. To be able to work with her, I had to understand what she believes. Scanning through the first couple pages, I stopped at the nuts and bolts of the book.

A Mother's Guide to Living

Step 1. Let Go of the Past
Step 2. Learn Gratitude
Step 3. Work with What You've Got
Step 4. Know Who Your Friends Are
Step 5. What Matters Most?
Step 6. The Art of Balance
Step 7. Living Right Now
Step 8. All You Need is Love

I read through the list, keeping an open mind. *Why did people need a book to change their lives?* If you didn't like something, change it. It seemed so logical and always worked for me.

Or did it?

I flipped back to the dedication.

To G & G, for teaching me about motherhood.

She dedicated this to Gordy and me? *Why didn't she tell me*? I assumed she viewed me as a reminder of a failed mother-daughter relationship.

I snapped the book shut and picked up the remote. Changing to CNN, pictures of teenage girls flashed on the screen. Straight, brown hair. Perfect, clear skin. Cheerleader uniform. The sound was drowned out by the echoing in my ears.

"… *letting him rule your life from a jail cell two hundred miles away.*"

I snapped the power off and threw the remote across the room. I couldn't look at the reality of what was going on in my life, and wasn't sure I ever would.

I needed a distraction.

On the way to Traverse City, I cracked the window and turned the music up loud. I brought my phone with me just in case my mom or Jeri needed me, and it sat in the passenger seat, buzzing. It was a Frankfort area code.

"Gracie?"

I'd know his voice anywhere.

"Hey Jimmy."

"How are you this morning?" His voice was raspy

with sleep.

"I'm hanging in there," I lied. "I'm actually on my way towards TC to pick up some things at Target."

"I don't want to bug you, but wanted to check in and see if you were okay." My stomach fluttered.

"That's sweet of you," I said. "I'm just trying to take it one day at a time. I wish I hadn't watched at the news this morning."

"That's one thing you need to ignore for the next couple months. By the looks of it, the trial is going to be a circus." He paused. "I know we didn't get to talk much last night, but I wanted you to know if you need anything, just ask. Charlie and I talked and want to help any way we can."

My heart swelled. "I may hold you to that. I'm going to need my friends more than I anticipated. That is if my mom and I don't kill each other."

"Yeah, Charlie told me about Jeri too," he said. "I am so sorry."

"There's definitely a cloud following me around. That's why I'm doing a little retail therapy and getting some things I'll need to help my mom."

"Well, I won't keep you. I was just thinking of you, and I hope you don't mind that Linn gave me your number."

"I don't mind at all. You and Charlie have been very sweet."

"You didn't exactly look thrilled to see me

Wednesday night. It's been a long time since high school, and I know I wasn't the nicest guy back then."

"We all grow up at some point, and high school was a long time ago."

He chuckled. "You couldn't pay me enough to go back to that age."

"Agreed," I said. "Although Linn and I had a few good memories last night."

"Yeah, she still can't hold her drinks, and I was trying to keep them light for your sake."

"What's the deal with her and Barry? I couldn't get a good read on them when I asked her about him."

"Not sure," he replied. "The only time I ever see her is at the bakery or on the rare occasion when she comes into Lakeside."

"Well, I just got the feeling she isn't happy. I probably should just keep my nose out of it and worry about my own problems."

He sighed. "Again, is there anything I can do for you?"

"Just keep asking," I said. "I'll let you know eventually."

"That I can do," he said. "So I have to get going, but just call me at this number anytime. Or maybe we could just hang out this weekend. I have Sunday night off…"

The question hung in the air. "That might work," I said, stalling. "Let me check and see what my mom needs first."

"Sounds good and no pressure," he said. "I'll let you go. Drive safe, Gracie."

"Thanks for calling Jimmy," I said. "I'll see you soon."

I disconnected, wondering what the hell just happened. Jimmy was notorious for moving quickly, but I couldn't be his next conquest. My life was too upside down for that.

I found myself at Target, giddy as a kid shopping for school supplies, buying my favorite pens, notebooks, and splurging on an iPad. Buyer's remorse would kick in eventually, but for now, it felt productive.

My mom had texted and said she would meet me at Bab's for lunch, and my stomach started to growl. My phone buzzed, and I answered it without looking at the caller ID. A recorded voice crackled, asking me if I'd accept this call from Andrew at the Ingham County Jail.

Without thinking, I accepted.

"Gracie?" It was Andrew.

My heart stopped, and I knew I should hang up, but I froze.

"Grace, I only have a couple minutes to talk," he pleaded. "I'm going crazy here without you."

"I don't even know what to say to you." My hands shook, and I pulled into a small gas station.

"I know it all looks bad, but Gracie what happened to 'for better or worse'? I know we can get through this if you just heard my side of the story instead of this media hype judging me before the trial," he said. "I thought you'd be back by now."

I scoffed. "Andrew, you're delusional, which is precisely how you got in this mess. You *never* thought you'd get caught." He didn't respond, so I continued. "And for the record, for better or worse only counts when your spouse isn't sleeping with teenage girls."

"Jesus Gracie, you're acting like one of their parents," he retorted.

How is it possible this is the man I loved?

"Andrew, I can't help you through this," I said, quietly. "I'm not sure why you called or what you want, but I am not going to be that person for you. I *thought* I made that clear at the jail."

"You're really not coming back home? What about your job?"

"I've been in contact with Tim, and he is in support of my decision to stay out of town. I'm not sure what I'm going to do, but I certainly won't be there for you," I said.

"What's going to happen to me?" His voice was deflated.

"Well, hopefully your lawyer has filled you in on those details, but after researching it, I'd say you'll get about twenty-five years for criminal sexual conduct, first degree." I wanted to hurt him.

"Wow, thanks for your support. Sure glad I called,"

he said. Passive aggression at its best.

"Actually, I am glad. Hopefully now we're clear about the future," I said. "I really don't have time for this Andrew. I'm hanging up."

He disconnected before I said goodbye. I sat there, in a cold sweat. My phone buzzed, a text this time.

MOM: *Where are you?*

ME: *Stopped for gas. Be there in 10.*

MOM: *Drive safe.*

I swallowed the feeling of helplessness creeping from my stomach. I couldn't break down out here in the middle of nowhere. I put the car in drive, heading towards Bab's, replaying the conversation in my head.

Linny and my mom were sitting at the table in the window and waving at me as I walked across the street. I smiled and shook my head. My mom greeted me with a hug, something new for both of us, and Linny just smiled.

"So…" I said, sighing. "Andrew called."

They gaped at me, wide-eyed.

"*And*?" Mom asked.

"I wish I had recorded it. He can't believe I won't come back home to help him through this."

Linny grabbed my hand, eyes blazing. "I hope you told him to go fuck himself." She glanced at my mom. "Sorry about my French, Mrs. D."

My mom smiled politely. "I think you two studied with the same teacher." She took a sip of water. "What did you tell him?"

"Just that I wasn't coming home and couldn't help him."

"Okay," Linny said, bolting up. "There's too much going on at this table on empty stomachs. Chicken salad on croissants?"

I nodded vigorously, and she took off for the kitchen. "That had to be difficult talking to him," Mom said. "How did he sound?"

"Lonely. Isolated. I'm sure most people are staying away from him right now, and he didn't have a ton of friends. other than at school."

My mom shook her head. "I can't believe he called you. I got your note, by the way. Did you get what you needed?"

"I did, and then some. It was nice to be among real people doing normal things again."

Linny carried a tray filled with sandwiches and lemonade for each of us. "So, how did Jeri's appointment go?" I asked, mouth full of chicken salad.

"About what we had expected. She is having surgery on Monday, and then she will start chemo four to six weeks afterwards, depending on her recovery." She sipped her tea and looked out the window. "I know she's putting on a brave face, but she's scared. Pete is coming home for the surgery and to help out next week."

"Doesn't she have a sister in Gaylord?" I asked.

My mom nodded. "Yes, Terese, but they haven't talked in years. Something about the will when their dad died, and they just don't talk now."

"Let's get back to dipshit," Linny said. "Can't we figure out how to block his calls?"

"Actually, that's not a bad idea," my mom agreed.

I shook my head. "I don't think I'm going to need that by the way things ended. Besides, I could've just declined the call at the beginning. He caught me off guard, but I made it pretty clear that I wasn't going to be there for him any longer." I took a big gulp of lemonade. "Which brings me to my next question. Linn, does Barry have a partner that specializes in divorce?"

"Oh good choice. There is one, but he's kind of a shark. Barry doesn't especially like him, but would agree he'd be the best for you."

We all sat there in silence, finishing our lunches. "Well, I guess I need to call Barry," I said to Linny. "Let's get this in motion."

Linny left the table and came back with one of Barry's business cards. "Call him this afternoon and he will connect you with Terrence."

I felt better after lunch, stronger.

"Ladies, this is the best lunch date I've had in a long time," Linny declared. "Even if I did have to prepare it myself."

"It was just what I needed today," I said, hugging her. "I feel ready to actually get through a day without a nap."

"There's nothing wrong with a little siesta," Linny said. "You need to take care of yourself right now." She hugged my mom next. "After last night, I think *I* need a nap today."

"Still can't hold your alcohol," I said. "Even after all these years."

"Yeah, yeah Dunham. I could still beat you at quarters," she countered.

My mom rolled her eyes. "I'll see you at home," she said to me. "Linn, thank you for lunch. It was perfection."

"Anytime, Mrs. D. Have a good weekend," she said.

"I'll call you," I said as we left.

"I'm going to stop at the grocery store and pick up a few more things for the weekend. I think Jeri might hang out with us tonight at home, if that's okay with you?"

"Of course," I said. "Is there anything you want me to get?"

"No," she said, sliding on her sunglasses. "You get home and relax for a bit with Rumi."

I waved goodbye.

Rumi greeted me at the door and followed me to the kitchen. Setting my bags on the table, I cracked open a window over the sink to hear the waves.

I heard tapping on the back door. Charlie stood there smiling and I waved for him to come in.

"You busy?" He opened the door a crack.

"Nope, just getting organized before Jeri comes over tonight," I said.

"Hang on a sec, I have to tie up Sadie."

She watched him, head cocked, ears perked up. He patted her head. "Good girl. Stay."

"We can sit outside if you don't want to leave her." She stared at us, unblinking.

"Hell no, it's chilly today, especially by the water," he said. "She'll be fine, but you'll have to ignore the doe eyes she'll give you."

I laughed. Her body vibrated with excitement. He shook his head. "You need to stop looking at her or she won't give up."

I did as he said. "Poor girl."

"That dog could convince a homeless man to give up a hamburger," he said, sitting down and eyeing my shopping bags.

"Welcome to my desk," I said. "Can I get you something to drink?"

"I'll just have water, thanks. I stopped to see if you were going to run today," he said, stalling. "Thought maybe Sadie and I could use the exercise."

"I've been so busy getting all this stuff together, I hadn't even thought about it." I set a bottle of water in front of him. "I could definitely use a run today. Do you run a lot?"

"Uh… not particularly, but I need to start doing something. Late nights and operating a bar isn't exactly doing me any favors."

"We can start slow and work our way up," I encouraged.

He took a long drink of water. "How is your day going? I see your shopping trip was productive."

I took a deep breath and blew it out. "It's been an interesting day. Andrew called me."

"I'm surprised it wasn't sooner," he said. "How did he sound?"

"Miserable… desperate," I said. "I don't know how to feel about it, even now. I talked with Linny and my mom about it over lunch, but I just keep replaying the conversation over in my head." I met his eyes. "Am I doing the right thing staying here, or am I just running away?"

He flinched. "Why do you think you're running from anything? If you stayed you would be dragged into this mess with him." His eyes locked on mine. "I know it's probably hard to let go of the idea of what you had, but Gracie, that was just an illusion. The reality is plastered all over the news."

He was right, but I couldn't shake the sinking feeling in my gut. "I saw the girls on TV this morning. Jesus, Charlie, they were so young. How I could have been so out of touch with reality?" I didn't want to cry, but the tears came anyways.

He chewed on his lip and didn't try to stop me.

"I'm sorry," I said. "Guess my mind has been working overtime." I wiped my nose with the sleeve of my shirt.

"Did you really just use your shirt to wipe your nose?" He grimaced.

"Maybe." Laughter through tears.

"How about you grab a tissue and change for a run? We need to get you out of these four walls."

"On it," I said, getting up. My mom walked through the garage door with more groceries. I grabbed a tissue, but she raised her eyebrows.

"I'm fine," I said, defensively. "I'm going to change, and we're going for a run." I stomped upstairs, hearing their whispers. This was comforting and annoying at the same time. I wasn't used to being the one that people worried about.

My clothes from yesterday were laying on the bed, so I threw them on. *Why didn't I get more clothes today?*

"We won't be too long," I said to my mom when I got downstairs.

"Take your time," she said. "Fresh air is the best thing for you right now."

I bit my lip. Her need to express what was best for me made my skin crawl.

"See ya, Mrs. D," Charlie said, following me out the door.

"Bye Charlie," she chimed, closing the door behind us.

I rolled my eyes, pulling my hair into a ponytail.

"What?" he asked, unwinding Sadie's leash. "You could cut her some slack. She just wants to help."

I walked towards the beach. When he caught up with me, he grinned.

"What?" I asked.

"I know you don't want anyone telling you what to do or how to feel," he said. "You've always been that way, but it's not a sign of weakness to let those around you help a little."

"My dad always said I was headstrong, and it felt like a good thing to me. I took pride in being the stubborn one in the family." I started to walk faster once we got to the hard sand, Charlie matching my pace. "I'm not trying to be difficult, but sometimes I push back just because I can. Does that make sense?"

He laughed. "You're forgetting I grew up with Jimmy. It makes perfect sense."

"C'mon, let's run," I said, and picked up the pace to a slow run. For the next twenty minutes we jogged side by side, not saying anything, but not needing to either. I rarely had running partners, liking the freedom of setting my own pace. But this was different. The steady rhythm of our breath was in sync with the water today. The waves were high, and the air was damp and cool by the water. The clouds had moved in to hide the sun. This was the Michigan weather I was used to.

I started to slow down, my legs tired from yesterday's run, and Charlie and Sadie were right by my side. He was breathing heavy and sweating profusely.

"You okay?" I asked, walking now.

He nodded. "Once I get the feeling back in my legs, I'll be great."

"You'll get used to that feeling, and someday you might even like it," I assured him. "Sadie seemed to like the run just fine."

Hearing her name, she looked up at me and wagged her tail. I found a stick and threw it down the beach. She sprinted and brought it back, tail still wagging.

Charlie smiled and shook his head. "That never gets old."

"Pretty soon she'll get used to these runs and you'll have to keep it up," I said. I wandered to my favorite log and sat down to stretch my legs.

Charlie followed, his eyes scanned my face. "You seem better after the run," he said. "Not as… tense."

"It's the endorphins," I said. "I have found if I don't run every couple days, I sink into bad moods that will last for weeks. My mom says I'm running away from something, but I call it mood management."

He looked out at the water. "I have a very bad

feeling that once I do feel my legs again, they are going to be really sore."

I smiled. "Probably for a couple days, but if you know what's best, you'll run again this weekend, even if they still hurt."

"I'll try," he said. "I may be crawling, but I'll try."

We sat in silence with nothing but the waves. They seemed moody today, like me, and I matched my breath with their flow.

He was watching the waves too. "The waves bring chaos and calm."

I shot him a side-eye. "What does that even *mean*?"

He had a distant look in his eye. "My dad was a man of few words, as you know. Always said a story could be told in six words, and he often did." Sadie sat at his feet, panting. "So, whenever I think of my dad, I try to come up with a six-word story for him."

"Wow, I have never heard of that before. Give me another one."

He returned the side-eye. "She runs fierce and without worry."

"Okay, you're starting to freak me out a bit," I said, laughing.

"You should try it," he said. "It forces you to choose words wisely."

I thought about how I felt in that exact moment. "I liked having a running partner." Not poetic, but truthful.

He continued watching the waves, but his face

relaxed into a smile. "Me too."

As hard as I tried, I couldn't nail down this feeling as I sat beside him. It was like sitting with Gordy, but not brotherly.

"What time are you working today?" I asked, breaking the silence that had fallen over us.

"I'll go in around four thirty till close. Fridays are busy during dinner time, but it will quiet down after nine or so," he said. "Just a few regulars come in after that."

"What made you come back and take over the business with Jimmy?"

"I did the whole corporate thing, suit and tie every day for three years, and when I moved back here, I knew I'd never wear another suit again." He shook his head. "It just wasn't me."

"You don't mind the late nights and bad karaoke?"

"It's strange, but I don't. I keep to myself, but I like to be there around people. It's less lonely that way." He petted Sadie, who was eyeing a couple sandpipers. "And when my dad died, it was just a natural progression to help Jimmy with the business."

I shivered thinking about my call from Jimmy earlier. "Well, I'm going to head in and try to warm up now," I said.

"Have you talked to Gordy yet?" he asked, standing up.

"We've texted back and forth, but I haven't talked to him yet," I said. I stood and stretched, my body stiffening in the cold. "He thinks he might come up next weekend."

"Cool, I haven't seen him since the funeral," he said. "Let me know for sure when you find out. We can all go out." He leashed up Sadie and started towards the parking lot. "Thanks for running with us."

I smiled. "We'll see if you say that tomorrow. Have a good night, Charlie."

Watching him walk away, I pushed down a feeling of need. I felt completely safe around him, like he would protect me from anything. Growing up, my primary goal had been to become as independent as possible. But here I was, wanting someone to save me.

Chapter Ten

After a long, hot shower, I picked up the dirty clothes on my floor and started a load of laundry. My mom had made a snide comment earlier about *some things never changing*, and I took the not-so-subtle hint.

Downstairs, a batch of chocolate chip cookies were cooling on a wire rack. The kitchen smelled of chocolate, and she opened the fridge to put the dough away.

"Hold on there," I said. "I need to test that and make sure it's not poisoned."

She smiled and set it on the counter for me. As long as I can remember, my mom kept homemade cookie dough in the refrigerator for when she needed a quick batch. When we were little, homemade cookies were always an after-dinner treat. It surprised me she carried on this tradition.

After testing the cookie dough and claiming it poison-free, I tested an actual cookie. They were warm and gooey in the middle, chocolate sticking to my fingers.

"Mmmmm," I said. "I need a glass of milk to go with this."

She watched me, smiling. "You always had a soft spot for the chocolate chip. Gordy, on the other hand, loved the oatmeal cookies."

"I never understood that, either," I said between bites, "I mean, they're good, but nothing beats these." The richness of the chocolate followed by the cold milk tasted decadent, like I was savoring it for the first time.

"After you're done with that, do you mind helping me cut vegetables for dinner?"

"Sure, what are we having?" I asked.

"I thought we'd do Mexican and have chicken fajitas, with rice on the side," she suggested, looking for approval.

"That sounds amazing, but I'll need to start running more if I'm going to live here indefinitely," I said.

"Oh good, I'm never really sure what you'll like," she said. "It's been so long since I've cooked for anyone but myself and Jeri."

"Ma, I eat anything and everything," I reassured her. "Honestly, we ate out a lot in Lansing, so home-cooked food is a welcome change."

She beamed. "I love cooking for people, and now that you're here I have a good reason."

I washed the chocolate off my finger tips and grabbed an apron hanging by the pantry door. "Okay, let's get this party started," I said. "I'm thinking peppers, onion, and… what else?"

"Usually that's it, but Jeri has to be different and likes mushrooms in hers," she said, setting the veggies in the middle of the table. "I'm going to start the guacamole and the rice. The chicken is already in a southwest marinade."

As I began slicing the onion, I couldn't remember a single time ever helping my mom with dinner. When I was in high school, afternoons and evenings were always dedicated to school work or soccer practice, and dinner was just on the table or in the fridge if we were late. When we did come home for holidays, it was never like this. She always made a point of having everything done so we wouldn't have to help her. Having Andrew in the house created more tension than anything else. My main goal was to eat and run, claiming we had somewhere else to be.

There was a knock at the door, then Jeri let herself in. "Well, this looks cozy," she said, smiling at the two of us slicing and mashing at the kitchen island. Setting her bag down by the desk, she noticed my iPad. "Well, well, well, someone's been shopping today."

Looking up, I smiled. "Guilty."

"Good choice," she approved. "I'd rather have the mini myself, but don't want to switch now. Do you have lemons?" she asked my mom.

"Bottom drawer, and there's a pitcher on the top shelf in the pantry," she said. "You know where everything else is."

"When you're given lemons, you make lemonade," she said, mostly to herself.

We continued on like that, cutting, cooking, and I

didn't think about Andrew or the trial. It felt like a movie, and I played the part of a girl who was content with her life. This scene was so vastly different from any other in my past. Connection and closeness weren't words I would use to describe my life with Andrew, but I never saw that until now. The difference in the two worlds was like switching from grayscale to vibrant color.

The fajitas tasted better than any I've ever gotten at a restaurant. After cleaning up, we gathered around the table again. This time with a single focus: to teach me everything about Jeri's job duties.

"I don't care how many calendars you have, sugar, if you don't look at them every single day, sometimes a few times a day, you're going to miss something important. Her calendar is now your most important priority," Jeri told me.

"Gracie, I don't want you to worry too much right away," my mom said reassuringly. "I know your life is upside down, and we will learn to work together. This won't happen overnight."

"However, there is a book signing on Sunday I want you to cover," Jeri chimed in. I swear they finished each other sentences. "You'll have to learn on the fly this weekend, but there are notes in the file as well. Easy peasy."

I ran my hands through my hair. "You will have to tell me exactly what you want, when you want it. You've had Jeri knowing all this for so long, and you're going to miss that," I said. "And I will try not to take anything personally when I do screw up."

"Oh, yes, never take it personally," Jeri said, sipping more lemonade. "She can be temperamental when things don't go her way. I learned a long time ago that she has an image in her head of what life should be like. If the image doesn't match reality then all hell breaks loose. Just try to figure out the image and you'll be fine."

I swallowed hard. This was going to be more difficult than I thought.

"You're both making me sound like a bull-headed witch!" Mom said.

Jeri patted her hand. "No, I'm just trying to make sure this transition is as seamless as possible."

"Okay, what about social media," I said. "Facebook and Twitter? Do you update those?"

"Absolutely, every day. I have the passwords for you, as well as some guidelines for what to include each day." She slid a file folder to me with several papers inside. "We use Google everything... Gmail, Google Docs, and everything is already updated in the calendar. The password for that is also in there, along with any other information you will need."

I started to flip through all the papers, seeing everything from passwords to bank account numbers and credit cards statements.

"I already requested a card in your name for expenses... hotel reservations, flights, gas...

whatever you need to get her where she belongs. On time, preferably. And by on time, I mean an hour early. Card should be here by Monday. Everything, and I mean *everything*, goes on one card, and it's paid off every single month."

"Do I pay all the bills as well?"

"She has all of her bills set up to be paid online through her bank," Jeri explained. "The only one you have to confirm is the Amex because the amount varies from month to month."

My mom sighed. "Now you're making me sound like an invalid who can't care for herself. I can pay my own bills."

"When is cable due?" Jeri asked.

My mom gave her a blank stare.

"Precisely. This is why we have everything on autopay, so you don't have to worry about it," Jeri said. "Believe me, I did this years ago, and have never had any issues." She took a sip of her lemonade. "Do you have any questions for me?"

"This seems pretty straight forward," I said. "But I do have one question: do I get paid for this?"

My mom blinked. "Of course, you do. I couldn't ask you to do all this for nothing."

"That's right. Gracie, I will need your bank routing and account number, so I can set up a direct deposit for you," Jeri said. "You'll get paid every Friday, but that won't start for two weeks."

"Okay," I said. "But what about my bank now? I

still share an account with Andrew, and I don't want him to know about this income."

"You should open a new account," Mom said. "Most banks are open Saturdays, so you can go in the morning. However, until the divorce is final, he technically could have access to that money."

I sighed and pushed the file away. "Is there ever going to be a time when my life doesn't feel like make-believe?"

My mom reached across and squeezed my hand. "There is nothing here that's make-believe, only different. You've been here less than a week and everything is different for you than it was a week ago," she said. "You are bound to have a moment or two when your life feels like someone else's."

"The only time I feel myself is when I'm running lately," I said.

"And it doesn't hurt when you have a handsome running partner."

I ran my fingers through my hair. "Oh my god, Mom. Are you really going there?"

She winked to Jeri. "All I'm saying is you're lucky to have friends around you right now. I know you're not looking for anything more than that."

Jeri smiled brighter. "Besides, I think it's the younger one that has the hots for you." They both burst into laughter. I couldn't help smiling myself.

"You're both whacked," I said, packing up my stuff. "No one has the hots for me, and it's going to stay that way."

"No offense sugar, but what would be wrong with that if it were true? Which it is."

"You don't know that. Charlie has been through a lot lately, and I really don't think he has a ton of friends. What's wrong with a running partner?"

"Oh honey, we're just giving you a hard time. We've been together for so long, and it's nice to have someone else around here to pick on."

"I am off-limits right now," I said. The last thing I wanted was to encourage any romance with anyone.

Maybe.

Later, after Jeri left and my mom went to bed, I curled up on the couch with a blanket and searched every channel, looking for an escape. *You've Got Mail.* I dropped the remote, finding comfort in lines I could recite myself.

A bouquet of newly-sharpened pencils.

We would never.

I wanted it to be you.

Unable to relax, I grabbed my iPad and started to plug in the passwords to my mom's Facebook and Twitter pages. Seeing how many followers she has was mind-boggling. *How did I not know how famous she really was?* I knew she had been on the morning network shows, and *The Tonight Show* tried to book her once. She declined.

The one show she wanted and never got was *Oprah*. I know the last year the show aired, she was hoping for that magical phone call that would change her life. In the last few days, I've learned she isn't doing this for the fame. She truly believes in what she's doing and wants to make other people's lives better.

I logged into the Google accounts to see what the email and calendar situation entailed. Jeri was a genius at organizing my mother's life. She color-coded appointments in red, speaking engagements in purple, class times in blue, book signings in green, and personal engagements in pink. Email automatically shuffled into the following files, depending on the subject: Personal, Students, Retreats, Random, Fan Mail, and Bookstores.

My eyes were burning. I set aside my iPad and turned the volume louder. It was a rare moment when I just sat and watched TV, so I was happy it was near the end.

Don't cry, shopgirl, don't cry…

Gets me every time.

Chapter Eleven

The drive to Leelenau for the book signing was uneventful and quiet. My mom seemed preoccupied, but I attributed it to nerves and left her alone. I didn't know what she went through to get ready for a book signing, but the silence had my nerves jumpy.

Being true to Michigan fashion, the weather outside was cloudy and cold. The high was going to be forty-two, and I was feeling sorely underdressed. The best I could come up with was a pair of dark wash jeans, white T-shirt, and a bright pink cardigan with black flats. I wore a simple silver necklace with silver hoop earrings. My mom, of course, looked like she just stepped out of a Banana Republic catalog, with her hair perfectly straightened and make-up done. How I grew up with this woman and didn't assume any of her style I'll never know, but it wasn't fair.

"So," I started, breaking the silence. "Once we get there, I'll check in with Claudia and make sure your table and books are all set up. Is there usually a reading done at these things?"

Whatever I said made her smile. "No, I don't usually do readings at any of my book signings. People are less interested in hearing self-help read to them. I'd be better off selling highlighters with the books." She laughed at her own joke.

"Well, what will you need from me once this gets going?"

"Just stand by the table so you can see if anything is needed," she explained. "Once, I had a person come up and recognize me from high school. Can you believe it?"

I smiled and shook my head, wanting her to get on with the story.

"So Jeri took her contact information so I could email her or get a hold of her some time."

"Did you ever see her again?"

"Sadly, no," she said quickly. "This was when I toured four years ago, and I think we were in Seattle at the time. It was just fun to see a connection from so long ago."

"Okay, so basically I'll just stand around and wait to see if something comes up."

"That would be perfect," she said. "Thanks for coming today Gracie. I know Jeri was worried about making sure everything would go okay, but really, these things run themselves, and the people are always so nice."

"It's not a problem," I said, glancing over at her. "And it's not like my life is getting any better by hiding out at your house."

She shook her head slowly. "I'm not sure how you keep blaming yourself in all of this mess, but I will just keep reminding you that you did nothing wrong.

You are doing the best you can right now."

"Can I ask you a question?"

"You can ask me anything, you know that," she encouraged.

"I think I accepted a date with Jimmy tonight, and starting to feel some guilt. Should I cancel?"

She smiled and had a twinkle in her eye. "So Jimmy is making the first move, huh? Jeri and I had our bets on Charlie."

"You two are betting on this?"

"Well, it's all in good fun, and they both seem sweet on you since you got back into town."

"But is it something I really need in my life right now? Shouldn't I be focusing on fixing my life?"

"Okay, tell me this," she said, turning in her seat to face me better. "Before Andrew was arrested, would you say your life needed fixing? Were you happy?"

"Honestly, I don't know. We kind of lead separate lives, and I wasn't unhappy, but I can't say I was in love with my life. I did like my job, but I think it was more about the people I was working with more so than the job itself. Andrew and I had just gotten comfortable and settled with each other." I kept my eyes on the road and didn't let my thoughts get away from me. "Other than his vacation time we didn't see each other a lot."

My mom nodded like she knew exactly what I was talking about. "Well, sadly, that is more common than you think. The women who come to the summer retreats often say the exact same thing. Their husbands are hotshot lawyers or ER doctors, and are literally never home. They're abandoned wives and don't have a clue what to do with their lives."

I nodded. This was the most honest conversation we've ever had.

"The only thing that's different is that you have a life," she continued.

"Correction. I *had* a life. I can't go back to that one."

"Well, *that* life yes, but the point I'm trying to make is you weren't sitting around waiting for him to come home."

I laughed. "Well, at least I'm thankful for that," I said, sarcastically. "That would've been embarrassing."

She gave me a sideways glance. "You are braver than you believe, stronger than you seem, and smarter than you think."

I had heard that before a long time ago. "I like that… Is that E. E. Cummings?"

She giggled, "No, it's Winnie the Pooh. But it's true," she said quietly. "I didn't want to tell you this, but yesterday there was a phone call from an Officer Marks about Andrew's case. He wants you to call him at your convenience, but I made sure he knew it wouldn't be until tomorrow."

"What did he want? Did he say how he found me?"

"I think Andrew gave him the home number,

knowing we'd be screening the calls. He just said he wanted to see how much you knew about the… case."

Great. This was all I needed to worry about now. The last thing I wanted was to be dragged into this mess. "Did he say I had to come back in town?"

"No, in fact I told him that if it had to be in person, he would have to come to you."

I smiled. "You're good, Mom. Thank you for telling me."

She waved her hand. "Oh, it's nothing. I'm sure he can just interview you over the phone anyways."

We drove a few more minutes and she directed me through the small town to the corner bookstore-cafe. It was a cute, brick building that looked like it had been there forever and recently remodeled.

"I love it already."

She glanced up from her phone. "It's sweet isn't it? Claudia has the best taste and isn't intimidated to modernize this store."

I gathered my bag and checked to see if she needed anything else for me to bring in with her. Walking through the doorway was like walking into a charming old house that happened to be filled with books. The walls were painted a buttery yellow, with quotes and pictures covering the walls. A woman, I assumed to be Claudia, poked her head out of the back room.

"Hey, you're here!" Her voice boomed towards the front of the store. "I'm so glad you made it early."

My mom walked towards the back of the store and hugged Claudia warmly. "It's so good to see you my friend," she said. "How are you? Business going well?"

Claudia waved her hand. "Oh you know business is mostly during the summer season and winters can be a bit slow. But that's when I get to catch up on my reading list."

She glanced up and saw me. "You must be Grace," she said, walking towards me, hand extended to shake. She had grey hair pulled up into a bun, held by what looked like chopsticks. She was wearing a black jumper dress that covered her soft, round body. Everything about her reminded me of Mrs. Claus. Not surprisingly, she had a hearty handshake.

"Nice to meet you... I've heard so much about you," I said. "Your store is absolutely charming."

She gushed. "Well, after all these years, it's nice to know I got something right." She looked at me as if she knew me. "Forgive me for asking, but have we met before? You look positively familiar to me."

My stomach clenched and I suddenly needed water. "Not that I know of. I haven't been to Leelenau since I was in high school, and I don't think we ever came here as kids."

"Well, isn't that something." She finally let go of my hand and headed towards the back of the store again. "I know I'm getting up there in age, but I never forget a face."

My mom looked at me and I swallowed. "Maybe I just look like someone you used to know."

"Maybe," she said. "If not, I'm sure it'll come to me." She led us to the back room, which I was surprised to find was another section of the store. Stacks and stacks of books lined the walls, and the left side opened up to a sitting area where she had placed a small desk-like table with a vase of pink tulips and more stacks of my mom's books on display. Bottles of water were on another small table behind the desk, as well as a mug of felt-tip pens.

My mom smiled. "It seems you have remembered me well," she said.

"Well, they didn't have any daffodils, so I went with the next best thing," she said, moving a few more books to her stacks. "So tell me, how's Jeri doing?"

My mom slumped ever so slightly, and I wondered how much stress this actually was on her. "Well, she has surgery tomorrow to remove what they can and check the lymph nodes. After that, she will start chemo and radiation once she has recovered."

"Oh, I'm so sorry," she said, shaking her head. "I'm sure with her spirit she will pull out of this better than ever."

We all nodded, not knowing what to say. "Well, I sure hope so. Not much keeps her down."

"So Gracie, what brings you back up North? I know you were living in East…" She stopped talking and looked closely at me. "Oh my goodness. It's you. Your husband–" She stopped again, not knowing what to say.

I bowed my head. "Yes, my husband is the teacher being accused of sexual misconduct with his students. I came up here to stay out of the chaos he created in our lives."

Her eyes were bugging out of her head, and shockingly she was at a loss of words. "I'm sorry, I don't know what to say," she said. "I must admit that up until now, I partially blamed the wife. How could you not see what was going on under your own nose?"

My face blazed. This was exactly the response I had been expecting from people. "I'm going to get a few pictures of the front of the store for the Facebook and Twitter accounts," I said. I backed up out of the room slowly and turned to get out of there.

I heard my mother picking up the pieces as the bell rang overhead on the front door. Everyone who knew me here had been supportive, but I didn't think about the ones who suspected I had been aware of his behavior.

I busied myself with my camera app trying to get the right shot of the store front. Once I got a few, I used another app to use a vintage filter to capture the quaint look I was going for. Next, I uploaded them to both Facebook and Twitter in a matter of seconds, naming the time, and checking in with both so people could find us more easily.

I decided I had stalled enough and went back in to face the fire. They were sitting down, Claudia sitting at the table for my mom, and my mom in one of the lounging chairs. My mom looked exhausted, but when she saw me, her face brightened up.

"Did you get the pages updated?"

"Mom, we can't pretend my husband is someone else." I sat down in one of the folding chairs. "I need to own this before I can move on. I've spent so much energy trying to hide, but I have to figure out how to deal with it now."

She and Claudia shared a look.

"Gracie, I'm sorry if I seemed judgmental earlier," Claudia apologized, sincerely. "It took me by surprise because I've been glued to the story on TV. And here you are in my store!"

"I know, and I've been avoiding people for this reason. I didn't know *anything* about what he was doing, but I'm so ashamed."

My mom sat up straighter. "What do you have to be ashamed about?"

I shook my head. "Nothing, but I feel like I should've seen something, just like Claudia said."

"Oh honey, we've been over this. What he did doesn't fit in with any reality of any kind, so how could you have seen something like this?"

"Again, I am sorry for my snap judgement. What he did was despicable, and he should be strung up by his you-know-what," Claudia chimed in.

My mom snorted. "Well, that about sums it up, and I'm pretty sure we're not the only ones who feel that way either."

We finished setting everything up before the fans arrived. I tried to stay out of the way, but be as helpful as possible. The nervous energy made me feel like I was in the newsroom again. I had forgotten what a rush it was to walk that fine line of being in charge, but at the mercy of someone else. It felt good.

When we left, Claudia unexpectedly wrapped me in a big hug. "Be strong," she whispered. Tears sprung to my eyes, and I nodded into her shoulder. As we separated, my mom smiled and winked at her.

"Claudia, I can't thank you enough for having me back every year."

"Oh nonsense. It's a privilege to have you here," she said. "And give Jeri my best. I'll make sure to send her a care package by the end of the week."

"She'd love that," my mom said, leaning in for one last hug. "Till next time…"

My mom was quiet on the way home. *Was my baggage getting to her?* She said it went well, but I hate she has to be associated with my drama. I didn't push her, because I couldn't do anything but apologize again.

Sometimes apologies just aren't enough.

Chapter Twelve

When we arrived home, my mom went straight to her room and I changed into running clothes.

My run felt amazing today. The clouds and cool air somehow mimicked my mood, letting me push myself into a faster pace than I normally take. I wanted to feel stronger with this run today.

On my way back, I heard the familiar dog bark alerting me Sadie was near. They were playing on the dunes, Sadie running up the sand hill to get the stick, then racing down back to Charlie. I slowed down to a walk, bringing my breathing back to normal. My forehead was slick with sweat and my shirt felt damp from running by the water. Why does he always see me at my worst?

He glanced my way and smiled. "Wow, that looks like you had some run." He stole a glance head to toe and quickly looked back down at Sadie. "So, how did it go with your mom today?"

I grabbed the stick from him and threw it up the dune. It flew out of sight and landed on the other side. Charlie cocked an eyebrow. I missed feeling strong.

"It went better than I anticipated, but the owner of the store recognized me. It upset my mom, although she wouldn't admit to that."

"Were there a lot of people there? I saw it on Facebook by the way. Nice picture."

"You're on Facebook?" I asked. "I had no idea."

"I think there's a lot of things you don't know about me," he replied, his eyes locked on mine. I remembered the first time Andrew looked at me that way. Like he was waiting to be noticed. My heart skipped a beat.

I looked away quickly, too quickly, and he went back to playing fetch. "Well, I should probably go in and get cleaned up," I said, unsure of what just happened.

He nodded, but the look was gone. I was Gordy's little sister again. "Do you have plans later?"

Do I tell him about Jimmy? It felt like I was going on a date, which it wasn't, but I didn't want Charlie to get the wrong idea.

"Actually, I do have plans," I said, vaguely.

"Well, if you want, I'll be working tonight. Sundays are slow, and I'd love the company."

I smiled, grateful he wasn't holding an awkward moment between us against me. "Well, if the plan falls through, I'll come by."

"Take care, Gracie."

I turned and walked across the patio and into the house. I slid my shoes off before going in, and tip-toed to the kitchen to watch Charlie from the window above the sink. Every now and then he would glance towards the house, but Sadie tugged on the leash

131

every time he stopped.

"Why didn't you stay out there with him if you're so interested?"

I jumped. "Why didn't you say something when I walked in? You scared me half to death!"

She was smiling now. "What? And ruin your spying?"

I took a final glance outside and noticed he was heading back to his car, head down. "I wasn't spying, for your information. I just wanted to make sure Sadie didn't follow me back to the house," I lied.

"Of course… it's Sadie you're looking out for. I had forgotten she was out there."

I poured myself a glass of water from the pitcher in the fridge and walked back to sit with my mom. "So, you're feeling better?"

She nodded. "I don't know why, but I was simply exhausted from this morning. I didn't sleep well last night, and I just needed to sit quietly for a moment."

I eyed her suspiciously.

"What? You run, I meditate. It's the same outcome."

I had to admit it made sense.

"I love to see the lightbulb go off in your head when something finally clicks with you," she said.

"I just never thought about it like that. I've tried to meditate and failed miserably. I can't sit still to save my life, but once I set myself in motion, I usually calm down."

She nodded. "I didn't think about it much until you came in from the rain yesterday. I couldn't understand how running in that weather could calm you down, but like you said, it's just weather. You needed to move to feel calmer."

"Exactly!" I sat back and relaxed deeper in the chair. "I feel like I just learned something about myself," I said.

"So, you want to own up to the fact that you were checking out Charlie, now that you're all enlightened?"

"I will own up to no such thing," I said, stubbornly. "Besides, last time I checked, he's still hung up on his failed marriage. I don't think he wants to get involved with someone with so much baggage."

"You really have blinders on if you believe that," she said. "He is very smitten with you. Both of them are. I know Jeri and I told you this, but you don't seem to be listening to us."

I took a deep breath and held it for a moment. All the good feelings I had were starting to feel like anxiety again. "Mom, I'm just not sure I want to be with anyone right now. Both of them are so sweet in their own ways, but breaking Charlie's heart would really send me over the edge."

"So you're not afraid of breaking Jimmy's heart? Or you don't think you will?"

"Honestly, I don't know. I just feel like Charlie is more fragile… more breakable. Jimmy just feels like a good time, and maybe that's why it's easier to be around him more right now. I don't see him as a long-term relationship kind of guy, and Charlie screams commitment." My mother listened to me, eyes genuinely interested in what I was saying. I don't remember her looking at me like that before. Ever.

"Well, the best thing is you don't have to make any choices right now. And if you do, you will be forgiven if they're the wrong ones because of your circumstances," she said.

"That's just it, bad choices will end up in someone getting hurt, and I don't want to risk that."

"But a life without risk isn't worth living," she said, getting up. "Taking risks means we still have a heart that cares. It's everything."

She walked to the kitchen and grabbed a coat from the hall closet. "I'm going to walk to the lighthouse and back."

I watched her go and scolded myself for letting her have the last word. Of course she was right, but there was no way I could break Charlie's heart knowingly. Jimmy would be fine, as he always is, but Charlie needed someone who could give him everything he deserved. Right now, I was not that girl, and the sooner he knew that the better. I would simply have to tell him the next time I saw him.

My phone rang as I was on my way up to shower and change for dinner. It was Jimmy.

"Hi Jimmy," I answered.

"Hey darlin'," he said. "How did your day go?"

I sat on my bed, cross-legged, like I did in high school. "It went well," I said, grinning like an idiot. "Surprisingly well."

"Huh, why surprisingly?"

"Oh, I don't know," I said. "I just didn't know what to think going into this. I've never even been to a book signing before, let alone help organize one."

"Well, I'm sure it was great. You still up for some entertainment tonight?"

"I'm not sure I'm up for entertainment, but I wouldn't mind hanging out tonight."

"Who says no to entertainment?"

"You have to remember I'm not the best company right now."

"Blah, blah, blah… just keep an open mind and dress warm."

Dress warm? "Are we cooking out?"

"Ah-ah-ah, no guessing," he said. "Besides, you'd never guess in a million years."

Dammit, I hate surprises. "Do you want me to meet you somewhere or what?"

"Actually, I'll be picking you up in about an hour if that's good with you," he said. "And don't eat anything. We'll have dinner too."

"Dinner and entertainment? This sounds interesting."

"You have no idea," he said. "See you in an hour."

I barely had time to shower, dress, and primp before he was here, ringing the doorbell. Still upstairs, I heard my mom answer the door. I couldn't hear what they were saying, but I did hear my mom giggle a couple times.

My mom doesn't giggle.

I finished up, wearing the same outfit I had on earlier, but grabbing my Northface coat to wear outside. They were chatting in the kitchen when I came down, and he turned when I came up behind him. His eyes grew wide, and he smiled.

"Well, you look… really good," he admired.

My mom bit her lip, and I blushed.

"Thanks, you too," I said.

He had on jeans, a blue plaid flannel button-down, and a navy pea coat. And he smelled divine, with just a hint of cologne. My stomach felt jittery, like right before a newscast I was producing. Nerves were jumping through my skin.

"Are you ready?" I asked.

"Yes! I was just catching up with your mom, but we can go." He sounded as nervous as I felt.

We headed out, saying goodbye to Mom, who was planning on visiting Jeri before she went into surgery tomorrow morning. She shooed us out the door and locked it behind us.

He opened the door of his pickup truck for me, and it smelled like him.

"Is your truck always this clean?" I asked when he settled behind the steering wheel.

"Not usually. I might have gone through the car wash today and spruced it up a bit."

The radio was set to a country station, and I could hear Kenny Chesney sing one of his early hits, one I hadn't heard since college.

"So," I said, "what big entertainment plans do you have for me tonight?"

He grinned and wiggled his eyebrows. "Well, you'll just have to be patient a little longer. It's not far from here."

We had turned onto Main Street, and looked like we were driving out of town. I tried to relax and just let the night go without getting too uptight. He turned right onto State Road, and then I saw it: the old ice rink.

"Oh no. No-no-no-no-no-no," I pleaded. "Please tell me we are not going skating." He played hockey as a kid and was on the high school team.

He laughed as he pulled into the empty parking lot. "Oh, my dear, yes we are." He parked in front of the entrance, but it looked dark inside.

"But they look closed!" I don't care what my mom said, I wasn't up for this kind of risk.

"That's why Jeff gave me the keys this morning. They're closed on Sundays for the summer and he trusted me with the building."

I sat in the truck, refusing to get out. "I don't think I can do it," I said.

"Suck it up, buttercup. We're going skating."

"But I have weak ankles. I can't skate."

"Says the girl who runs three miles a day."

"How about I just keep my shoes on, and you can show me all your hockey moves?"

He had walked around the truck to open my door and was waiting for me now. "Oh, I'll show you my hockey moves all right, but you'll most certainly have skates on."

I bit my lip, arms crossed.

"While you look adorable sitting there being all stubborn, I will hoist you over my shoulder if I have to," he said, laughing. "Let's go, chicken."

Nobody calls me a chicken. I slid down the seat until my feet hit the ground. He didn't budge. He wiggled his eyebrows again, but I stood my ground waiting for him to move. When my eyes met his, my stomach did a flip-flop.

"Ready?" he whispered.

I nodded, not trusting my voice. He had a duffle bag over one shoulder, a cooler with him in one hand, and he grabbed a different set of keys out of his pocket as we walked to the front doors. After letting us in, he locked us inside.

The lobby was dark but we could still see from the row of lights left on in the rink. It was quiet and peaceful, but not much warmer than it was outside. If the lobby was this cold, what was the rink like?

He walked through the office door like he owned the joint and flipped on one set of lights in the lobby.

"What size shoe are you?"

"Eight," I said.

"Hockey or figure skates?"

"Are you really going to make me do this?"

"Hockey it is then."

"No! I've never worn hockey skates. I want figure skates," I said.

"Excellent choice. You sit there on the bench, and I'll bring them right out." A few minutes later he came out with my skates and two hot chocolates.

"Here, have some hot chocolate. It'll calm your nerves."

I took a sip and tasted Bailey's in the mix. It was strong but delicious. A warmth immediately spread through my chest. He took a sip of his own drink and walked back to the office. A moment later Rascal Flatts filled the lobby.

"Dare I say you almost look relaxed?" He sat down on the bench next to me and took a sip of his own drink.

"It's the Bailey's, although I'm not sure we should be drinking and skating."

"Would I get you on the ice without it?"

"Not a chance," I said, taking another sip. "You still might not."

He turned to face me. "When was the last time you did something that scared you?"

"Last week. I packed everything I needed and left my husband."

His shoulders slumped. "I'm sorry. I didn't mean to dredge up crappy feelings." He kept looking at me, but I just stared at my feet.

"I know running away seems like the easiest thing to do, but every day I wake up and remember why I'm at my mom's house. It's like trying to let go of something that you loved, knowing you'll never have it again."

"Wow, do I suck at this whole cheering you up thing," he said, shaking his head. "Look, if you just want to go back to your mom's and hang out, that's fine with me. I just wanted to get your mind off it for a night, and, well…"

"No, we are not going home," I said, interrupting him. "You didn't dredge up anything. *I* did. And I thought you were going to teach me how to skate."

We sat, facing each other on those old carpeted benches. If I didn't feel like I was in high school earlier, I did now. He reached for my hand and raised his eyebrows to see if it was okay. His eyes locked on mine. My heart was racing, and my mind could only think about kissing him.

He smiled. "My, my, my, I do believe you're thinking impure thoughts right now." His voice was raspy and came out more of a whisper. "Do you know the sexiest moment is always that anticipation of the first kiss?"

I nodded, knowing he had me when he took my hand.

"Well, we're going to prolong this moment, because there is no way I'm kissing you before you get on the ice."

What?

"Now I know you are going through a range of emotions since you got back. As much as I'd like to take advantage of that, I'm not going to. Tonight is about getting you out of your head and doing something completely different."

I shook my head in embarrassment and took my hand back. "I'm sorry, I don't know what came over me," I said, turning away from him. "You're right, I am going through so many emotions and I really should just stay focused on getting my life back together."

"Don't go pulling away from me," he scolded, playfully. He knelt down in front of me, resting his elbows on my knees. "For the first time in my life I don't want to rush anything and ruin something that feels really good right now. I don't want to scare you away."

I wasn't sure what came over me, but I put my hands on either side of his face, leaned in until our lips were almost touching. His breathing quickened, and I relished the feeling of being that close to him.

"So you think this is the sexiest part?"

He nodded, his eyes were darting between my eyes and lips.

"Well okay then," I whispered, pulling away. "I just wanted to make sure."

His head fell in my lap while he laughed. "Woman, you have a mean streak in you."

"And don't you forget that."

"Trust me, I won't," he said, getting up. He sat back down and started to take his shoes off. "Let's go. My lesson rate is probably more than you can afford, and you're wasting time."

Picking up one of the skates, I wondered how many other people had had their feet in them.

"Best not to think about all those feet. Just slide them on," he said. "Let's go. Chop chop."

He stood in front of me with his skates on. I took my time tying them, trying to stall every last minute of peace that I could. Once they were both tied, I stood up and felt both of my ankles being squeezed. "Jeez-louise, these are uncomfortable. Don't they have softer ones?"

He rolled his eyes and grabbed my hand. "Let's go already."

I followed him through the set of double doors that led to the rink. The music was on out here as well, but was quieter. With only one set of lights on, it was so dark and peaceful, and I could see my breath. I tightened my grip on his hand as he stepped onto the ice.

His eyes lit up. "Are you ready?"

I shook my head no.

"C'mon, give me your other hand. I promise not to let go."

I gave him my other hand and felt stiff as a statue.

"Just try to relax a little. You look so uptight," he said. "And just try to keep your feet closer to each other. Don't let them slide away."

The ice was so smooth, and with the music and cold air, it felt like a winter night. It was magical.

"Let's try to just move in a general direction together," he suggested. "Give me your hand again." I did, and we started to head towards the end of the rink. There was a digital clock on the score board giving off a glowing red light, but it was dark otherwise. I just kept taking steps and clung to his hand like I was going to fall. He peeled his hand away from mine and started to skate circles around me, literally. I held my feet still but they kept moving out of my control.

"So, tell me, Dunham... what do you think of skating?"

Gliding to a stop, I attempted to relax my back muscles and stand still. "I think I have a new appreciation for hockey players now," I said. "I don't know how you do it."

He had skated away from me but was quickly coming back towards at me now. I closed my eyes and braced myself for an impact. Instead, I heard a *whoosh*, and when I opened my eyes he was standing there, close. He wrapped his arms around my waist. I had chills down to there, and buried my face in his shirt. Eric Church was singing quietly, and we began swaying with the music.

"I think what we're doing would be an insult to any ice dancers," I whispered. He finally pulled away from me and held both hands with a gleam in his eye.

"Do you trust me?"

I was shaking my head no, yelling for him to stop, but he started to skate backwards. Slow at first with my resistance, but then he built up speed, and soon I was just hanging on for dear life. The sound of my laughter echoed through the rink, and I was flying down the ice with him. The rush of air made my eyes water until tears were streaming down my cheeks.

He stopped us quickly, and I felt his arms circle me. I didn't have time to react as he put one hand lightly on either side of my face and kissed me. It was light at first, just a brushing of lips, and when I didn't stop him, he pulled me in a little tighter. Weak in the knees, I clung to his waist.

If I were blindfolded, I'd know these weren't Andrew's lips. I dreamed of this moment every night in high school and now, ten years later, here I was... kissing Jimmy Darnell... in an ice rink.

Linny was going to die.

I broke the kiss and pushed him back. "Whoa," I

blurted. He dropped his hands and reached for mine again to keep me balanced. "What happened to 'just getting my mind off things for a night?'"

"Whoa is right," he said. "How come we never did that in high school?"

"Because you were too busy kissing all the other girls," I teased.

He cringed. "Was I that bad?"

"You know you were," I said.

He looked down at our hands. "Let's skate, or I'm going to keep kissing you to shut you up." He tugged and pulled me along again.

"Can we keep the speeding to a minimum from here on out?"

He let go of one hand so we were both just skating along, hand in hand. "Is this okay? I don't want this to be your first and last time skating with me."

I smiled at the thought of coming back with him. "I give you no promises, but yes, this is better." We skated along while the music played for us, and even though I knew I was slower than what he was used to, he seemed pleasantly relaxed. "Do you still skate a lot?"

"During the fall and winter I play every Sunday night. Our team isn't very good, but we have a lot of fun," he said. "And after the games we go to Lakeside and tear it up a bit. Boys being boys."

Gordy and Charlie were like that in high school. Andrew was never a guy's guy and didn't seem to have many friends. We had a few couples we'd hang out with once a month or so, but no one too close. I thought of Linny again and couldn't wait to call her when I got home.

Smiling, he lifted my hand and kissed it.

I hadn't had this much fun in a long time. "In case I forget to tell you later, thank you."

"Believe me when I say, it's been my pleasure," he said, looking up at the digital clock. "It's almost time for dinner though. You hungry?"

I was starving and not afraid to say so.

"Well, let's get our skates off. I have pizza coming in a few minutes."

"They're bringing it *here*?"

"Yup, and I brought a few beers so we could make it a meal," he said, leading me off the ice.

"It seems you thought of everything," I said. Andrew would never have thought of a date like this in a million years.

Sure enough, as soon as we got our skates off, there was a knock at the entrance doors. He didn't have his shoes on yet, but he went to get the pizza in his socks.

He set the box down in the middle of our bench and went to get his cooler and napkins, still shoeless. I tried not to think of the dirt getting on his socks.

We ate, picnic style, on the bench talking easily about everything: how my day went, how afraid I was to fail my mother, his fear of owning Lakeside, and various people from high school and what they were doing.

"That was so good," I said. "I haven't had pizza in a while. Thank you for keeping this low-key."

"Well, I'm glad you enjoyed it," he said. "And I hope I was able to take your mind off life for a while." He closed the box, one slice left, and threw it in one of the garbage containers in the lobby. I took one last drink of my Bud Light and set the bottle down.

"I have to admit I was pretty skeptical when we got here, but it really was fun. Definitely a night to remember."

"Good, that's what I was going for," he said. "What time is surgery tomorrow?"

"I think she has to be there at seven to go over all the pre-surgery prep. My mom wanted to be there with her all day, so I figured someone needs to be there for my mom too."

He gave me a lopsided smile. "I know this isn't how you planned your life, but your mom has to be so glad you're home right now."

I was starting to believe this was where I was supposed to be, but found myself missing the old me. The anxiety and nerves tonight were a blatant reminder of work in the news room.

He grabbed my hand on our way out, and it seemed as natural as breathing. The drive home was quiet and he opened his window a crack to let cool air in his truck. He was silent, and I didn't want to force any conversation. I just wanted to enjoy a few more minutes with him. My mind kept looping back to Charlie, and wondering what he would have thought about tonight. Sure there were a couple kisses and some serious flirting, but Jimmy has always been like this. I'm not sure he ever did relationships for very long, so I wasn't going to get hung up on this.

We pulled up in front of my mom's house and he put the truck in park.

"What are you grinning at now? Every time I look over you're smiling," he chuckled.

"You say that as if it were a bad thing," I said. "I had fun tonight… more fun than I've had in a long time."

"All part of my master plan." He got out to walk me up to the front door. I found my keys in my purse as we walked up.

"So, thank you again for… everything," I said. I leaned in and brushed my lips against his cheek, and he smiled. He reached for my fingers and brought them up to his lips, keeping his eyes on mine.

My heart began beating out of my chest.

"Call or text tomorrow and let me know how it's going," he said. "I have to open, but I could stop in and bring coffee if you wanted."

"I'll keep you posted." I wanted to stand out here with him all night. Reluctantly, I opened the door. "Sweet dreams Jimmy."

He stood there looking at me through the glass,

faint smile on his face. I locked the door, shut the lights off in the kitchen, and peeked out the front window to see if he was still out there. He waved to me as he pulled away from the driveway, red taillights getting smaller and smaller.

Sleep would be elusive tonight.

Chapter Thirteen

The air was calm tonight, eerily still, and the lake appeared glass-like. I sat here for an hour, maybe longer, and hadn't notice a single wave. Every so often, a fish would jump and plunk back into the water causing ripples, but otherwise it was flat.

My mom was sleeping upstairs after I insisted she take a Xanax this afternoon. The doctor, pale and direct, wasn't completely sure what had happened in surgery. His guess was a cardiac arrest or an allergic reaction to the anesthesia. They were going to do an autopsy to find the cause of death.

I was on the outside looking in, watching everyone's reaction but not feeling anything myself. My mom collapsed on the waiting room floor, falling to her knees as if she had forgotten she was standing up at all, and I had been trying to pick up the pieces ever since. Jeri's son, Peter, was also there with his girlfriend, thinking this was just a routine surgery to remove the lump and checking the lymph nodes. In a matter of months Peter had become an orphan.

I had taken the reins and made an executive decision to cancel all of my mother's classes for the week. She had another book signing for the coming weekend in Charlavoix, and I canceled that too. The owner of the store was heartbroken and gave us her best.

I sat outside, sipping the remainder of a cabernet, and I let the tears slide down my face without wiping them away. Thoughts ran through my head about this morning and the past few weeks. Snippets of images rushed through my mind.

Me collapsing in Tim's office.

My mom falling to her knees.

Charlie's look yesterday on the beach.

Peter's face today while his girlfriend wept beside him. It was blank, not comprehending the words being said.

Visiting Andrew in jail.

Seeing the girls on the news, each of them prettier and younger than the next.

My mind went to the dark corners, reminding me how alone I was. The images kept rolling, and I couldn't stop them. I embraced it like it was a blanket, wrapping it around my shoulders. I leaned forward, resting my head in my hands, and sobbed. Coming here was supposed to be helping me, and life was falling apart all over again.

I heard footsteps coming close and felt two hands lift me up into a hug. I knew it was Charlie before I opened my eyes, and a part of me had been waiting for him, wanting him to hold me until I felt normal again. He just kept stroking my hair whispering it was all going to be okay. Over and over again. "Shhhh…

It's going to be okay…"

The more he said it, the harder I cried. I couldn't stop and wanted to cry until I was empty of all these tears that have plagued me since I arrived. He held me so tightly my feet were barely on the ground. In that moment, I didn't want to be with anyone else. Charlie understood what I was feeling and knew what I needed. I would carry this moment in my memory forever.

Feeling empty, he slowly released me, but kept me close. I notice several bags on the table from Lakeside that he had brought with him.

"You brought food?" My voice was scratchy and hoarse.

"It's the least we could do," he said quietly. "Can I get you something to eat?"

I sat down heavily and sighed. "I don't know what I want," I sniffled. "But I'm not hungry right now. I've probably had too much wine."

A sad smile played on his lips. "Well, you have to eat something. I'll just get you a couple things to pick at." He grabbed both bags and took them inside. A few minutes later he came out setting down a small plate of cheese and crackers and joined me at the table.

I knew I was going to regret it in the morning, but I reached for my wine instead of the food. Somehow, I didn't think cheese and crackers were going to help me feel better.

"Is your mom okay?" He kept his eyes on mine the whole time.

"I finally forced a Xanax on her and sent her to bed a few hours ago," I said. "I imagine she'll be up soon."

"And Peter? How is he going to handle this?"

I shook my head. "He has lost both parents within a few months. I can't imagine what he's going to do now."

Time passed as we sat there in a thick silence. I stared the water even though it was so dark the water looked black. I could feel Charlie's eyes on me. The lapping of the water should've been calming, but I wanted to scream at the top of my lungs and make it all go away.

I set my wine down, unfinished, and stood. I walked off the patio and across the sidewalk towards the beach. The sand was cold between my toes, and it felt good for my legs to be moving after a day of sitting.

"Gracie…" he yelled after me. "Don't go out there."

Ignoring him, I kept walking, a clear path to the water. Suddenly, I stopped and turned to him.

"Why?" I screamed at the top of my lungs, the screech of my own voice foreign to me.

He jumped up and ran towards me. I turned and ran away from him, knowing he could never catch me. I didn't want to be caught and shushed.

I knelt down in the water and screamed again,

shaking from the freezing lake. Charlie was lifting me up within seconds and carrying me back to the sand where he set me down and held me again. I buried my face in his chest and screamed again, my entire body shivering. To his credit, he held me tight and didn't try to quiet me.

"Let's go," he whispered. "You're going to freeze out here." He reached down, picking me up and cradled me into his chest. I wrapped my arms around his neck and leaned into him. My mom was watching from the kitchen window.

He set me down once we got inside and went to hug my mom. I left them to go change into something dry and warm. I couldn't bear to see my mom break down again. I changed and brushed my teeth.

When I came back down they were both sitting at the bar, talking. He stood when he heard me. "Well, I need to get back to Lakeside," he said, walking over to me. He leaned down and pressed his lips on my forehead, whispering he'd see me tomorrow.

I didn't move from the spot, even when he walked through the door. I wanted to stop him and ask him to stay, but I didn't have the right, and I needed to help my mom now.

"Are you okay?" she asked me. I just looked at her, thinking I should be the one asking her.

I shook my head, "I'm fine." I went to the refrigerator and grabbed a bottle of water. "Can I get you something? Charlie brought so much food."

She just stared out the window from where she was. "I'm good. Not really hungry."

I took the barstool next to her and sat. I reached for her hand resting on the table, and she squeezed my fingers. "What on earth am I going to do without her?" she whispered.

We eyed one another when the garage door came to life. "Mom, who knows the garage code other than us?"

Dazed, she shook her head. The door opened to the kitchen, and in walked my brother Gordy. He had gained a few pounds since I saw him last, but on his six-foot-one frame, he still looked lean. He hadn't shaved and sported a Detroit Tigers baseball hat on backwards.

"Oh Gordy," my mom cried. She got up to hug him. He closed his eyes, holding my mom tight. She wrapped her arms around his neck and didn't look like she was ever going to let go. "What are you doing here?"

"Jeez Ma, did you think I wouldn't be here?" He looked in the fridge and grabbed a beer. "Jeri was part of the family." He took a long drink as if he hadn't had anything to drink in days. "Charlie called me this morning."

I walked over to hug my brother whom I hadn't seen in over a year. He held me tight. "You holding up okay?" he whispered in my ear. "I know these last few weeks have been shitty."

I smiled at the simple understatement. "I'm okay," I whispered back, even though we both knew it was a lie. Mom needed to be our main priority now.

"Let's sit where it's more comfortable," my mom suggested, leading us into the family room. I grabbed my water and Gordy grabbed his beer. "I can't believe you're both here."

Gordy sat next to mom, and I sat in the oversized chair across from them. Rumi immediately jumped in my lap and started to purr, circling to find a comfortable spot.

"Well, I was planning on next weekend, but when I heard the news this morning I knew I needed to be here. Cindy was fine with it, and I'm just taking my vacation days early." He took another drink and set his beer on the coaster.

"Did you check in with Peter? Do we know if he's okay?" my mom asked.

"I called over there about five thirty and he was waiting for his aunt to come into town," I explained. "He said people had been bringing food over all day and wondered if we wanted any of it."

My mom shook her head. "God no, we have enough from what Charlie brought over."

The doorbell rang and I dumped Rumi on the floor. Peeking out the window I saw it was Linny holding a giant rectangular white box.

I opened the door and pulled her into a side hug. Her eyes were wet. "I just can't believe it," she said, walking into the kitchen and setting the box down on the bar. "How's your mom?" she whispered.

I nodded towards the couch where she and Gordy were, and her eyes widened. "Gordy…"

He jumped up and came around to hug Linny.

Since when are they so close? She broke the hug and went to sit with my mom who looked too exhausted to greet her. Linny put her arm around her shoulders and my mom leaned into her. I had the distinct feeling of being on the outside looking in, but I was so physically and mentally overwhelmed it didn't even matter.

While the three of them caught up, I went to the kitchen to get some Motrin and noticed my phone buzzing on the counter. It was a Lansing area code, and I thought it might be the detective in charge of Andrew's case. As soon as I answered and heard the recording from the prison, my heart sank.

I snuck out the front door and sat on the porch swing, trying to stay out of earshot of my mother and Gordy.

"Gracie? Are you there?" He sounded breathless.

"Dammit Andrew, I told you not to call."

He paused, hearing my voice. "I… uh…" he stuttered. "I got some news today, and I just wanted you to know."

As soon as I heard his tone, I knew it was going to be more bad news.

"Well," he continued. "Sarah, the one who is

pregnant... well, they did a prenatal paternity test, and I was a positive match."

"*What*?" I snapped. My heart began beating rapidly. I knew I heard him correctly, but my brain wasn't processing it properly. "*What*?" I said louder.

"The baby is mine. It was positive," he repeated. "I just wanted you to know before it was on the news tomorrow morning."

I started to shake. "How could you do this? How did this ever happen Andrew?"

It was the one question I had never asked him and now I wanted to know. I wanted to know why he ruined our lives.

"Gracie, please. I don't know, it just happened." His voice cracked, full of guilt.

"*Accidents* just happen, Andrew," I said, raising my voice. "Getting young girls pregnant is a pretty fucking deliberate."

"Please, please forgive me, Gracie. Please," he begged.

"I wouldn't even begin to know how," I said. "Don't call me again." I hung up with the sound of him calling my name. I knew this would be the last nail in his coffin. I shook my head at the insanity of what my life had become.

The door opened and Linny peeked her head out. "There you are," she said, coming out and sitting down on the swing with me. "What's going on? You look like you've seen a ghost."

I nodded slowly. "I wish that were all it was."

"Uh-oh, what happened?"

I sighed. "Andrew called."

"*And...?*"

"He called about the young girl who's pregnant. They did a paternity test, and the baby is his. It was positive," I said.

She had been holding her breath and blew the air out in one whoosh. "Oh fuck." She tipped her head back. "Jesus Gracie, what the fuck kind of day is this?"

I shrugged and looked over at her with tears in my eyes. A fat tear rolled down my cheek, and she pulled me into a hug.

"Just when you think a day can't get worse, this happens," she said. "What can I do? Do you want me to spend the night? My mom is with the kids, she can stay."

"No, no, no. You don't need to spend the night, but I don't want to tell Mom tonight. Can you just keep this under your hat?"

"I can, but I imagine the news will be all over this tomorrow."

"I know, that's why he wanted me to know before tomorrow morning. He was 'doing me a favor.'"

She barked out a laugh. "That fucker. He's lucky I don't go down there and cut his balls off."

I giggled and wiped my eyes. "Let's go back inside before my mom knows something is up." I stood up and slid my phone in my pocket of my sweatshirt.

She didn't get up right away, but just looked at me. "In case you didn't know this already, you are quite possibly the bravest person I know." She stood. "And don't think for a second you're not going to tell me about your date last night."

I smiled through the tears but didn't say anything.

"Oh. My. God. Something happened, didn't it?"

I shrugged again and opened the front door. "Maybe," I said, letting her follow me into the kitchen. Gordy eyed both of us carefully.

"Why don't I put some of this food on the table and we try to eat something?" Linny said, unwrapping the trays Charlie had brought over. She reached for a platter in the cupboard and started loading it with food.

"That's a good idea, Linn," Gordy said. "I'm actually starving now. C'mon Mom, let's eat something." He grabbed her by both hands and pulled her off the couch. They both came over and sat down at the table.

Mom mostly picked at the food. Conversation was light, and Linny and Gordy did their best to make sure we didn't go into anything about Jeri or Andrew. We talked about Gordy and Linny's kids, one story funnier than the last, each of them trying to prove themselves to be unfit parents. After about an hour, my mom started to yawn, and I suggested she go back up and try to sleep. Thankfully she agreed, but insisted on getting fresh bedding out for Gordy in his room.

"Just leave it on the bed, Ma. I can make it myself," he reassured her. She nodded and kissed each of us on the head before going up, even Linny.

Linny went to the freezer and took out a bottle of Absolut. She held it up and Gordy immediately nodded yes.

"I had too much wine earlier and I think I'm hungover now," I said.

"Even more reason," she said, grabbing three tumblers from the cupboard.

"How do you know where everything is in this house? I didn't even know she had vodka," I said.

She poured three shots and passed them out. Gordy slammed his down and then Linny did the same, both of them looking at me, eyebrows raised.

I shook my head. "I really don't want any right now."

"Are either one of you going to tell me what was going on earlier when you were on the porch?"

Linny and I shared a look, and I nodded for her to tell him. I was exhausted from my own story.

"Well, Andrew called Gracie to tell her he's going to be a proud papa," Linny said sardonically, pouring them more shots.

Gordy's eyes widened. "The baby's *his*?" I nodded. "That sonofabitch," he swore. "Why didn't you say something?"

"Mom doesn't need more drama in her life, in case you didn't notice," I said. "Besides, I just want to forget he even called tonight." I picked at one of the oatmeal cookies Linny brought over. It reminded me of sitting with Jeri at Bab's. "Look, I am just going to bed. I'm sorry, I can't sit and think about this day anymore," I said.

We said our goodbyes, and I promised Linny I'd call in the morning. I thought Linny would leave, but she was sitting back down as I headed up the stairs. I couldn't wait to crawl into bed and wait for the sound of water carry me off to sleep. I hugged my pillow, thinking of Charlie. I wanted him to be here, holding me again, telling me everything was going to be all right.

Would I ever feel that safe again?

Part Two

"The secret to change is to focus all of your energy, not on fighting the old, but on building the new."

Julia Dunham,
A Mother's Guide to Living

Chapter Fourteen

Step 1: Let Go of the Past

The beauty of going to bed with a hangover is feeling completely normal the next day. I had a dream about Jeri. We sat together on the patio, drinking a glass of champagne and smiling. The sky lit up in pink and orange as the sun set into the lake. I woke up feeling like a different person, stronger.

The sun was shining, and even the waves were back to normal, crashing on the shore. I threw on some running clothes and couldn't wait to get on the beach.

My mom was watching the news, mouth gaping, as I entered the kitchen. She quickly powered off the TV when she heard me, but I raised my hand to stop her.

"I already know. He called me last night," I said.

"What? Well why didn't you tell me?"

"I thought letting you sleep with only one tragedy on your mind was enough."

She shook her head. "What is going to happen to him now?"

"Well, he's looking at ten to twenty-five years as far as I can tell from researching it online," I said. "I'm sure this news won't help him at sentencing."

She shook her head again. "I just can't believe it. I mean I knew he had done those things, but this makes it so much worse."

"Well, I'm going for a run to clear my head," I said, slipping by her to kiss her cheek. "How are you today, by the way. Did you sleep okay?"

"Yes, but I woke up at five and couldn't sleep. I've been down here wondering who will handle all the arrangements this week."

"I'll call Peter when I get back and find out what's going on. I know Jeri's sister was coming to town yesterday, so maybe she will? If not, you and I can help with whatever they need."

My mom eyed me suspiciously. "You seem different this morning. I thought this news would break you."

Opening the door, I smiled at her. "Well maybe I'm more like you than we thought." A small smile crossed her lips as I closed the door behind me.

Just as I suspected, the run was empowering. I looked at the spot where Charlie held me screaming last night, and knew the week would be tough – but I was tougher. There's something to be said for facing your problems head on instead of running away from them. Despite the chill this morning, I was sweating hard by the time I got back. I had seen the sunshine reflecting on the water a million times, but this morning it stopped me in my tracks. A cool breeze blew through me as I took in the scenery with fresh eyes.

Thank you, Jeri.

My mom was sitting with Gordy in the kitchen, both drinking coffee and watching the news. "Gracie, did you ever call Officer Marks?"

"No, I didn't," I admitted, getting a glass for water. "I didn't feel like getting into that yesterday."

Gordy stared at his coffee. "Gracie, I really am sorry about all this mess," he said. "Is there anything I can do?"

"Nope. I talked to him last night and made it clear that he didn't need to call me anymore," I took a long drink of water, gulping it down. "I just want to focus on moving forward at this point." They both raised their eyebrows at me.

"Gracie, it's like you woke up a different person today. What on earth is going on?"

"Step one: let go of the past," I said, smirking.

"Oh Good God," she said. "Please don't tell me you're going to start listening to me *now*."

Gordy chuckled. "I don't know Ma, she does seem a little different this morning."

I poured a cup of coffee and pulled up a barstool on the other side to face them. I clinked mugs with him. "Thanks Gordo," I said.

"I just think it's a little too much for you to just let go of, don't you think?" She stood up to dump her coffee in the sink. "I mean, you're just going to let go of the past few weeks and move forward like it didn't happen?"

I opened her book that was laying on the bar and

flipped to the quote I had highlighted. "*Maybe the past is like an anchor holding us back. Maybe you have to let go of who you were to become who you will be,*" I imitated my mom. Gordy erupted in laughter.

"Oh, well of course, let's just base everything on a quote I found from *Sex and the City*. Carrie Bradshaw would be so proud," she quipped. "I just think it's going to be more difficult than you think to just let go of the past."

"And I don't have blinders on, Mom. I know this is an uphill battle, but I'm tired of running away and hiding," I said. "I thought you'd be happy."

"I am, we both are," she said. "But healing is a process, and I feel like you're just thinking it's going to be onward and upward. Have you gone through the whole chapter? Are you prepared to do the exercises in them?"

I took a deep breath. "Yes, I have, and while I'm not looking forward to writing all the stuff down, I am going to do it. And one of these nights we'll have a little bonfire and watch it go up in flames."

"Oh I'd love a bonfire. Can we invite people?" Gordy asked.

"Of course, the more the merrier," I said.

She pursed her lips and shook her head slightly. I would've thought she'd do back flips knowing I was actually going to follow her advice for a change.

Gordy broke the tension, "So, how 'bout them

Tigers?"

I smiled, thankful he was here. "Well, they blew the series against Boston."

"Yeah, but Boston is hot right now," he said. "They can't keep that up all season."

"I hope so. They started off well, but lost some easy games in the last week. And at home too. What's gonna happen when we go on the road this week?"

My mom had wiped down the counter and waited for us to finish. "I'm going for a stroll," she said sliding into her flip-flops. "Anyone want to join me?"

"I'll go with ya Ma," Gordy said. "Let me refill my coffee."

"I'll call Peter while you're out and see what the plans are for Jeri." My mom's shoulders drooped at the sound of Jeri's name.

"Will you see if there is anything we can get them?"

"Of course I will," I promised.

"Whatever they need, I don't care the expense," she said.

She and my brother left and the house seemed quiet. Too quiet. I grabbed my phone and dialed Charlie's number.

"Good morning, sunshine," he answered.

"You must have erased last night from your memory."

"You are allowed one breakdown per disaster, so I think you were just catching up," he said, smiling. "I'm just glad I was there to help you. Swimming in

April isn't for wimps."

"Yeah, the water was a little chilly."

"I think our definitions of chilly are vastly different," he said. "I've never been in the water before June, just so you know."

"Well, I'm sorry you had to break that rule for me. It won't happen again. But I did call to thank you again for rescuing me last night."

"Yeah, next time you're SOL, I'm staying dry."

"Please. If I went in again today, you'd come in with me," I said, smiling.

He sighed. "You're probably right, but let's just stay on the beach."

"Deal," I said. "Hey, did you know Gordy was coming to town? I wish you had said something."

"I did, but he wanted me to keep it on the down-low in case Cindy had an issue with it. He texted me last night and said all seemed to be well," he said. "And then I turn on the news this morning and all hell has broken loose again."

"Yeah, Andrew called me last night to warn me about the baby."

"As if the affairs weren't enough, now *this*?"

"I know, I know. He should have it cut off," I said. "Or at least dip it in acid."

He gasped. "You have a mean streak in you I didn't see before."

I chuckled. "Yeah, some of my thoughts even scare me a bit."

"Duly noted," he said. "So, not to change this enlightened topic, but how are things with Jeri's family? Have they done an autopsy yet?"

"I haven't heard, but I'm calling over there soon. I think Mom is a little anxious about not being in the loop, but Peter would've called if he had heard anything by now."

"Probably, but you have to remember he's just a kid," he said. "And a kid with no parents now."

I sighed, knowing how hard it was going to be for him. "I know Mom was already planning on making sure he knew he was a part of our family too."

"Life is crazy, isn't it?" he said. "One day everything is normal, and the next, everything's different."

"I know. I feel like someone is trying to tell me something," I said. He was silent on the other end. "Hey, are you okay?"

"Yeah, just thinking about how much we've all lost in the past couple months," he said.

"If you don't have to work this morning, why don't you come over? I know Gordy would love to see you."

"Jimmy is opening, so maybe I will. Do you guys need anything?"

"We're all set. After you and Linny, there's more food than we know what to do with."

"Ok, I'll be over with Sadie soon," he said. "She is in need of some beach time."

"Perfect day for it then," I said. "See you soon, Charlie."

"Later," he said, before disconnecting.

The memory of last night wandered into my brain again. I've never been the knight-in-shining-armor kind of girl, but today I can see the allure. I'm not sure I ever felt that safe in Andrew's arms – not that I ever let myself break down with him. I always needed to be the strong one.

I shook my thoughts loose and dialed Jeri's home number. My heart raced as I waited for Peter to pick up. He answered on the third ring.

"Hey Peter, it's Gracie."

"Oh, hi Gracie," he replied, his voice heavy with exhaustion. "I'm glad you called. I just got off the phone with Dr. Gray, and they got the results from the autopsy."

"Oh," I said. "What did he say?"

"He said that even with the extensive pre-op testing, she had an allergic reaction to the anesthesia. He's sending the results of all tests to a hospital in Lansing to find the missing link."

"Oh Peter, I am so sorry," I said. We lost her due to a mistake. "Is there anything you need?"

"Well, they released her body, so we're going to the funeral home at two today. Would you and your mom want to be there with us? I think it's something my mom would have wanted."

"Of course," I said. "Is your aunt there?"

"Yes," he said. "She got in last night and is a total disaster."

"Well, maybe we can help with her too. Bring her today, since she'll want to be part of the arrangements this week."

"I know, she was already planning on it. I have to warn you though, she's a little pushy."

"Oh Peter, have you met my mother?"

"You're right," he said, sounding relieved. "I know your mom will take care of everything. I just hate that she's already wanting to call lawyers to sue the hospital over this. I mean, my mom is barely gone twenty-four hours and her sister is already making waves."

I sighed and rubbed my eyes. "Listen, focus on what your mom would have wanted and leave the rest alone. Let us handle your aunt today."

"I will," he said, sounding more hopeful. "I don't know what I'd do without you."

"Okay, we'll see you at two. Hayes Funeral Home?"

"Yes, she will arrive there this morning," his voice cracked. "Thanks again for everything, Grace."

I poured another cup of coffee and turned on James Taylor. I understood the pull his voice had over my mom. It was soothing, and the lyrics were like a balm. Maybe that was how my mom felt too.

Charlie said it best... life certainly was a crazy thing.

Chapter Fifteen

At 1:30 we headed over to Hayes Funeral Home to meet with the funeral director before Peter and Jeri's sister, Terese, arrived. My mom wanted to make sure all of the arrangements were paid, so Peter wouldn't have to worry about them. Once we were done, we were given bottles of water and asked to wait until Peter and Terese arrived.

At 2:10 they walked in, Peter scowling. "We would've been here sooner, but she wouldn't get off the phone," he said. "I am so sorry."

My mom stood and wrapped him in a hug. I turned away as he broke down into sobs.

"So, should we get this show on the road?" Terese asked. My mom didn't respond, and I shot her a look.

The director came out with more bottles of water.

My mom peeled Peter off and they turned in his direction. "I know this is such a difficult time, but we really need to handle a few details this afternoon. If you could follow me," he said, turning towards the main showing room. "This is where we will have the visitations and where she will rest before the funeral."

Terese gave a low whistle. "This is some big room," she said. "Are you sure we need all this space?"

My mother's eyes narrowed. "Regardless of what

you think of your sister, she was a beloved part of this community and I anticipate this room will be filled to capacity."

"I was just saying," she snapped. "I'm not sure how Pete here is going to foot the bill for all this."

"Let me assure you that Peter will not have to worry about a thing," Mom said.

Terese frowned as if she was sucking on a lemon. My mother stared, challenging her. The air was thick with tension.

The director cleared his throat and continued walking again back to the lobby to his office. "So, we will need to go over a few details about her life for the obituary. Would you all have a seat?"

His office was enormous, more like a waiting room than anything else. Several large leather chairs were facing his desk, and there were chairs lining the walls. We each took one of the leather chairs closest to his desk. He opened his laptop and began typing immediately.

"So, I have some details from the hospital about your mother," he said, speaking to Peter. "But I'd like to gather some personal information so we can recognize what an amazing person she was."

We all nodded at him so he continued. He peppered us with questions, with a reporter-like quality, and continued to type our answers out as we spoke. My mom and Peter answered most of the questions as Terese sat, looking annoyed. After about ten minutes he told us to relax a moment while he finished up. He then read to us the obituary that would appear in the paper the next morning. It never occurred to me that this was how it was done. I'm twenty-eight years old, have been in the news industry for five years, and I never knew how an obituary came to be. At one point, he spoke of my mother, calling her Jeri's special friend and co-worker. My mom stopped him mid-sentence.

"You make it sound like we're, uhhh, more than just friends," my mother said, blushing. "We were lifelong friends, best friends, even cherished friends, but please let's not say special friend."

Peter shifted and covered his mouth, not sure if he should find anything funny at this point, but I couldn't help it and started to giggle. The director turned several shades of red and began deleting that portion of the obit. Mom decided "lifelong friend" was the best choice, and he continued on without any stops from her. Once he finished, we all agreed it was well-written and a beautiful tribute to her life.

"Well, with that finished," he said, closing his laptop, "the last order of business today is to pick out a casket."

He led us through another doorway, into what could only be described as a casket showroom. Caskets of every shade, size, and texture were lined up like TVs at a Best Buy. He asked us to narrow it down by choosing the outside (steel, hardwood, or the least expensive veneer) and then we would decide the lining (velvet, silk, or taffeta). Peter's eyes glazed over. Terese wandered the showroom, looking at each of the caskets with a vulture's point of view.

"I think she would want to be buried in this one," she announced, pointing to a steel grey monstrosity with black silk lining.

My mother flinched. "Did you even know her at all?"

Peter finally spoke up, "I really think she would've liked one of these wood ones with a white lining. Something simple."

My mom nodded. "I think that sounds perfect," she agreed, moving closer to him. "What color wood do you think? The oak? Cherry?"

"Actually, the white-washed one over here looks like the floor in our kitchen, and she loved it in there."

"Yes, she did. I remember when she got that floor put in two years ago. She loved that kitchen."

Peter started to cry and my mom held him close. "Mom, why don't I take Peter and Terese outside and get some air. You can help finish up here."

She nodded and Terese looked at me, eyes narrowed. "I think I should stay here and see what else she is going to decide for us."

"Well, if you plan to contribute something useful, then by all means please stay. Otherwise get the hell out. Why you are trying to weasel your way into planning her funeral when you couldn't stand to be around her when she was alive is beyond me."

"Thanks Mrs. D," Peter said, wide-eyed. "I think I will go outside."

Terese followed us out and went straight for the car. Peter and I sat on a bench in the shade. "I know the next few days are going to be tough, but Mom and I are here for you. You know that, right?"

His head was down, but he nodded slightly. He reached in his back pocket and pulled out a folded envelope. "I found this by the phone this morning," he said, handing it to me. "It has your name on it. I think my mom knew something was going to happen."

I unfolded the envelope, my name written in Jeri's loopy handwriting. I tucked it in my purse. "Was that it, or was there one for my mother?"

"That was all I found," he said. "What am I supposed to do with Aunt Terese? She's such a bitch."

"Well, you're right about that. Not sure how those two were sisters, but it explains a lot of why we never met her before."

"I think she used to come around when I was little, and I knew there was a fight between them. Never really knew why."

"Well, being blunt works with her. She just needs to go back home if she's not going to be respectful of what your mom would've wanted."

He sighed. "I just want this all to be over with. I still keep waiting to wake up from a bad dream."

I put my arm around his shoulder and leaned into him. At that point, my mom came out and slid on her sunglasses. "Where is your aunt?" she asked Peter. He nodded towards the car, and my mom walked over to her side, rapped on the window, and waited for her to roll it down. She said something to Terese, but we couldn't hear. After a minute, she came walking back to us.

"Well, that should be that," she said, looking in her purse for her keys.

"What did you say, Mom?"

"Nothing Jeri wouldn't have said," she smirked.

"Uh-oh. That leaves the door wide open," Peter said, smiling.

"Either way, she won't be bothering you again this week. She promised to be on her best behavior."

I looked sideways at Peter, and for the first time today, he looked relaxed. He stood and hugged my mom. "Thank you again, for everything," he said. "My mom loved you both so much and loved being a part of your family."

"And don't forget we're still your family. We are going to get through this together."

We said our goodbyes and got into our separate cars. I drove home so Mom could relax a little. We kept the windows down and let the wind blow our hair around. When we got home, I offered to get us a snack for the patio, but she declined. I didn't ask when she went upstairs and shut her door. She needed to process all of this her own way. I grabbed a Diet Coke and went out to the patio, pulling out the letter from my purse. It was dated from two days ago.

Gracie,

If you are reading this, then my gut feeling came true. I didn't want to worry anyone about the surgery and this little thought in the back of my head, but now there's not much we can do about it. There are just a few things I need from you:

1. Make sure Peter is looked after. He will be set for life, but please encourage him to finish school and find a job that brings him happiness and fulfillment. I know that's a tall order in this day and age, but maybe not having to worry about money will help him choose something close to his heart. Beware of my sister, and be clear with my lawyer that I do not wish to leave her anything from my inheritance. She is going to come sniffing for money before I'm even cold, so set her straight.

2. Take care of your mother. She seems to have an extremely tough exterior (believe me I know!), but underneath, she is all heart. She has wanted you in her life for as long as I can remember, so I hope this new adventure you two are on will only bring you closer. I know leaving her business in your hands is the best for everyone involved. If you have any questions about anything, there is a "Jeri" file on her computer that explains everything from taxes to publishing. Oh, and the password to her computer is "happiness" but you didn't hear that from me. Be gentle with her for a while now. She is going to retreat into her room and you will have to make sure she stays among the living. Above all else, love your mother for who she is and stop being angry for who she isn't.

3. No matter what else happens, be true to yourself. After living and breathing self-help for the past twenty-five years, these are the only words to live by. Stop worrying about what everyone is thinking and just care about what you think. All the other advice your mom gives is good too, but if you can look in your heart and know what you truly want or don't want in your life, then that is all you need. Don't make anyone else's life more important than your own, and learn to be grateful for every second of every day, because it really is a gift.

That's it. That's all I have for you. I want you to use the wings God gave you and fly through this life. Don't think your life is summed up by the recent events, and for the love of God, enjoy those two men who seem to be courting you right now. I have a feeling I know which one is for you, but you will need to find your way to him in your own time. Know that I couldn't have loved you more if you were my own family... Give your mom the strength she is going to need (along with her precious space), and keep Peter close to you.

God bless you Gracie.

Love, Jeri

Tears pricked my eyes. I slid the letter back into the envelope and folded it into my back pocket. Should I show my mother?

The slider door opened and Gordy and Charlie walked outside. Charlie squeezed my shoulder as he sat down next to me.

"So," Gordy said, "how was it?"

"It was hell. Jeri's sister is a bitch," I said, wiping away the remaining tears.

They both raised their eyebrows. "She's that bad?"

"Worse. Peter is going to need our help over the next few days."

"And Mom? How was she?"

"Actually, she was solid," I said. "I don't know how she's handling any of this, though."

"Let me guess... she's upstairs?"

"As soon as we got home. Can't say that I blame her. Writing an obituary and picking out a casket for your best friend is exhausting."

Charlie tipped his head to the side. "How are you holding up? I'd be drinking something stronger than a Diet Coke if I were you."

"I thought about it, but after last night's fiasco, I'll just stick to this."

"What happened last night?" Gordy asked. "Did something happen before I got here?"

Charlie locked eyes with mine. "Let's just say red wine was not her friend," he said.

"And I was a hot mess."

"So you weren't kidding when you said you were hungover last night when we got the shots out?" Gordy asked.

"Oh no," I laughed. "I don't kid about hangovers."

"With what you're going through, it's no wonder you're not drinking more," Gordy said. "What the hell was Andrew thinking?"

I ran my hands through my hair. I have asked myself this question more than I care to count, and the answer is always the same. I don't know.

"Do you think you'll have to testify at the trial?" Charlie questioned.

"I still have to call the detective in charge of the case. I can't imagine I will actually have to testify, but who knows at this point? Nothing has made sense for weeks."

"Gracie, nothing is going to make sense for a while, if ever. We're gonna help you through this any way we can," Charlie said.

Gordy's eyes darted from Charlie to me. "Is there something I'm missing? Are you two hooking up?"

I choked on my Diet Coke. I glanced at Charlie and

he was blushing.

"Holy shit, you two are totally hooking up, aren't you?"

"No, jackass, we're not hooking up, although I think Jimmy is up to his old tricks," Charlie said. "Gracie and I are just helping each other through some tough times." He winked at me.

Gordy looked skeptical but dropped the subject. "Well, keep Jimmy away from her if you can help it."

"I'm sitting right here, in case you didn't notice," I reminded. "And I can *hook up* with anyone I choose at this point. I think I'm entitled. Stop trying to be my big brother."

"There she is," Gordy said, laughing. "I've been wondering where my stubborn sister was."

"Well, congratulations," I said. "You found her."

"Now *this* feels like home. I've missed the bickering."

"Well you'll have front row seat for the rest of the week," I said. "Speaking of, don't you have to work?"

"Yep, going in at six, though. You two should bring your mom in tonight. Get her out of the house. It's 'Half-Off Pizza' night."

Gordy nodded. "That actually sounds like a good idea."

"I'm in," I said. "Not sure if Mom will want to, but she's dragged my ass out when I didn't want to, so I may just have to force her." I yawned and stretched. "I think I'll take a page out of Mom's book and go take a nap."

"You better rest. Last night you were just lame," Gordy said. "You want me to call Linn?"

"You have her on speed dial or something?"

He shrugged one shoulder. "Something like that." I knew something was up.

"Well, sure I guess. She's good for keeping things light," I said.

I closed the sliding door and listened for my mom upstairs, but all was silent. I tip-toed up the stairs and closed my door quietly.

I woke myself up from another dream about Jeri. Just like the last dream, we were outside, here at my mom's. I followed Jeri out to the lighthouse, but the rain made it hard to see. Every time I called her name, she would turn and smile, but continue on.

Rubbing the sleep from my eyes, I went downstairs to find Jimmy, Gordy, Linny, and my mom sitting in the living room talking. Jimmy stood and came over to hug me, and everyone gaped at us.

"Are you holding up okay?" he whispered, and I just nodded into his shoulder. Their looks were making me squirm, especially Gordy's. I pulled away, and he grabbed my hand to bring me over to the couch. He sat down next to me, and they were still looking at us.

"What?" I snapped.

"So, as I was saying," my mother said. "The visitation will be tomorrow and the funeral on Thursday with another short visitation before the service."

"Is there a meal or some sort of gathering after?" Linny asked. "I can help with that if you need."

My mom paused to think. "Actually I was planning on having it here, so if that's something you could cater that would be lovely. With everything happening so fast, I hadn't thought that through yet."

"Can do. And just give me an estimate of a head count and I'll figure out the food. You don't have to worry about a thing."

"But aren't you still short on workers this week?"

Linny shook her head. "I got two of them back today, so I'm all set. Don't worry about a thing. Except do you mind if we prepare some of the food here?"

"Well my kitchen doesn't compare to yours, but absolutely, it's all yours," Mom said.

While I listened, Jimmy rubbed small circles on my hand with his thumb. It was as comforting as it was confusing. My stomach growled and Gordy smiled.

"Some things never change," he said. "You have always had the loudest stomach in town."

"Hey," I countered, "I had a Diet Coke for lunch, so I'm due a meal about now."

"We were just waiting for you, so we can go now," my mom said, getting up. "I could use a nice meal myself."

I found my flip-flops by the back door and slid them on. Linny and Jimmy were heading towards the front door.

"Want to ride with me?" Jimmy asked me.

Gordy chimed in. "Actually I thought the girls could go in one car and we could ride together."

Jimmy raised his eyebrows, but didn't complain. "Sure, let's roll."

Linny and I followed my mom out to the garage, and I offered to drive. Once we got in the car, Linny started to grill me from the backseat.

"So, Gracie-girl... what's the deal with Jimmy? You guys look pretty comfortable together."

My mom smiled, but stayed silent.

"He's just being a friend," I said defensively.

She chuckled. "Riiiiight, and I'm your friend, but not going to sit there and hold your hand or give you the world's longest hug," she said. "And that was full body contact, I might add."

My mom smiled bigger.

"Jeez, Linn, stop it. He's affectionate is all." I wanted to bring up Gordy to her, but not in front of my mom. I would have to wait until later.

"And is it me or does Gordy seem a little uncomfortable with all of that? He was giving Jimmy daggers and obviously didn't want you riding with him." She added finger quotes to riding, and now I laughed.

"Oh my god, stop," I said laughing.

"I'm just sayin'…" she grinned. "If I were single, I'd be all over that."

My mom barked out a laugh.

"See? Even your mom can see the chemistry between you two. Why are you fighting it?"

"Have you seen her with Charlie?" my mom asked. "That's why she's fighting it."

"What is *that* supposed to mean?" I asked.

"I'm just sayin'," she said, mimicking Linny. "There's a lot of chemistry going on around our house."

"Are we all forgetting the fact that I'm still married?" I said.

"Oh stop," Linny said dismissively. "He's a cheating scumbag, and the only reason you're not divorced yet is because you haven't called Barry."

"Which you need to do tomorrow, by the way," my mom said. They were finishing each other's sentences.

"Sure thing Mom, I'll fit that in right between the visitations. Anything else I need to do?"

"Call Officer Marks," she said, without missing a beat. I rolled my eyes. "You're the one who is needing to let go of your past. It's best to rip the Band-Aid off sometimes."

Linny met my eyes in the rear-view mirror, hers

reflecting humor with sympathy.

Jimmy and Gordy were already sitting at the bar when we walked in. I met Charlie's eyes and he winked at me.

"I know the view is much better at the bar, but would you ladies mind if we sat at a table tonight?"

"Not at all, Mrs. D. The boys can be boys for tonight."

A waitress led us to an empty table in the back and took our drink orders.

"Ladies, we're going to do some homework tonight," my mom said, grabbing a napkin from the middle of the table. She then gave one to each of us. "Since Gracie is going to make a list of things in her past that she would like to let go of, we all are... here, tonight. And tomorrow night after the visitation, we will have a bonfire and burn them."

Linny's eyes lit up, "Oh I love this idea! I have a few things in my past I'd love to see go up in flames."

"Mom, I can do this later or tomorrow morning," I said. "We don't all have to participate, especially here."

"What have you got to hide? Your whole life has been on *The Today Show* every morning for the past few weeks," she said, taking a sip of water. "It's time to let it go."

I nodded, feeling more exposed than I had since I found out. Tears welled up in my eyes, and I tried unsuccessfully to blink them away.

"Hey, what's going on? This is supposed to help you feel better, not worse," my mom said.

"I just need a moment," I said, getting up.

The bathroom was empty. I took my time washing my hands with cold water, and slowed my breathing down. *What was holding me back*? I knew I could do this, *had* to do this to move on. I wish Jeri were here to help kick my ass into gear.

I walked back to the table feeling Charlie's eyes on me. I was grateful they were sitting at the bar. My mom and Linny were writing on their napkins, and Linny's was almost covered. I took a sip of wine and another deep breath. Calmer, the words flowed out of me without hesitation. Linny had finished and was eating a breadstick, and my mom seemed to be pondering her list.

"I can't believe you have anything in your past you regret," I said to her.

"Oh honey, we all have a past filled with things we want to forget," my mom said. "I am no different than anyone else, and sometimes it's good for me to follow my own advice every now and then to see if it really works."

"My past is a shit-show," Linny said, laughing. "I literally can't wait to burn this fucker tomorrow."

I shook my head and laughed. With my napkin safe in my back pocket, I felt my shoulders begin to relax. More words would come after my run tomorrow, but they could wait tonight.

The waitress came with three shot glasses filled with something pink. "Ladies, these are from the boys at the bar," she said, setting them down. We turned to find all three boys raising their own glasses to us.

"I'm too old for this," my mom said.

"Like hell you are, raise it up." Linny already had her glass raised, and Mom and I lifted ours too.

"To Jeri!" Jimmy yelled.

"To Jeri," we all said in unison before tossing the drink back. It was the same one Jimmy made us that first night here.

"Oh yum," Linny said, licking her lips. "That was fabulous. Bartender, another round on me this time."

Charlie shook his head, smiling, and took out the silver shaker.

"We're getting dinner, right?"

"Yes," I said. "Should we get a pizza?"

We agreed on the veggie special, and sent the meat lovers over to the boys. Mom and Linny finished their list before dinner came and started to go over the food list for after the funeral.

I kept one eye on the boys at the bar and noticed that Charlie was doing the same with us. Jimmy and Gordy were drinking beer faster than Charlie could pour them. My head started to pound, and I could only pick at the pizza.

When our plates were cleared, Jimmy and Gordy came over to sit with us. Jimmy sat next to me and rested his hand on my knee. I wasn't sure it was what

I really wanted or needed.

I excused myself and went to the bathroom, Linny following me.

"You know, if you keep hiding in the bathroom, people are going to think you have bowel issues," she warned.

I shrugged. "No they won't. Everyone is aware that I'm hiding. Besides, I really have to use the bathroom this time."

She waited till I was done, leaning against the wall, arms crossed. "What's going on? Jimmy is looking pretty friendly tonight. What ever happened on your date?"

"Not what you're thinking," I said, washing my hands. "He did kiss me, but that was it."

She raised her eyebrows, "And how was the kiss?" She sighed. "A girl like me has to live vicariously through you."

"One kiss isn't going to erase the past few weeks of my life. Do you really want to walk in my shoes?"

"It depends," she said. "Are you kissing Charlie too? Because if you are, then hell yes."

I blushed and shook my head. "Charlie is a different problem all together. And not that he's a problem at all. He is the one who seems to be picking up my pieces lately, but I just don't know... he seems torn. Like he's still hung up on his ex or something."

"Why don't you let me be the judge of that. Let's go sit at the bar and chat with him for a bit."

"Like that's not too obvious."

"Just follow my lead," she said, heading out towards the bar. She sat on the end and I took the stool next to her. I looked over and my mom seemed to be deep in conversation with Jimmy and Gordy.

"So, bartender," she began. "How is life going?"

He set down two waters in front of us.

"Well, Linny, I'd have to say that life can be confusing lately. Nothing seems to be going the way it should be, in my opinion."

She looked at me sideways. "In your life, or like life in general?"

"Both." He wasn't giving her the answers she expected.

"Huh, well we all seem to be in that same boat," she said. He looked over at me when she said this. "So tomorrow night, after the visitation, we're going to have a bonfire on the beach and set the past on fire."

He cocked his head to one side. "Forgive me Linny, but what the hell are you talking about?"

"Well, actually it's Gracie's past we're setting on fire, but while we're there, I'm going to burn mine too," she said, winking. "Not all of it, just the shit I don't want to worry about anymore."

"Are you going to explain, or just let her keep rambling?" He looked at me, tapping his fingers on the bar.

"According to my mom, we have to let go of the past in order to move forward in life. We've decided to make it more of a celebration and say goodbye." I took a sip of water. "So, I'm making a list of things I want to leave in the past, and I'm going to ceremoniously burn it tomorrow night. I hope you'll be there."

"Do I have to burn my past too?" The corner of his mouth twitched up.

"Not unless you want to. This is my battle, and I just want to have my friends and family with me," I said. "Honestly, I think Linny is more excited to burn my past than I am."

His eyes softened. "I think we all want to help you burn your past," he said. "At least the bad stuff."

I nodded, taking another sip of water.

"And let's not forget we need to help your mom with Jeri too," Linny remarked. "I think your mom is actually looking forward to this more than we are."

"So you'll be there?" I asked Charlie.

He nodded. "Jimmy will be pissed because he's closing, but I'll be there," he said. "Wouldn't miss it for anything."

Gordy drove us home since Jimmy stayed to help close. The air was so calm we rolled the windows down and turned the music up. A thick silence came over the car, and I thought of Jeri. Linny reached over to grab my hand, and when I looked at her, she had tear streaks on her face as well.

"We're gonna get through this," she whispered. "We are."

I nodded, swallowing a sob.

"You're damn right we are," my mom said from the front seat. "And when we do, we're going to have a party."

I wiped my tears away and peeked up at her. She winked and smiled at me, but her eyes were still sad.

How did we get to this place, and more importantly, how are we going to get out?

Chapter Sixteen

The first visitation was physically and mentally draining. I didn't need to be there the whole time, but wanted to be supportive for my mom and Peter. I saw friends from my past, and could tell some of them had put the pieces together by the familiar look of pity in their eyes when they greeted me. Gordy was by my side most of the morning, making inappropriate comments to keep my mind off my problems.

While everyone went to Jeri's home between visitations, I went back to our home to make the two phone calls I had been dreading. Barry was understanding and helpful, letting me know that Terrence was the divorce attorney in his practice, and connected me with his secretary to make an appointment for following Monday at 9:00.

Next, I called Officer Marks back in Lansing. He answered on the second ring, sounding cold and official. I explained who I was, and he quickly softened the tone in his voice.

"I've been waiting for your call, and was actually going to try again today," he said.

"I know. We've had a death in the family, so I've been preoccupied," I explained.

"Oh, I'm sorry you have to deal with that on top of

everything else going on."

"It is what it is," I said. "And to be honest, I don't know how helpful I'm going to be for your investigation."

"Well, I've talked with Tim Jacobs from the station, and he was pretty adamant that you knew nothing about any of this."

I smiled. Tim still had my back. "That's true," I confirmed. "In fact, he was the one who had to tell me."

"Well, the more we find out, the worse it gets. It seems most of the encounters were at your home while you were at work. Sometimes there was an occasional lunch hour in an undisclosed location at the school, but many of the girls could describe your bedroom right down to the items on the nightstand."

My stomach lurched. I knew he had sex with these girls, but I never thought about where it took place.

"Uhh, Mrs. Foster? Are you still there?"

I cleared my throat. "I am." My voice cracked. "What else do you need from me?"

I could hear a door shut in the back ground. "Hey, I'm sorry. I should've known better than to spring that on you like that. I forget that you haven't been part of the investigation."

"Whatever, it's fine. Were there other questions?"

"I just would like to know if you had noticed anything out of the ordinary in your relationship in the past two years."

"That's how long he's been doing this?"

He sighed. "This would be so much easier if you were here," he said. "But yes, one plaintiff made a statement that she and your husband started a sexual affair in July before her sixteenth birthday, lasting over six months. She claims that it began with after school tutoring your husband gave her."

I sat at the table and watched the waves coming in. *Two years?*

"Honestly, Officer Marks, I don't know what to think anymore. Do you think I would stick around with him if I had known or suspected *anything*?"

"No, ma'am, I don't," he said, quietly. "Did you notice any charges on credit card statements that didn't seem to belong there? Bank statements that had the wrong balance?"

"Andrew handled all the finances in our relationship," I said. "I never really even looked at any statements of any kind. I could go through them now, but at this point I don't know what I would remember or not."

He sighed again. "Ma'am, that won't be necessary. We have all the statements, and dates and places match with some of the statements we've gotten from the plaintiffs. Mostly I just wanted to verify that you had no idea of his actions, which is clear to me you didn't."

"Am I going to have to testify or anything?"

"I don't see why you would, but that would be up to

the attorneys. I specifically told them they couldn't contact you until I had a chance to talk with you personally," he said. "I will give them my report, and let them make their own conclusions." He paused, then continued. "Can I just say how sorry I am that you have to go through this?"

"I appreciate that, but I'm sick about what he has done to those girls and their families."

"Will you ever come back to Lansing?"

"I don't see how I could. I no longer have a life there, and I'm trying to rebuild back at home."

"So you're up north? Frankfort is it?"

My stomach did a flip. "How did you know that?"

"Andrew had mentioned that's where you're from, and I remembered because my mom's family was from there too. When I questioned him, he said you had gone home. It's not in any report where you grew up, although I know with Google these days, that information isn't hard to find. It really is just a matter of time."

"I know, but I'm just hoping to keep the focus on Andrew and not on me at this point. I never asked for any of this."

"Well, I think that's about all I need from you. If you think of anything that will help with the case, I hope you'll trust me enough to call me."

"Believe me, if I had any information to keep him in jail longer, I would call you."

"Thank you for your time, and I hope you can get

back to some sort of normalcy soon."

"You and me both, Officer Marks," I said. "Feel free to call if you need anything else."

We hung up, and I sat there for a moment wondering if that conversation really just happened. How could I have been so blind?

Every instinct in me wanted to go for a run, but I knew I didn't have time. I started to pace around the kitchen, but I needed air.

The clouds hung low today, threatening rain. The waves were high and white tipped. Sadie appeared out of nowhere, running to me as if she had been searching for days. She leapt up with her two front paws, landing right on my chest, covering me with dirt and sand.

"*Sadie!*" Charlie came running towards us. "Sadie, no! Get down."

I eased her down and continued to pet her. "It's fine, she's just excited to see me," I said, standing to assess the damage.

He shook his head as he walked towards me. Lines formed around his eyes, and his five o'clock shadow was going on day two. "Bad girl," he scolded Sadie. "Look at you… you're covered."

It was true, I would have to change before I went back, and I didn't have a clue what I would wear. My clothes were limited at best. "It's fine, Charlie. Stop yelling. You're scaring her."

"I'm sorry. Your dress is ruined, and you look so

pretty." He gave Sadie the stink eye, and she wagged her tail, thumping my leg. Charlie clipped her leash onto her collar and pulled her away from me.

"What are you doing out here all dressed up? Aren't you going back?"

I didn't even know where to begin. I started to walk out towards the lighthouse, and he followed. I tried to brush off the sand, but the dirt only smeared deeper into my dress. He shook his head.

"Please stop doing that, you're making it worse," he said.

We walked in silence, until I thought I would burst. "Do you want to know what I just found out?"

He startled, his eyes darting.

"Andrew has been screwing teenage girls for almost two years now," I blurted out.

He stopped walking, but Sadie pulled on the leash to come closer to me.

"*Two years*. For the last two years he's been fucking other girls," I said, and he flinched.

"Who have you been talking to? How do you know this?"

"I finally called the officer in charge of the investigation. He also informed me that the plaintiffs claimed the main location was at our home, in our *bed*."

His eyes grew large and his mouth dropped open. "I swear, Gracie, he is never going to hurt you again. If he were here right now, I'm not sure what I'd do to him."

"Why would he do this to me? That's the one thing I don't understand. If you want out of a marriage, fine, ask for a divorce. But I can't for the life of me figure out what I did to deserve this."

He stepped closer. "This is not about you. He is just one of those guys who gets off on young girls, and you couldn't have stopped him if you tried. It has nothing to do with you."

"But I was so stupid. How did I not see any of this?" Tears were streaming down my face, and I didn't bother to stop them.

He came so close to me I could hear his breath, feel it.

"You can't possibly blame yourself in any of this," he whispered, wiping the tears away. "You are not at fault, and you didn't notice anything because you trusted him."

The waves were echoing in my ears and my heart was beating out of my chest, rising and falling as his eyes locked on mine.

He took one more step forward and gently reached for my face. He leaned in and kissed the tears trailing down my cheek, one side then the other. His eyes met mine, and he pulled me in to his lips. They were warm and soft, searching mine for something more. I reached around his waist and pulled him closer, wanting every part of him to be as close as possible. I wanted to get lost in him.

He pulled away, breath ragged. "You were saying something?" He leaned in to kiss me again. Sadie barked and we both looked down at her. "Damn dog."

I smiled, feeling my heartbeat start to calm down. My skin tingled as he grabbed my hand and led me back towards the beach.

"Can I ask you something?" His voice was raspy.

"Are you wishing you could take that back?" I asked, looking up at him.

He smirked. "Gracie, I will remember that kiss till they bury me," he said. "But I am wondering what is going on with you and Jimmy. He seems to think you two are a couple, and I've had my heart broken once this year. I don't need to go through that again."

I stopped walking and took both his hands into mine. I took a deep breath, looking into his eyes. "I know he's interested, but a part of me just feels like this is classic Jimmy, and he just wants the chase." He looked away, nodding. "Please believe me when I say that I am not leading him on in any way. And I would never break your heart."

"You don't get it. My heart has been breaking for you since you got back. Hell, I remember the first day I saw you at Lakeside and I was too nervous to come over because you looked so sad. Then watching you break down the other night? All I want is to take your pain away, and I don't have a clue how, or even if you want me to." He tugged on Sadie's leash and ran his hand through his hair.

I rested my forehead on his shoulder and wrapped my arms around his waist. "Charlie, I can't make many promises right now, and I get it if you want to turn and run as fast as you can from me. The only thing I can promise is that I don't want to lose this feeling I have when I'm with you."

"So you feel it too?"

I smiled and started walking again. "It's… it's like nothing I've felt before. Not even with Andrew," I admitted. "At first I thought it was just a crush on my brother's friend, but it's more than that. When I look in your eyes, it makes me feel like I'm home."

He smiled and looked out at the lake. "I can't believe this is happening."

"Me neither," I said. "But I guess nothing should surprise me anymore."

I looked down at my dress again. "I really need to change and get back to the funeral home."

"I can get that dry cleaned for you," he said apologetically. He tied Sadie's leash to the door handle and we went inside.

My phone was ringing, my mom's ID on the screen.

"Hey Mom," I answered.

"Are you coming to have something to eat or meeting us at the funeral home?"

"Why don't you just go, and I'll meet you there. I'm going to grab a quick bite first."

"Did you make your phone calls?"

"I did and everything will be handled. I meet with

an attorney on Monday morning."

"All right," she said. "You okay?"

"Yes, Mom, I'm fine," I said. "Charlie is just leaving, and I will see you soon."

"Oh, well, why didn't you say so? Love you, honey."

"Love you too Mom."

Charlie smiled. "You two seem to be getting along better these days," he said.

"She can still bug the shit out of me like no one else can, but yes, we are getting along far better than we used to."

"Well, I'm gonna let you get ready and I will see you there," he said, leaning down to kiss my forehead.

I studied his face, landing on his lips.

"If you keep looking at me like that, I'm going to help you change out of that dress." He leaned in and kissed me again, his hand at my back pulling me against him. His lips lingered on mine, as if they were looking for a soft place to land. "You're killin' me here," he whispered, breaking free.

I touched my lips, still tingling, and watched him walk out and untie Sadie. He gave a little finger wave and turned to go.

What am I doing?

Chapter Seventeen

The second visitation was busier. A long line of friends trailed out the main entrance. Everyone who knew Jeri also knew how close she was to my mom. By the end of the night, Peter's eyes were red and took on a hollow expression. Jeri's sister spent more time reapplying her red lipstick than she did greeting people. Charlie and Jimmy each came to visit separately while the other one watched the restaurant. Jimmy had to close, but reminded me he was just a phone call away.

Linny stopped by briefly. I gave her the keys to our house so she could start prepping for the food tomorrow. Charlie and Gordy were standing with me, and she gave Gordy the once over before leaving.

"I feel like she just undressed you with that look," Charlie teased.

Gordy blinked.

We were in a side room for family members to take a break from the visitors.

"What is the deal between you two?" I asked. "I've been getting this vibe from both of you like you're closer than you're leading on."

He shook his head. "I don't know what you're talking about. Linny and I have always been friends, even way back when."

I looked at Charlie, he gave me the side-eye.

"What I want to know is why are you two so chummy lately? Every time I turn around, you're huddled together, and don't tell me 'nothing,' because Jimmy sees it too."

"Nothing against my brother, but he's not really one to be judging us," he said. "And for the record, nothing is going on. We are just helping each other through some shitty times."

Gordy seemed to be studying us. "You just said that yesterday, and I'm still not buying it."

I wasn't completely sure nothing was going on. In fact, I was hoping something would develop.

"See?" Gordy pointed at me. "She looks like the cat who just ate the canary. She only looks like that when she's hiding something."

Charlie looked at me straight-faced and eyebrows raised. "I'll agree with you that she looks guilty, but it's not because of me." He winked. "Maybe it's Jimmy you should be asking."

Gordy rolled his eyes. "I'm going home," he said. "Can you let Mom know?" He hugged me and planted a kiss on my cheek.

Charlie and I went back out and he stood with me while my mother and I helped Peter greet Jeri's friends. Peter and his girlfriend declined our invitation to the bonfire, and we breathed a sigh of relief when his aunt said she would be leaving after the funeral.

The weather was excellent for a bonfire. Temps in the low fifties made it ideal for jeans and a sweatshirt. I finished my list this morning, and had it folded up in my back pocket.

Charlie and Gordy had a cooler filled with beer on the beach and started a fire big enough for a small crowd. They had towels and beach chairs for everyone to gather. With the clear sky, stars, and crescent moon, everything felt right.

Linny was cleaning up all her prep for tomorrow, sipping a glass of red wine while she organized the kitchen.

"Got your list?" she asked me.

I pulled my folded list out of my back pocket to show her the evidence. "Do you have yours?"

She grabbed a tattered planner out of her purse and found it amongst fifty-eight sticky notes.

"That is the planner of someone with multiple personalities," I said. "How can you possibly organize anything with that?"

She stuck her tongue out at me. "This, my dear, is planner perfection. I've had it since college, and I have never used anything else."

"I can tell."

"I'll have you know this Kate Spade was a graduation present from my grandma," she said.

"I think it's vintage Kate Spade now. You should burn *that* tonight."

She gasped. "Bite your tongue. This is my life line, and until it falls apart, I'm keeping it."

"Are you about done fiddling around here? Let's go outside already."

"Why yes, is there a certain tall, dark, and handsome man waiting for you?"

I rolled my eyes. "No," I said, defensively. "I have a past I'd like to burn." We shut the overhead lights off and slipped on our flip-flops. "So were you able to get your mom to babysit and have Barry come over?"

Her eyes clouded over. "Actually, yes, my mom is sitting, but Barry is still working. He was going to call on his way home and see if it was worth coming out."

I nodded. The slump in her shoulders said it all. As we got closer, I heard Jimmy Buffett playing on an old boombox we had from high school. I couldn't believe it still worked.

Linny and I sat on a towel centered between Charlie and Gordy. I assumed the boys had planned it this way. Gordy took out a beer for each of us, and offered Charlie another. Charlie scooted his chair closer to me, and I leaned against his legs. A warmth spread through my body.

My mom cleared her throat. "Well, before we get started, I'd like to read something I found today from one of Jeri's favorite books. She had tried to get me to read it so many times… and I never did."

She opened John Irving's *A Prayer for Owen*

Meany, and began to read:

> *"When someone you love dies, and you're not expecting it, you don't lose her all at once; you lose her in pieces over a long time – the way the mail stops coming, and her scent fades from the pillows and even from the clothes in her closet and drawers. Gradually, you accumulate the parts of her that are gone. Just when the day comes – when there's a particular missing part that overwhelms you with the feeling that she's gone, forever – there comes another day, and another specifically missing part."*

She closed the book, wiping a tear from her cheek. "I know Jeri is watching over us right now, and probably pissed she's missing a good bonfire."

I wiped away my own tears. "That was beautiful Mom," I said. "Really sad, but beautiful."

She smiled, her eyes twinkling in the fire light. "And now it's your turn, young lady. How do you want to run this show?"

"I'd like to start by raising our drinks to Jeri. I think she was a second mom to all of us, and her gift was showing us what real friendship looked like. I have always admired the two of you and how close you were," I said. "So, to Jeri."

"To Jeri," everyone repeated, taking small sips.

I took a deep breath and found my list in my back pocket, and I could feel Charlie squeeze my shoulder for support.

"I wasn't really sure how I was going to do this tonight. I've never wanted to live with regrets, and it's not that I have so many regrets, but just this overwhelming need to let go and move on." My voice quivered, and I knew more tears would be coming. "After losing Jeri so suddenly, I realized that life is simply too short and we have to figure out how to live and love every day. And to quote the great Julia Dunham, '*If you can't stop living in the past, you will never have a future.*'" I unfolded my list. "I think we should all do this together. If you have a list, get it out now, and we will all put them in the fire at the same time."

Everyone shifted, looking for their lists. My mom pulled hers out of Jeri's book, and even Gordy and Charlie had a sheet of paper in their hands. Everyone sat and waited for me.

"Does anyone want to add anything?" I asked. All eyes focused on the fire. "Then let's do this."

I stood, waiting for everyone else to circle the fire with me. Charlie grabbed my hand, and Gordy put his arm around my mom and held her tight. We held our lists above the flames, and one by one let them drop. The papers crackled and sent charred pieces flying in the air as they shriveled into tiny black pieces. We watched until the very last list was scorched and gone. No one moved except Gordy who brought his other arm around Linny hugging her close. I thought about Andrew and knew he would always be a part of my life, my past, but he couldn't affect my future anymore. A warmth spread through my entire body.

I leaned into Charlie and felt his lips brush my hair, sending chills down my back. I was overwhelmed with gratitude for the people standing by my side, helping me through this. My heart swelled, and I felt Jeri was here with us.

Well done, sugar.

"Well, I don't think I could've come up with anything more fitting than that," my mom said, winking at me. "Thank you for letting us be a part of this."

"I'm just thankful you're all here with me. This is such a blessing," I said. "Jeri would've been so happy to be here, and I think somehow, she is."

We all talked, laughed, and cried for a while longer. Linny and I were in charge of roasting marshmallows and making s'mores, and Charlie and Gordy kept us laughing.

As the night progressed, Charlie became more affectionate, keeping his hands on my shoulders or arms. Every now and again, he would kiss the top of my head. I loved every minute of it, but I kept looking for signs of judgement from the others. Linny would wiggle her eyebrows or wink at me, but Gordy remained tight-lipped. The Linny-Gordy vibe was strong tonight, evident they were closer than they should be.

Linny was the first to get up, wanting to get home to her family. Barry didn't show, but I never expected him to. My mom and Gordy got up to go inside as well. I knew I was treading in deep waters out here with Charlie, but with the fire and the music, I wanted more.

We all hugged goodbye, and the three of them walked into the house. I turned to look up at Charlie, and he had a small smile and twinkle in his eye from the firelight. He brushed the hair out of my eyes and tucked it behind my ear. My butterflies had butterflies.

"I am so proud of you," he whispered. "I know how hard this was for you tonight, and here you are, smiling up at me."

"I think my smile has more to do with you than anything else."

He tipped his head. "I wouldn't be so sure about that. Tonight took courage and heart, and not many people would've been able to do it so graciously."

"Are you ready to go in, or do you want to stay out here for a bit?" I asked him.

He shook his head slowly, eyes scanning my face, landing on my lips. He took my hand and placed it on his chest. "Can you feel my heart racing?"

I nodded. "Mine is too," I whispered. "I've never felt like this before." My heart was beating out of my chest.

"Oh hell," he said, leaning in, nose to nose. His mouth was so close to mine, teasing. Lightly he brushed my lips with his, smiling. "I don't want this feeling to end."

I stood still, breath shallow, wanting more.

"We should walk," he said.

I blinked and my stomach clenched.

"Trust me, your mom and brother are looking out the kitchen window as we speak."

He grabbed my hand and pulled me away from the fire, towards the water.

"Want to go swimming?"

"Why don't you ask me in a couple months," he said. "I will gladly jump in the water with you then. In fact, I'll probably be dragging you in there every night."

He glanced behind towards my mom's house, then turned around to face me. "I think we're out of their line of vision now."

He brought one hand into my hair and pulled me towards him. His lips found mine with intensity and hunger, and a soft groan came from his chest. His arms circled my waist as I reached around his neck, and he lifted me off the ground without breaking the kiss.

My skin felt electric, alive, and every cell vibrated.

"Sweet baby Jesus," he whispered in my ear, breaking the kiss. My feet were still off the ground. I clung to him and rested my head on his shoulder.

"I'm not sure my heart rate will ever return to normal," he said.

I kissed his neck, finding my way to his earlobe. A boldness took over, and I wanted him to feel what I was feeling. Breathless.

"Just so you know, I will not be responsible for my actions if you continue to do that. I will take you, right here on this beach if I have to," he said.

A throaty laugh escaped me. I moved around to his other ear, planting kisses around his neck on my way.

"I. Am. Not. Kidding." He set me down on the sand. "Are you trying to kill me?"

I circled my arms around his waist and pulled him close, hip to hip. I leaned in and kissed the hollow of his throat lightly. He lifted my chin and planted his lips on mine again. This kiss was slower and deeper than the last one. Our lips parted and his tongue circled mine, never resting. He groaned again, pushing me away.

"Gracie," he said, holding me arm's length away. "Honey, we gotta slow it down a bit."

"I'm sorry," I murmured, covering my face with my hands. "I don't know what's come over me."

He let me go, and sat down on the beach, tugging on my hand to join him. "I can't even look at you right now without wanting to... well, you know."

I nodded, and we just sat there listening to the waves come in. The sand was cold and a shiver ran down my spine.

My breathing started to return to normal, and his did too. "Can I ask you something?"

He smirked. "After *that*? Yes, Gracie, you can ask me anything."

"Why did your marriage end?"

His head dropped. "She didn't seem to think we were in love anymore, but it was just her. She was with someone else… someone she worked with."

I leaned and rested my head on his shoulder. I took his hand in my and held it. "I'm sorry," I whispered.

"It's fine. Whatever. I just wish she at least had the decency to be up front with me instead of lying. She made me feel like I was going crazy, because he was married and had kids. She told me, *promised* me, nothing was going on, and for the longest time I believed her. They would go on business trips together and text all the time when they weren't at work."

"Did you just get tired of it? How did it end?"

"When my dad died, I came home for the week, and she couldn't because of work. I came home a day earlier than expected and found them in bed together."

I squeezed his hand tighter.

"She cried and screamed at me, asking why I was home so early. She was screwing someone in our bed, and she had the balls to be mad at me."

"I'm sorry," I said quietly. "I shouldn't have

brought it up. You don't have to go on."

He shook his head. "You're the only person I've told other than Jimmy. Gordy doesn't even know. I just wish I had trusted my instincts."

"You're preaching to the choir."

His breath was steady as he looked out at the lake. "If we knew then…" he said.

"What we know now," I finished his thought. "Would you do anything different?"

He smiled and shook his head. "Honestly, I don't know. I feel like life isn't just rainbows and butterflies. You have to take the good with the bad," he said. "But it seems we've been dealt more bad than most people."

His fingers curled around mine, squeezing gently. "It would be so easy to say that I should've listened to my mom when she told me not to marry Andrew. None of this would've happened. But in my heart, I know that going through this, *owning* it, is what life is really about."

He wiped a tear that was trailing down my cheek. "I wish I could stop these tears from falling," he said. "Today, when you had just found out those details about Andrew? All I wanted was to stop you from thinking about him."

I gave him a sideways glance. "So you didn't really want to kiss me? You were just distracting me?"

"Uh, no. I have wanted to kiss you since you were in seventh grade, and I saw you in those little shorty pajamas for the first time," he said, smiling.

I giggled.

"It was the Fourth of July, and you and Linny came out on the beach to watch fireworks. I knew Gordy would knock me out because three years was a lifetime, but I'll never forget those pajamas."

My mind was spinning. "I had no idea, but I was just trying to get Jimmy's attention back then," I said. "I just can't get over how good this feels. It was never like this with Andrew."

He looked serious for a moment. "You know we will have to tell Jimmy about us, right?"

I took a deep breath and blew it out. "I know. He'll be bummed for a night, then move on. But yes, you're right, he will have to find out."

"Gordy seemed okay tonight with us though."

"More so than with Jimmy," I said. "He was so mad when Jimmy hugged me the other night."

"So was I," he admitted.

I looked at Charlie. "He did kiss me, last Sunday when we went out. Nothing else happened, but we did kiss."

He chewed on the inside of his mouth, the muscles in his jaw working. "Did it feel like this?"

"Not even close. Like I said earlier, this feels... different from anything I've ever felt. Maybe it's because we're both hurting and not wanting to trust again."

"And you're sure you don't want to be with him?"

He was giving me an out.

My eyes locked on his. I brushed my hand on his cheek, still unshaven and sexy, and kissed him ever so lightly. "I want to be right here, with you."

He smiled. "As much as I'd like to stay out here all night, I am going to be the gentleman and take you home." He stood and pulled me up with both hands. "Tomorrow is going to be a long and crappy day, and we will both need to get some sleep."

"Speak for yourself," I said. "I'm not getting any sleep tonight."

"Yeah, me neither, but I thought it was worth saying."

The fire was merely glowing embers by the time we got back. We packed up the towels, chairs, and radio, carrying it back to the patio.

"Thank you for coming over tonight."

"Wouldn't have missed it for anything," he said.

We walked inside to find Gordy and my mom had already gone to bed. I walked him to the front door, trying to be quiet, and slipped my arms around his waist.

"Six words," he said, kissing my forehead. "On this night, we started us."

I closed my eyes and listened to his heartbeat. "Six words," I said. "I loved your lips on mine."

Gone was the anxiety I felt earlier. Calm replaced it, and I gave him one last squeeze before he left.

As I lay in bed that night, I thought about the week

and how it wasn't really about letting go of the past as much as it was about choosing a future. I knew I still had loose ends to take care of, but the fact that I had already started to move on instead of dredging it up made all the difference. I wouldn't have been able to do this without my mom, Gordy, and of course Charlie. Jimmy had been there too, but he was also a part of my past that I needed to let go of. I had such strong feelings for him in the past, and laying here it dawned on me that I let go of those too. By choosing Charlie, I had let go of Jimmy, and I smiled to myself in the dark. After weeks of questioning everything in my life, something finally felt completely right.

I rolled over, closed my eyes, and let the sound of the waves carry me off to sleep.

Chapter Eighteen

Step 2: Develop an Attitude of Gratitude

The house felt quiet, too quiet, as the sun set into the lake. Charlie was working, Mom was resting, Gordy had already gone home, and Linny was with her family. Jimmy wanted to stay with me, but I didn't want to face him just yet. I spent an hour cleaning the kitchen and another going over my mom's plans for next week. I didn't want to push her, but we would have to make arrangements if she needed more time off.

I questioned how she was going to ever get back to normal. Her business— her *life* — was built around Jeri, and now that was all gone. After the chaos of this week, she would have so much time to think about what she was missing. With Gordy gone, it would just be me and her again, and I knew loneliness would kick in for her.

My phone rang, Charlie's number popping up on the screen. "I hope you're calling to tell me you're closing early for the night," I said. I could hear him smile on the other end.

"I wish that were true," he said. "And for the record, I wouldn't call to tell you. I'd just show up."

"Oh, thanks for the heads-up."

"What are you up to tonight?"

"Well, the house is back to normal after the luncheon. Linny had to leave early, so I've been trying to put all the pieces my mom's life back together."

"Well, I have a barstool here with your name on it if you're needing some company."

"As much as I'd love to see you, I think I'm just going to stay in tonight with Mom. I don't want to leave her now that Gordy's gone again."

"Okay, just thought I'd check. Maybe we can do dinner or something tomorrow night?"

"I am already wishing it were tomorrow," I said, smiling.

"Me too." I heard a waitress call his name. "Hey, I gotta go. I will check in with you later."

"Sounds good," I said.

We both disconnected, and I sat there smiling.

"It looks to me like you made some decisions."

I jumped. "Ever think of wearing a bell around your neck?"

"I think you were just preoccupied with your phone call." My mom pulled her sweater tightly around herself.

"Maybe just a little," I conceded. "I have to admit it's a little strange to be feeling butterflies again."

Her whole face softened. "Well, I am happy for you. Jeri and I were hoping for this, but obviously didn't want to sway you one way or another."

I held my hands up. "We're trying not to rush anything, though. Both of us have been through hell and back this year, and the last thing we need is to get in over our heads so quickly."

"Well, just so you know, you have Gordy's blessing too," she said. "Not that you need it… you're both adults, but he seemed genuinely comfortable with the two of you together last night."

"Yeah, I could tell he didn't want Jimmy involved with me."

"Well, you know Jimmy has always had that 'ladies' man' reputation, and still does for that matter," she said, pouring a glass of wine. She looked at me to see if I wanted one, and I nodded.

"More than anything, no one wanted to see you get hurt."

We carried our wine over to the family room and settled in. She flipped the TV on and set it on the cooking channel. A guy with bleached, spiky hair was eating a sandwich bigger than his head.

"So what are you going to do about Jimmy? He doesn't know yet, does he?"

"We need to talk to him. But that's a conversation I'm not looking forward to."

"It'll be easier now than if you wait any longer," she said. "I'd nip that in the bud if I were you."

My stomach tightened. *Would this resistance always pop up when she told me what to do?*

"And now I have to ask your opinion about

something," she said.

"What could you possibly need my opinion for? I'm not up for giving anyone advice, let alone you."

"Well, I want to know what you think about me going to Florida for a week," she said, pausing. "This week."

"You want to go to Florida this week? Mom, I'm not sure I'm up for that."

She ran her fingers through her hair. "I want to take this trip solo. I need to get away, recoup, and just take some time to myself."

Our family has had a condo down in Pensacola for almost twenty years now, long before it became popular. It has always been her safe haven.

"Well, if you think you need to go, then you should."

"Will you be okay here by yourself? I'd hate to leave you knowing all the divorce stuff is going to come up this week. Not to mention, you'll have to move classes and appointments for another week."

"Mom, it's fine. When's the last time you even took a vacation? I've looked at your calendar and noticed it was last summer."

"I don't need vacations like everyone else does. I love what I do, and I'm lucky enough to live here. To most people, my life *is* a vacation," she reasoned.

"Well, I completely understand your need to get away, and I say go for it. Florida shouldn't be too hot yet, and it will be perfect for you."

"And you'll be okay?"

"Mom, I'll be fine," I reassured her. "I haven't been alone since my life fell apart, and it'll be good for me too."

"You're really okay with this?" I nodded, and she blew out a breath. "That's good, because I already booked the ticket when I was upstairs."

"Mom, please remember I'm here crashing in on your space. Don't feel like you need to clear your life with me. Obviously, if it's affecting the business, we need to settle things, but otherwise, pretend I'm not here."

She looked over at me, looking serious. "Can I tell you how much I've enjoyed actually being a mother to you again? For so long, you haven't needed me, and even when you needed me, you didn't want me. Now, it's like I'm getting a second chance to make things right."

Tears were welling up in the corner of her eyes.

"Mom, I know I wasn't the daughter you expected," I said. "I'm sorry I made it my mission to prove that I didn't need you, and always being the most stubborn one in the room."

Her hand reached for mine. "You don't have to apologize for anything. Remember what we did last night? No more regrets. I am just so glad you're here with me now."

I squeezed her hand. "What would I have done if I didn't have you to come home to? It's sad my life had to implode to get us to this point, but at least we're here now."

"Well, I leave first thing Monday morning, and will be home Sunday afternoon," she took a sip of wine. "And when I come back, we are getting back to business."

"Alrighty then," I said. "I will go through appointments and schedules tomorrow to see what can get pushed back or rescheduled. It will be handled before you go, so you know what is going on."

She shook her head. "Jeri would be so proud of you. Hell, *I'm* proud of you. Not many people would be able to handle everything that has come your way in the last few weeks."

"Well, it's the support staff I have around me," I said. "Never could've done it on my own."

"Are you hungry? Can I get you something to eat?"

"Good God, no. I picked all afternoon, and of course had a couple of Linny's cookies while cleaning up."

"Well, I'm going to see if there's some chicken salad left," she said.

"Bottom shelf in the fridge."

She got up to get some. "You know if you want to go see Charlie, you can. I'm okay here, and the last thing I want is for you to feel like you have to babysit me."

The mention of his name gave me goosebumps. She looked over at me and smiled.

"I have to say, I never saw this kind of reaction when you met Andrew. I know you were in Lansing at that point, but still, you are positively glowing when someone even mentions his name."

"I told him last night, I don't remember feeling like this before," I confessed, following her into the kitchen. "It came on so quickly and just feels like I'm falling."

"Well, it shows, and I can see it in his eyes too. He looks at you like you're the only woman in the room."

I smiled and sipped more wine.

"So go, get out of here, and go see Charlie. I know he asked you to come out tonight."

"Mom, we have plenty of time to hang out," I countered. "I don't need to go tonight."

"Well, I'm going back up and reading when I'm done here. This week has knocked me out, and I am not good company for anyone."

"Well, I guess if you're going upstairs…" Surprising Charlie sounded like a good idea.

"Now you're talking," she said, with a mouthful of chicken salad. "I know you don't want to rush, but really, what can happen in a bar?"

"You're right, and maybe if Jimmy is there we can talk to him."

"Heartbreaker," she said, joking.

"I hardly doubt I will break his heart," I said. "He will move on in no time."

We sat and chatted easily for a few more minutes before she cleaned up and excused herself. She grabbed Jeri's book from last night and headed upstairs, but not before giving me a hug. "Thank you for everything this week," she whispered.

I patted her back, surprised by her sudden affection. "Thank you for the past few weeks," I said.

—

The bar was crowded, and I found a spot at the end closest to the bathroom. Charlie and Jimmy were both behind the bar pouring beers and mixing drinks. Jimmy glanced up and did a double take. He wiped his hands on a towel hanging from his jeans. He grabbed a bottle of white wine and poured a glass, setting it in front of me.

"Well, that's service," I said. "Thank you."

"How's your mom holding up?"

I took a sip. "Surprisingly well. She wasn't up for socializing though."

"I'm glad you are," he said.

Charlie walked up behind Jimmy, smiling. "Look who's full of surprises," he said. "You alone?"

"Yes, Mom wasn't quite up for it, but insisted I get out of the house."

Someone on stage was killing a Beatles song, but the crowd seemed to love it. A waitress came up beside me with an order, and Jimmy quickly started getting what she needed.

"Busy night," I said to Charlie.

He rolled his eyes. "But I am glad you're here."

"Me too," I confided, sipping the wine. "Do you think we should break the news to Jimmy tonight?"

He turned back to look at him. "I think he may already have suspicions, but yes, we have to clear the air."

"Well, don't let me keep you. Go help your brother."

"I suppose I have to," he said, an edge to his voice.

Coming to Lakeside was exactly what I needed, although I did miss having someone by my side to laugh with. I was able to be alone with my thoughts, but completely entertained at the same time. Most of the people singing were pretty bad, but every now and then someone would really stun the crowd.

A group of girls called Jimmy to the end of the bar and huddled close. He eyed Charlie and nodded towards the stage, then rang a bell. The crowd erupted in chants for both of them. Jimmy sang the lead and owned the stage. Charlie played the backup singer and looked embarrassed the entire time. He spotted me once and shook his head. If I hadn't seen it, I wouldn't have believed it. They were magnetic on stage, and I suspect this is why the women kept coming back.

After the song ended, they scooted back behind the

bar to the sound of every customer clapping and yelling for more. I stopped an urge to grab Charlie and kiss him.

He squeezed my shoulder on his way past me. "Just so you know… at some point every customer has to get up there."

I smiled sweetly and batted my eyelashes. "Not a chance, bartender. I don't even sing in the shower."

He wiggled his eyebrows. "I guess I'll have to fix that, someday," he whispered in my ear.

My mouth dropped open, and he smiled like the Cheshire cat. Who knew Charlie could flirt?

"All I'm saying, is if you're gonna hang out here on Thursdays, you will be expected to perform sometimes. Perhaps you'll want to wait until Linny is with you?"

I nodded, dumbfounded. I hadn't seen this side of him yet, mostly because he was picking up the pieces of my broken heart. It was like getting a present and finding and even better present inside.

Jimmy came up behind him. "Gracie, he's not bugging you, is he?" he asked, smiling. "'Cause I can kick him out if necessary."

Charlie gave him a smirk. "Yeah, you and what army?"

"The girl at the end of the bar, pink shirt, wanted a drink from the 'hot backup singer,'" he said.

He looked behind him, and she gave a little finger wave. He looked back at me, and I shrugged my shoulders.

"Nice song choice," I said. "You guys do that every week?"

"Usually. They have to tip twenty bucks for that to happen though," he said. "That was one of my dad's favorites, and we started out singing it for him. He loved it."

"Well, it was the best part of the night," I said. "You guys were great."

He excused himself to help more customers. It was just after 10:00 and customers were still walking in. I tried to imagine if this would fit into my old life. Andrew hated karaoke bars and refused to go. Officer Marks' words echoed through my head, and I tried to think back over the last two years to see if anything was different. I had noticed he lost interest in sex, but now I know he didn't want sex with *me*. I figured it was a natural progression in a marriage to lose that spark, but we never really had that spark. I believed that sex was part of a serious relationship. An obligation, really, because that was the next step, but I never felt like I did now.

My experience with relationships was limited when I met him, but I didn't act like my roommates, who couldn't get enough sex. I judged them harshly because I was in a grown-up relationship. Andrew and I were so comfortable just being together, and I thought that's what it was supposed to be like. Thinking about it now, I wondered if Andrew was ever attracted to me.

"What's going on in that mind of yours?" Charlie asked, breaking my thoughts.

I shook my head. "Just putting the pieces together," I said. "I should get going."

"Wait," he said, grabbing my hand. "What is going on? You were just fine five minutes ago, and I look over here and you're clearly upset about something. You can't just leave."

I took a deep breath and remembered the past is in the past. I looked into his eyes, those deep blue eyes, and sat back down. "I'm sorry, my mind just got away from me. I'll be fine."

"You want to talk about it? Bartenders are supposed to be good listeners," he said, taking a sip of water he had sitting under the bar.

"Is he upsetting you?" Jimmy joked, pouring me another glass of wine.

Charlie glared at him. "You do realize she drove here, right?"

"It's fine," I reassured them. "I'm barely drinking it."

"Besides," Jimmy said, "one of us can always take her home."

Charlie shook his head and walked away. I couldn't stand the friction between them over me anymore. "Jimmy, can you come over here and sit with me for a minute?"

His smile faltered, but he came around and sat close

to me, his hand resting on my thigh.

I sighed and took his hand in mine. "As much as I would've jumped at this ten years ago," I said, looking him in the eye, "this isn't going to happen."

He looked at the bar. "Is it because of Charlie?"

I leaned forward to meet his eyes. "It's because of me, not anyone else."

"But you two are getting together, aren't you? I can feel it."

I looked up at Charlie, and he was keeping one eye on us. "I think because of what we have both been through, we're able to help each other. It was *never* a competition between the two of you."

He shook his head. "I have the worst timing."

"I was so not prepared for you ten years ago. I think we both knew that, and that's why you never asked me out."

"So you two are official or something?"

"I think we're still trying to figure out what we are. For obvious reasons, both of us are a little nervous and just going to take things slow."

He cleared his throat and stood. "Well, thank you for telling me," he said, kissing my cheek. "He is a lucky man."

My heart melted and I stopped him to give him a hug. "Thank you Jimmy."

He walked back behind the bar over to Charlie and shook his hand. Charlie nodded, and pulled him into a brotherly hug. A couple girls at the other end of the bar tipped their head at the moment, swooning. I smiled at Charlie, his eyes warm with gratitude, which reminded me of my week two challenge.

I stood and reached around the bar for a napkin and a pen. At the top of the napkin I wrote 'I am grateful for:' and continued to write five things I was thankful for at that moment.

1. My mom and for second chances for both of us.
2. Jeri.
3. Being back home, and creating a new life.
4. Linny and her crazy friendship.
5. Charlie making me feel like it's all going to be okay.

"If you keep that up, I'm going to charge you extra for napkins," Charlie said, smiling. "What are you working on?"

"Step two is all about gratitude, and one of the challenges is to write a list every day of what you're grateful for." I turned the list so he could read it.

"I'm beginning to think this book of your mom's is pretty cool," he said, smiling. "I think I'll have to make my own list later on tonight. And thank you, by the way, for talking with Jimmy. I didn't realize how uncomfortable I was feeling until he knew."

"It had to be done. I could feel tension between you two and didn't want to be in the middle of that. If we're going to do this, then it has to feel good."

His eyes twinkled. "I couldn't agree more."

I folded my napkin and slid it in my purse. "I think I'm going to head out. I'm exhausted, and want to get back home."

He nodded. "Let me walk you out."

I waved to Jimmy on my way out and he winked. It was so quiet outside, and the chill in the air made me shiver. Charlie wrapped his arm around my shoulders and pulled me close as we walked to my car.

"I'm glad you made it in tonight," he said. I was leaning against the door, and he put one arm on the car and held my hand with the other.

"Me too," I said, butterflies flaring. Would every moment alone with him feel like this?

"You have a funny look on your face again," he said, kissing my hand. "What are you thinking?"

"You make me feel so out of control," I confessed. "It's like butterflies, but a thousand times stronger."

He leaned in and kissed me, long and slow, pressing me into the car. I reached for his waist and pulled him tighter.

"Get a room," someone yelled across the parking lot.

He broke the kiss, smiling, but kept me pinned against the car. "Damn customers," he muttered.

"You better get back inside," I said, breathless. "Or I won't be responsible for what I'll do."

"That's my line," he said, leaning in for another kiss.

I giggled. "I'm not kidding. Control flies out the

window when I'm alone with you. I need to get going."

He backed away, but took my hand and kissed it again. "To be continued..." he said. "Perhaps tomorrow?"

I nodded. "But I'm not sure how long I'll have. My mom is leaving for Florida on Monday morning, and she might need help getting stuff organized."

"Florida? Are you going too?"

"Nope, she wanted a week to herself, and seemed pretty adamant about it. It'll be good for her."

"Okay," he said. "Well, I'll just check in tomorrow at some point and see what's going on."

"Sounds good. I'm sure it'll be fine, since we have all weekend to plan," I said. I reached up to kiss him one last time. His hand pressed into my back pulling me into him.

"Jesus," he swore. "You are relentless."

I giggled, opening the car door and sliding in. I waited for him to walk back to the bar before backing out. I wondered if this is how my roommates used to feel about their boyfriends. I shook my head, touching my lips. If kissing him felt this good, what was everything else going to feel like?

Chapter Nineteen

We spent Friday morning helping Peter with thank you notes and cleaning up his house. Plants and flowers from the funeral sat everywhere, a constant reminder of what was lost. He had more food in his freezer and refrigerator than he would eat in a lifetime. I packed up the food in the refrigerator and drove it to the homeless shelter on the other side of town. When I got back, he and my mom were sitting in the kitchen talking about his plans. He would finish this year at school, then come back home for the summer.

He hugged each of us as we left, promising to text if he needed anything.

"Anything I can do?" She stared out the car window.

"I don't think so. Unfortunately this is the part that hurts the most. When all the commotion ends, and you're left to carry on with the rest of your life without the *one* person who could make it all better."

I blew out a long breath. "Maybe a little work would be good for you right now."

She didn't say anything right away. "That might be good. And God only knows how little I've written lately. My publisher is expecting a first draft next month, and I'm not even halfway through it."

"Mom, I'm sure your publisher will be able to grant you an extension, given the circumstances," I reassured her. "Either way, I'll call them today and see what can be done."

We got home late afternoon, both needing space. "I'm going for a run before we get into any work if you don't mind."

"Not at all, I may head outside myself."

I had texted Charlie earlier letting him know my plans for the day, and realized he called an hour ago. I called him back before changing into running clothes.

"Hey," he answered. "I was just thinking about you."

I smiled. "A girl could get used to this."

"That's what I'm planning on."

"Today took forever. His place was a mess, and he has more flowers and food than he knows what to do with. Honestly, I bet he can't wait to get back to school."

"Poor kid. When is he going back?"

"Probably this weekend. Mom and I brought some of the plants here so they wouldn't die, but we donated a ton of them along with a fridge full of food. I'm going for a run, and then working with Mom for a bit," I said. "She's pretty upset after being over there all day."

"That's understandable," he said. "Just take care of her. We have plenty of time to hang out."

"But I was really looking forward to seeing you tonight," I said. "Maybe if she goes to bed early you could come over and we could watch a movie or something?"

"As long as it's not a chick flick, I'm cool with that."

"And what makes you think I watch chick flicks?"

He chuckled. "Let's just say it wouldn't surprise me if your favorite movie was something like *Sleepless in Seattle* or *You've Got Mail*."

"Don't forget *Jerry McGuire*," I said.

"*You had me at hello*."

I sighed, content. "Well, if you don't want a chick flick, then you better come prepared with other options."

"Deal," he agreed.

"I love that I can hear it when you're smiling on the phone," I said. "How is that?"

"Probably because I'm always smiling when I'm on the phone with you?"

"Cheesy, even for you, but I'll take it because it's been such a bad day."

"I hope to see you later, then," he said.

"Just count on it. I'll let you know what time when we finish up around here."

I changed into running clothes and made a mental note to buy some more clothes this week. There was no way I was going back to my home to get any, and besides, most of them were work clothes. Sliding my headphones on outside, I turned the music up a little louder than usual, Lady Gaga filling my ears, keeping the voices in my head at bay while I ran.

I slowed my pace down a bit on the way back, wanting the run to last longer. I started to make a mental list of things I was grateful for. Running was at the top of my list. Then phone calls, Lake Michigan, chick flicks, and music. I would write them down when I got home, but for now I wanted to keep thinking of what made me happy.

My mom was sitting on the log when I got closer to our house. I slowed to a walk to bring my heart rate down before I sat down. I peeled off my long-sleeved jacket so I was just wearing a sweat drenched T-shirt now.

She snickered at me walking up. "You were never a girly-girl growing up."

"True," I agreed. "I was always trying to prove myself to Gordy or his friends."

"And now? Are you trying to prove anything now?"

I stopped, looking out at the water. "I don't think so. Mostly I just love this feeling I get after a run."

"The infamous runner's high," she said. I couldn't tell if she was mocking me or not, so I let it go.

"Are you ready to go over some work stuff?"

"I am if you are," she said. "Why don't you cool down a bit and I'll go put on some coffee. I could use a boost right about now."

I nodded, watching her walk off. The beach was

empty again with the exception of our elderly neighbors power walking. She gave me a brief wave without breaking stride.

I continued my grateful list in my head while I sat there cooling off. Sand, lighthouses, runner's highs, coffee, and freedom. For the first time in weeks, I felt free and wasn't afraid of what was going to happen to me. I had been through hell and had come out on the other side. In that moment, I was even grateful for the hell.

Maybe there was such a thing as fate. Maybe my mom has been right all along, and it was me who never had a clue.

Just maybe.

—

The coffee didn't help my mother, and she just was tired and unmotivated to get anything figured out. She told me several times to just handle it when I brought up another appointment or engagement needing attention. I suggested we table all decisions until the morning when we both had clearer heads.

"I've had enough of today," she said, sighing. "I'm going to turn in and read a bit."

"Okay, Mom. Get some sleep," I said. "Do you mind if Charlie comes over to watch a movie?"

"Not at all," she said. "Tell him I said hi."

I texted Charlie, and ten minutes later he was knocking on the back-patio door.

He had basketball shorts and a hoodie on, and I wanted to crawl inside that sweatshirt with him.

"No movie?" I asked. "Maybe there's a *Harry Potter* marathon this weekend."

"Not so fast," he said, reaching in the pocket of his sweatshirt. He pulled out the movie *Gladiator*.

"You've *got* to be kidding," I exclaimed. "There has to be middle ground between my movies and yours. That's all blood and gore."

"So you've seen it?"

"No, but I've heard. You can put it on, but I'm not going to see much of it," I said.

"Actually, this is three-parts gore, and one-part chick flick. It's a bit of a love story in the end." He shrugged one shoulder.

I agreed, grudgingly.

"Popcorn?"

"Absolutely," he said. "Can I help?"

"No, but you can keep me company," I said.

"Deal. What would you like to drink?"

"I just want water," I said. "Help yourself to whatever's in the fridge though. I know there's plenty of beer from the luncheon. Gordy insisted people would want drinks after the funeral."

"Have you talked to him since he's been home?" he asked, twisting the top off a Bud Light.

"I haven't, although we've never been real chatty."

"Maybe that will all change now. Things seem different around here."

I smiled. "You have no idea," I said, pouring oil and popcorn into the pan.

"Wait, you're making *real* popcorn?" he asked, peeking over my shoulder.

"As opposed to fake popcorn?"

"No, smartass," he replied. "Most people have microwave popcorn on hand."

I giggled. "This is how I like it, with a little Parmesan cheese."

"This will be a first for me, I guess. I don't remember this when we were younger."

We carried the popcorn and drinks to the family room. He slid the movie into the DVD player and turned off the lamp beside the sofa. I raised an eyebrow.

"You can't watch a movie with the lights on. It's ambiance."

"Well you and your ambiance better be prepared for me to hide my face in your chest."

"I suppose I can accommodate that for you, if I must."

We sat down and I snuggled in as close as I could without actually sitting on his lap. He peered down at me. "Comfortable?"

I nodded. "Very."

The movie started and the first scene included spearing, clubbing, and beheading. But as promised, the actual story sucked me in. That and Russell Crowe. In the end, I found myself wiping away tears.

I looked up at Charlie and he kissed the tip of my nose.

"This is where I get to say I told you so."

"I will admit that it wasn't exactly what I expected, but it was just as violent as I imagined."

"How would you even know? You hid your face through most of it!"

"Do you know why I hate movies like that? I sat through *Silence of the Lambs* with you and Gordy once." He started to laugh. "That's why I can't watch anything scary now."

"I forgot all about that. We tricked you into watching it with us," he said. "I think Gordy was just as scared as you were, if it makes you feel any better."

"It doesn't," I said, arms folded.

"And you can't compare the two. I'll give you that one was pretty bad, but this one was just killing. Nothing really scary about it."

"Well, that demented son was scary."

He squeezed me, and I snuggled in closer, his heartbeat calming my nerves.

We sat there for a moment, in the quiet, listening to the house creak. Rumi sauntered over and jumped on his lap, purring. He instinctively started petting him, and Rumi started to knead his stomach.

"What in the hell is he doing?"

"He thinks you're his mama. He's just trying to find a soft place to sleep."

"And he's thinking that my stomach is that place? I'll have him know I have a six-pack under this sweatshirt."

"I'm sure you do, but the cat is thinking otherwise."

Rumi plopped down on his lap and looked up at Charlie. "What if I need to get up?"

I sighed, grabbed Rumi off his lap and set him on mine. The stupid cat was kinda growing on me. Charlie stretched out, folding his arms behind his head.

"You just wanted me to take him, didn't you?"

"I absolutely did," he said, leaning in. "So I could do this." His lips brush the side of my neck and goosebumps erupted over my entire body. I shivered.

"Are you cold?" he whispered.

I tipped my head back and looked at the ceiling.

"Huh... I was just trying warm you up." He found the same spot and kissed again, nuzzling his way up to my ear.

I slid away from his lips. "What are you doing to me?"

He cocked an eyebrow. "I believe you were doing this to me the other night and seemed to think driving me crazy was hilarious."

I was breathless and flushed, and knew we'd be on the floor if my mom wasn't here.

"I can't believe I'm saying this, but I should

probably go," he sighed.

I bit my lip and shook my head slightly. Sliding Rumi off my lap, he eased me back the length of the sofa. The weight of him on me felt like he belonged there.

"I promise I won't let this go too far, but I can't help myself right now."

I nodded, and he brushed the hair from my forehead, heat in his eyes. His lips met mine so softly I wasn't sure if I imagined it. Soft kisses along my jaw and neck, trailing up to my ear again.

The quivering started in my stomach and spread throughout my body. I couldn't breathe or think, and all I wanted was to keep kissing him.

"I'm going to make myself crazy doing this," he said. "I don't think I've ever wanted anything more than this right now."

I sighed. "Me too, but we have to at least wait a couple days until my mom is out of town."

His eyes widened. "Your mom is going out of town?"

"I told you that last night," I reminded him.

"Well forgive me, I wasn't thinking of *this* when you told me."

"Look, I know it's making you crazy and all, but can you just give me one good kiss before you get up? Just one?"

He smiled, looking at my mouth. Slowly, he came closer, eyes on mine now, and his lips made full contact, suddenly hungry. His tongue was circling mine and his hand started to slide up inside my shirt, resting on the bare skin of my stomach. He broke away, breathing heavy, and rested his head on my shoulder.

"Damn," he mumbled. "You are going to be the death of me."

I pulled up his sweatshirt and found his bare skin with my hands. I could feel his head shake.

"No," he said. "No-no-no-no." He sat up, pulling his sweatshirt down.

"Just one more kiss." I wanted his body on mine again.

"Just one more kiss, and we will be doing it on the beach. I'm not kidding."

I covered my face with my hands. "What are you doing to me, Charlie?" I sighed heavily. "If I tell you something, will you promise not to laugh at me?"

He eyed me carefully. "I promise, but is this a trick to get me to kiss you again?"

I sat up. "No."

"Okay, then what?" He sat back and leaned against the arm of the sofa, opposite me.

I ran my fingers through my hair, gathering my thoughts. "Would you believe me if I told you that I have never really liked sex? With Andrew it was so – I don't know – uninteresting? He couldn't get me this bothered if he tried. I'm not exaggerating when I say that I literally have never felt these feelings before."

He sat there with a smirk on his face. "Well that explains a lot. I just thought it had been a while for you."

"Yeah, like… never," I confided.

"So you're basically telling me that the two of you had sex, but you never got… *aroused*?" He grimaced. This was new territory for both of us.

"Well, if this is aroused, then no, he didn't do it for me. And the problem was, I didn't know any better because he was my first. I just thought I was one of those people who doesn't like sex."

"Sweet baby Jesus," he said. "Have you ever–"

"If I did, I wouldn't know it."

"Oh boy," he whispered.

I covered my face again. He crawled towards me and nudged my hands away. "I want you to trust me when I say there will be no doubt in your mind when we are done. It will be a new beginning for both of us."

He kissed me softly to seal the deal. "But that is not happening until we're alone."

I sat up, mortified.

"Don't go looking all embarrassed," he gently scolded, standing and pulling me up into a hug. "I'm glad you had the balls to be honest with me. That was not an easy thing to admit."

I loved how safe I felt in his arms. I didn't know where it would lead, but for now, this was all I needed.

"Thank you," I whispered. "For letting me be honest with you. Although a part of me is slightly terrified now."

"It's gonna be fun," he promised, kissing my forehead.

"You have to go before I sneak you up to my room."

"See? Now, that's not fair. Do you still have the pink striped wallpaper up there?"

I giggled, leading him to the back door. "No, Mom redecorated the room years ago. Slightly more grown-up now."

"Damn, I loved that wallpaper."

I slid my arms around his neck and kissed him. "Goodnight," I whispered. I didn't want to let go.

"Don't forget sweet dreams," he said, smirking. "I can guarantee there will be some sweet dreams at my place tonight."

"You're such a shit." I slapped his butt.

"I know, but you can't wait to take advantage of me now," he said. "That's the funny part."

He kissed me one more time and walked out to the sidewalk. *What the hell I had gotten myself into?* When he was gone, I carried a blanket and a notepad to the patio, so I could work on my list to the sound of waves. I looked at the stars, knowing Jeri was probably watching my every move.

I smiled while writing my list...

Today I am grateful for:

1. *Making out on the couch.*
2. *The power of running in my life.*
3. *The sound of waves.*
4. *Helping Peter.*
5. *Seeing the faces light up while donating the food and flowers.*
6. *Acceptance.*

Chapter Twenty

Step 3: Work with What You've Got

It was 5:30 on Monday, and Charlie would be here at 6:00. The knots in my stomach tightened with every tick of the clock. Linny insisted we go shopping in search of something sexy for the occasion. I insisted we didn't need lacy underwear for tonight. Linny won.

I had met with Terrence Davis this morning to find out what needs to be done to file for divorce. Terrance assured me that he would walk me through all the paperwork necessary to serve Andrew this week. If uncontested, it would take six months to finalize, and that would be the end. I couldn't imagine Andrew would have the balls to drag this out, but Terrence did warn me to expect the unexpected, given his history.

Needing a serious attitude adjustment, I grabbed my notebook and began to write a list of adjectives to describe myself. Week three was all about self-acceptance and working with what you've got. Two subjects out of my comfort zone.

intelligent
efficient

hard-working
loyal
athletic

By the looks of it, my qualities also described a working-class breed at the dog shows. Unable to sit still, I poured a glass of wine to calm my nerves and put on John Mayer.

I decided to make fajitas instead of something heavy, and began the process of cutting the veggies and slicing the chicken into strips. They didn't take long to cook, so I just wanted everything ready to go when he got here. I was gutting an avocado when I heard a tapping on the patio door. I wiped my hands on my hand towel and slid the door open. He was holding a grocery bag in one hand and flowers in the other.

"I can't remember the last time anyone got me flowers," I said, taking the bag from him. I buried my nose in the bouquet and inhaled.

"Since the menu is Mexican, I thought I'd get stuff for margaritas," he said. "Hope that's okay."

"Don't they just make margarita mix?"

He chuckled. "Oh honey, you're dealing with a professional. We make margaritas from scratch, and this is one drink I can make better than Jimmy."

"These flowers are beautiful," I said. "Thank you." I stood on my tip-toes to kiss him on the cheek. My stomach fluttered and nerves kicked into overdrive. "Why don't you start the drinks, and I'll get dinner going."

"You okay? You're acting a little funny."

"I'm fine," I assured him, mashing the guacamole. I kept my attention on cooking. I added oil to the pan, turned the stove on, and added the chicken.

I did anything that would prevent me from looking in those blue eyes. I reached for a measuring cup and felt his hands on my hips. He turned me around to face him.

"Just stand for a second." He reached over and turned off the burner, and focused on me again. My heart was thumping out of my chest. "Talk to me, what is going on with you?"

"I'm nervous," I admitted, biting my lip.

His eyes softened and a smiled played on his lips. He lifted me on the counter so we were eye to eye now, his hands resting on my thighs. "What are you nervous about?"

I looked over his shoulder, at my hands, anywhere but those eyes. "I don't know, I've just been wound up all day about this."

"About me? Are you having second thoughts?"

"God no, that's not it. It's just I'm scared as hell about what we're doing tonight, and I just don't want the first time to be bad. And then I started thinking about how I should've gone to a doctor after I left Andrew just in case, and maybe you should too because your wife was fooling around. And Linny has been going on and on about how hot you are and made me go to Victoria's Secret today, and everything there is so not me, and I got something and it's pretty and all, but I don't want to change who I am because of you. I've done that long enough and this time, I want you to be with me because you like me, and how will I ever know if I'm distracting you with lacy things."

I covered my mouth to stop the words.

He blew out a breath and rested his head on my shoulder. "Woman, you just scared the hell out of me," he said, laughing. "By the way you were acting, I thought you didn't want me here."

"Linny just got in my head today, and I just feel like the reality isn't going to fit the fantasy."

He lifted my chin. "You went to Victoria's Secret for me?"

I nodded, not taking my eyes off of his. "She said what I had wasn't sexy enough."

He smiled and rubbed his stubble. "Just so you know, something lacy couldn't possibly make me want you any more than I already do, but we don't have to do anything before you're ready. We can just hang out and sit on the patio with a pitcher of margaritas," he said. "I'm not going anywhere, so there is no need to hurry up and get the first time over with. I'd much rather it just happened." He squeezed my hand. "And as much as I'd like to see what you bought today, I'll wait. In the future though, Jockey is just fine with me."

"That's exactly what I told her," I said. "She insisted you would want something... well, something else."

"What am I going to do with you?"

He leaned in and kissed me. Long and slow, winding his fingers through my hair. I could taste peppermint as his tongue mixed with mine, going deeper. He broke the kiss and smiled. "Better?"

"Much," I sighed, feeling out of breath. "I'm sorry. This is new to me, and I don't want to screw anything up."

"You have to stop worrying," he said soothingly. "And for God's sake, stop listening to Linny. She couldn't possibly know what I want from you. Trust your heart when it comes to me."

I took his face with both of my hands. "How do you always know what to say to make me feel better?" I pulled him in for a kiss and wrapped my arms around his neck, pulling him even closer. His hands slid under my shirt warming the skin on my back with his touch.

"We..." he kissed my neck. "Should probably get dinner started..." He kissed a trail down my chest. "Or I'm going to start looking for what you bought today."

"It's pink," I whispered. He dropped his head on my shoulder again.

"Has anyone ever told you that you don't play fair?"

"I'm beginning to think I have split personalities around you. You definitely bring out another side of me." I nibbled his ear and continued to kiss his neck, wrapping my legs around him at the same time. A warmth spread through my body as he groaned.

He backed away. "Okay, we have to set some boundaries," he declared. "The ears and neck are off limits. It makes me crazy."

"Setting me on the counter should probably be off limits too," I said, sliding down. "How about we just get dinner going and make some margaritas?"

He came towards me again, eyes dark, pinning me to the counter. "I could just skip dinner and have the margaritas," he whispered, kissing me again.

"We are so bad at not doing this," I said.

He nodded, moving to my neck, while his hands slid up my shirt again. My head was telling me to stop and pull away, and my heart was singing for the first time in my life. Regardless of what I felt ten minutes ago, I wanted him, and I heard a voice in the back of my head.

Let go…

He must have heard the voice too, because he lifted me back on the counter. I wrapped my legs around him and pulled him closer. I pulled his T-shirt up and over his head and his eyes widened. I leaned in kissing his collarbone and saw goosebumps erupt on his shoulders. He closed his eyes as I left a trail of kisses up his neck.

"Are you sure?" he whispered.

I nibbled on his earlobe and nodded. He lifted me off the counter, legs still wrapped around him, and carried me upstairs to my bedroom.

With everything that has happened in the past month, it was hard to believe I was here with this man who wanted me just for me. And only me. From the moment he walked in tonight, Charlie made it his mission to heal me.

Later, as I lay beside him with my head on his chest, listening to his heartbeat, I smiled knowing that what we did tonight was more about me than him. I used to think sex is all about the man, but tonight it wasn't. There were feelings and emotions that I will never be able to explain to anyone but him, because we're the only two people who knew what I needed. And for the first time I allowed myself to let go and gave in to the feeling of utter joy.

Andrew had never given me this chance. He had taken so much from me, but it didn't matter any longer. I was free.

And maybe, just maybe, Victoria's little Secret was worth every penny.

Chapter Twenty-One

Step 4: Know Who Your Friends Are

I woke up alone, in bed, with a flower on my nightstand and a note attached.

Good morning sleepyhead!
I went to get Sadie and will be back for a run
before breakfast. See you soon...

Charlie

I lifted it to my nose to find a trace of his scent on the paper. I jumped out of bed and threw on some running clothes. The kitchen was empty but the coffee was made. Instead of turning on the news, I opted for music this morning.

I poured a cup of coffee and waited for Charlie and Sadie on the patio. The temperature was in the sixties and felt balmy for early May. Beams of sunlight reflected on the water. I had to shield my eyes to look across the lake, and breathed in the first sign of summer this year. I sipped my coffee and heard the pitter patter of Sadie's nails on the sidewalk. She got to me and jumped up like a lapdog, giving me kisses all over my face.

Charlie rounded the corner of our house and yelled. "Sadie! Get down!" I was laughing and pushed her off me.

"Sadie has some unnatural tendencies towards you," he said, leashing her. "I'd apologize, but I think you're gonna to have to get used to it."

"She's fine. You obviously don't give her attention."

He rolled his eyes. "Yeah, that's it." He leaned down to kiss me.

"Mmm, you taste good this morning," he murmured. He tied the leash to the door handle. "I'm getting a cup... you need anything?"

I touched my lips and shook my head. It was surreal to be having coffee with him after he spent the night in my bed. I couldn't wipe the smile from my face if someone paid me.

"So, have you heard from your mom yet?" he asked taking a sip.

"She called me yesterday once she got settled in, but I haven't heard from her today," I said. "I'm sure she's just walking on the beach, or sitting with a cup of coffee like us."

"What are your plans for the week?"

"I just have to square away some stuff for her business, and make a brochure for the retreat weekend."

"Yes, the 'lonely-lady weekend,' as we like to call it around here," he said. "They are usually a funny group of women. You should have fun with them this year. I know Jeri always loved the retreats."

"Other than that, I'm open to anything. It's kinda nice to have some space to myself for a change."

"Well, if you get sick of me, just kick me to the curb," he said. "Otherwise, I think I could get used to having coffee on the beach."

"I think I could get used to having you here too," I said. "But we'll see how you feel after a run. You may prefer to have coffee at your own place."

"You don't scare me," he said.

My phone rang, the caller ID showing Tim's face. I hit ignore and set the phone back down.

"What's with the face? Was that your mom?"

I took a deep breath. "No, just someone I used to work with in Lansing. He's been updating me on Andrew and I want nothing to do with it." I looked out at the water wondering when the thought of Andrew would ever stop hurting me.

"Six words," he said. "Let's leave the past behind, today."

"Six words," I replied. "What we know now, is everything."

His head tipped. "I like a girl who pays attention."

"Let's go," I said. "Let's get moving."

"A sailor can't even finish his cup of coffee before basic training? Tough base you run."

"Ha ha, get your dog."

In the short time that Charlie had been running, I could feel he was gaining strength and stamina with every run. We started slow and quickly moved to a nine-minute mile pace and held there for thirty minutes. We could've gone faster but we had all summer to do that, and I didn't want to scare him off early on. When we finally started to slow down, relief crossed over his face, and I smiled. We slowed to a walk to prolong the moment.

"It's a good thing I like you already," he said, hands on his hips.

I giggled. "What happened to '*you don't scare me*,'" I said, imitating him.

"One, I don't sound like that, and two, I lied. You're starting to scare the hell out of me. Are you sure you're not part Kenyan?"

I laughed and Sadie started to jump up and down, wanting to play. "Who's a good girl?" I cooed, picking up a stick and throwing it.

We stopped in our tracks, noticing two men standing on the lighthouse walkway. One, dressed in jeans and a T-shirt was holding a news camera filming the back of my mom's house. The other was facing away from us, crouched down looking for something in a bag. Most likely it was a mic, since I knew they lost them all the time in the field. He stood up and turned, and I gasped. The camera man panned his way around to find us in the lens.

"Charlie, go. Take Sadie and just leave," I ordered.

"Like hell I am." He stood in front of me to block their vision.

I peeked over his shoulder. "That's my old boss,

Tim," I said. "I don't know why he's here, but I will get rid of him."

I charged towards him, Charlie by my side. Tim had jumped off the walkway and was coming towards us in the sand. He held his arms out for a hug as he came closer. Sadie ran towards and jumped, sandy paw prints covering him.

"Sadie! Down!"

Tim eased her down and stood petting her. He straightened up and I hugged him. "What are you doing here? And turn that fucking camera off."

He turned and gave the cut signal. The camera guy did a double take and pulled the camera off his shoulder.

Tim gave Charlie the once over, both of us sweating profusely. "You are a sight for sore eyes, Gracie," he said. "And wow, this place is amazing. I can see why you wouldn't want to come back."

I crossed my arms over my chest. "I'm not sure what you're doing here, but I can't help you with anything. That part of my life is over and you have to go."

He looked at Charlie again. "I see you didn't waste any time getting… settled."

"You heard her," Charlie fumed. "You need to go."

"Look Gracie, I'm sorry we just showed up here, but I did try to call first. Andrew's trial is the biggest story out there, and he gave me rights to an exclusive interview – but only if you agreed to do one as well.

Not at the same time, separately of course, but still, this is a career-maker."

I shook my head and turned towards the water. "You must be out of your mind to think I would *ever* go on camera and discuss my life with you."

"Please, Grace," he begged. "Andrew gave me the address up here. He thought you'd do it for me, since we were so close in Lansing."

I could feel Charlie stiffen beside me. "Charlie, this is Tim, my old boss," I explained. "Tim, this is Charlie, and I promise you he will dismantle that camera faster than you can say 'action.' That is not a threat, just a warning, so please pack up your things and go. I have absolutely no interest in helping you or Andrew tell this story, and quite honestly, I am sickened that you would invade my privacy like this."

"Well, you have my number. I think we'll stay in town for the day and see if you change your mind."

"Man are you *deaf*? She isn't going to do the interview, and she has asked for you to go back home."

He patted Charlie on the chest, and then wiped his hand on his coat. "I think I can make my own decisions, big guy." I wanted to punch him. "Gracie, can I have a moment with you... alone?"

"No, you can't. Anything you say can be said in front of him," I said. "And honestly I'm done talking. I can't believe how much you've changed – or were you always like this?"

He tipped his head. "Gracie, there was a time you would've done this same thing. Don't you remember the thrill of chasing a story?"

"Only difference is I wouldn't fuck my friends over for that story, but apparently you will." I starting to walk back to the house. I stopped and turned. "Get off my beach, or I'm calling the police."

I started to shake before I even got in the house. Charlie tied Sadie up and followed me in, keeping one eye on them.

"They're packing up," he said, coming over to hug me. "You're trembling."

I couldn't talk and just wanted to be held at that moment. Everything I had done since I had gotten here, all the progress I made, had just washed away with the waves. I was right back to where I was when I arrived. Broken.

"Hey, say something," he said gently. "You're scaring me."

I shook my head in his chest, clinging to his waist.

"What a tool that guy was. You used to be friends with him?"

"He was one of my only friends in Lansing. He was the one who broke the news to me about Andrew," I said. "I have a bad feeling about this, Charlie. He's not going to let a chance like this go."

"Why don't you call Barry today and see what kind of rights you have or if you can get any restraining orders or something."

"That's not a bad idea," I said, reaching for my phone. I peeked out the window and there was no sight of them. "Why does this keep happening to me?"

He wrapped me in a hug again, kissing the top of my head. "Do you want me to call Jimmy and have him cover today? I can stay here with you if you like."

"No, that's not necessary," I said. "I'm going to try and get some work done. I'll call Barry after I take a shower."

"Need help with that shower?" He raised his eyebrows, smiling. "Being a sailor and all, I'm really good with water."

I blushed. "It's nice to know you're here for me in a crisis... or a shower."

"I take my job seriously." He kissed my forehead. "Ok, I'm going to try and wash this lovely paste of sweat and sand off my body, and I will text you later. Call me if you need anything."

He stepped out and untied Sadie. I leaned through the door and kissed him. "Thank you for last night," I said. "I'm sorry about this morning too. He was such an ass to you."

"I'm tough," he said. "And apparently you are too. I don't think the news business brought out your good side."

"It's weird to think that was my life a short while ago."

"I like this version better," he said and kissed me again. "I'll catch you later."

I watched him and Sadie walk around the corner. He turned and gave me a final wave before he disappeared. Pouring myself another cup of coffee I headed upstairs to shower and wash away the remnants of the past hour.

Chapter Twenty-Two

The day passed quickly once I settled down to work. I called my mom and left a message on her voicemail. When I didn't hear from her by 5:00, I left a text message. It nagged at me that she wouldn't answer.

Linny texted me at 6:30.

LINNY: *Met your friend Tim today!*

ME: *What? You didn't tell him anything, did you?*

LINNY: *I don't think so. We just talked about high school and how you were doing now.*

ME: *He's no friend. Please don't talk to him again.*

My phone rang thirty seconds later. "What do you mean you're not friends? He said you used to work together and said you were close," she sounded panicked.

"We used to be friends, until he came here today to interview me about Andrew."

"Shit, I wish I had known that," she said. "I invited him to go out with us tonight."

"Linny, you didn't," I gasped. "I will text him and tell him it's a no-go."

"Goddamn it. The way he talked about you, I

would've sworn you would be okay with it."

"I thought Charlie was going to knock him out on the beach today," I said.

"Well, I'd pay money to see that," she fumed.

"I was going to call Barry to see if I had any legal rights to keep him off my property, but realized the beach is public, and he was behaving just like any other paparazzi, so I didn't."

"Shit," she cursed. "Shit, shit, shit. He's going to Lakeside tonight. Supposed to meet us there at eight thirty."

"Okay, I'm going to text him and tell him it's off. Thank God you called me," I said. "He and Charlie can't be in the same room."

I hung up and texted Tim.

ME: *Just talked to Linny. Not meeting you tonight.*

Please leave me alone.

TIM: *I'll still be there if you change your mind.*

Leaving in the morning. Hope to see you there.

ME: *Not changing my mind.*

Next, I called Charlie and left a voicemail explaining the situation, but he didn't check his phone that often. Maybe Tim wouldn't even see him at the bar. I texted Jimmy to call me, hoping he would at least be at the bar and could help from his end. My phone rang a few minutes later.

"Jimmy, thank you for calling back so soon," I said.

"What's going on? You sound upset."

"Well, did Charlie tell you my old boss is in town?"

"He did say something about that, but he thought it was handled," he said.

"Well, it's not, and he thinks I'm going to meet him there tonight. Linny didn't know any better and set up the meeting," I explained.

"Okay, well I'm here and will keep an eye on things. I think you should just stay home though. Do you want to talk to Charlie?"

"Do you mind? I left him a voicemail, but I know he doesn't check them."

"Hang on, he's up front," Jimmy said.

Charlie got on. "Gracie?"

"Listen, Linny didn't know any better and set up a meeting with Tim for tonight. I've already texted him and said I wouldn't show, but he's going to be there anyway."

"Where is the meeting supposed to be?"

"There, at Lakeside," I said.

I heard him blow out a breath of air. "Okay, you stay put, and whatever you do, don't come here."

"Okay," I said, a little more relieved. "Don't let him get to you... please."

"And miss coming to see you after work? Not a chance," he said. I could hear his smile. "Honestly, Jimmy is here and we can handle this tool."

"You're coming over after work?"

"Do you mind?"

"I can't think of anything I'd want more right now."

"Good, I'll call you later to keep you posted, but don't worry. We'll be fine."

We said our goodbyes, and I called Linny.

"Please tell me I didn't totally screw everything up," she answered.

"Why don't you just come over here later when you can? There's no way I'm going to Lakeside, and Charlie said they would handle Tim."

"Cool beans," she said easily. "I gotta go, Charlotte is beating the crap out of Trevor." She hung up with the sound of screaming in the background.

It was now 7:00 and I still hadn't heard from Mom, so I called Gordy.

"Hey Sis," he answered.

"Hey there," I said. "Have you heard from Mom today? She hasn't responded to any of my messages."

"I know she was meeting a friend for dinner tonight, but other than that, not really. I talked to her early this morning."

"Huh, okay. I guess I just thought she would've checked in more."

"I know she's happy to be there. She sounded the most relaxed I've heard her in a long time."

"Yeah, she was really looking forward to taking some time off," I said. "Okay, that's all I really needed. How's Cindy?"

"Eh, about the same." I knew they had been having issues. I suspected Linny was part of the problem.

"Is there anything I can do?"

He paused a moment. "I don't think so," he said, quietly. "Hey, I need to go. If you talk to Mom, tell her I love her."

"Okay, take care," I said and he disconnected.

I curled up on the couch and turned on *Entertainment Tonight*, hoping a celebrity had more drama in their lives than I did.

I woke up to a tapping at the back door. Looking around, I saw Charlie at the back-patio door. The clock in the kitchen said 12:30.

I let Charlie in and grabbed my phone sitting on the counter.

"Well, hello to you too," he joked.

I looked up from my phone. "Oh jeez, I'm sorry," I apologized. "I'm completely out of it."

"I should've just gone home," he said, kissing the top of my head. "You look like you needed some sleep."

I snaked my arms around his waist. "You are exactly where I want you to be."

"Looks like you missed some messages," he said, pointing to my phone.

"Yeah, Linny is going to kill me," I said. We walked into the family room and settled into the couch together. I scrolled through my messages piecing together that Barry never made it home, so she couldn't come over. Her last text simply said "*Going to bed, bitch.*" I smiled.

"So, Tim is really a piece of work," he said.

"Oh shit, I totally forgot about that. What happened?" I sat up and turned to face him.

"Well, long story short, we asked him to leave the bar when he wouldn't stop asking questions about you or your mom. Wanted to know what she did, what you were doing now, and if you and Andrew were still talking," he said. "He wouldn't stop. And when Jimmy and I would ignore him, he'd just ask customers at the bar. Completely obnoxious."

"Oh fuuuuuck," I breathed out. "This is the one thing that I was afraid of more than anything. My mom's name is going to get dragged through the mud."

He took my face in his hands. "Stop," he said, slowly. "You did nothing wrong."

"I know, but the press has been waiting for me to pop up somewhere, and now that they know, this town will be filled with them. Especially with the trial coming up in a few months."

"Didn't you say you and this guy were friends back in Lansing? Maybe he'll just go back home and realize there's no story here."

"You don't know news people. Once he finds out my mom is the Queen of Self-Help, it's over. He will use that to boost ratings before the trial starts, and I wouldn't put it past him to use the fact that I used to work for WKND to build his story."

A wave of nausea rolled through my stomach. I

clenched my fists.

"You look like you're going to throw up," he said with concern. "Can I get you some water or something?"

I nodded, not knowing what I wanted. I followed him into the kitchen and sat at one of the barstools. He set a glass of water down in front of me and came around to rub my shoulders.

"Everything is going to be okay," he whispered. "I'm not going to let anyone hurt you or your mom."

I smiled at the thought, but in the pit of my stomach, I knew. If I was right, there would be press here from every major station by tomorrow afternoon. I wouldn't be surprised if he had run stories about me on the six and eleven o'clock news tonight. Exclusive stories were the home runs in the news world, and he was looking for the grand slam to get some ratings boost.

I turned to look at Charlie. "Before you say anything else, just hear me out." I said. "You are going to get dragged into this, and he is going to dig up your past, your marriage, *everything*. It would be best for you to just keep your distance from me."

He blinked a couple times. "You're probably right," he said with mock seriousness. "I'll just forget everything we've gone through this past month, not to mention last night. Every moment is only *seared into my brain*. But I get it, we'll just move on... like nothing happened." He leaned in and kissed me, then whispered, "Nice try, but I'm not going anywhere."

"I don't want everyone I care about getting hurt now, and it will happen. If I don't help him, he's going to make me pay one way or another," I said, feeling hopeless. "I thought he was my friend, but ratings take precedence over everything else. I can see that now."

He grabbed my hand and pulled me over to the couch, setting me on his lap. "Do you really think I care what anyone says about me? I get you're upset about your mom, but honestly, she'll be fine too. And luckily she's not even here right now," he said soothingly. "This could all blow over by the time she comes home."

I thought about it and sighed. "Why is it not possible to just go through one day without drama of some sort? Is that too much to ask?"

He studied my face and chewed the inside of his lip. "Do you remember going to Cedar Point?"

We went to Cedar Point every summer until my dad died. "You came with us once."

"A very wise person once told me that life is like a roller coaster, and the only thing you can count on is it never goes in a straight line until the end," he said. "When you're on top, you can almost guarantee that the bottom is going to drop out, and when you're at the lowest point, there is nowhere to go but up."

"But how can you ever be happy knowing that the bottom is going to fall out at any moment?"

"It's a matter of savoring those moments and always knowing that the low points won't last long. Look at this past week for instance."

I thought about Jeri and her letter. I thought about Charlie's first kiss and watching *Gladiator*. I thought about Linny and Gordy and the bonfire. The past week had so many downs and ups, I couldn't count them all.

"See? I know there has been some bad stuff, but look at all the good we've had too. If we hadn't been grieving so much, we wouldn't have connected so quickly, I'm sure of it."

How could I disagree with logic? Every heartbreak had blindsided us, and this is one would hurt everyone I wanted to protect.

I grabbed his hand and brought it up to my lips. "I'm glad you don't scare easily, because I don't think I could do this without you. I wouldn't blame you for running though," I said, kissing the tips of his fingers.

"I couldn't walk away from you if I tried." In one swift move, he flipped me on the couch and covered my body with his. He kissed me hard, not wasting any time with soft, sweet ones. "I couldn't stop thinking about you today."

My stomach did a flip-flop, as I slid my hands under his shirt and wrapped my legs around him. "So, tell me," I said, trailing kisses down his neck, "is this the top of the roller coaster, or are we at the bottom right now?"

"I'm gonna let you figure that out for yourself," he said, pulling my shirt off.

We made love on the couch. Mom would sanitize it if she knew, but I couldn't stop the moment. Letting Charlie take control was the most natural feeling in the world, and I didn't want my own rules or judgements running my life. This intimacy, this feeling of being cherished, overwhelmed every sense.

I wanted it to last forever.

Chapter Twenty-Three

Step 5: What Matters Most?

I woke up to my phone ringing on the nightstand. It was Mom.

"Hey," I answered, my voice gravelly.

"Have you seen the news?" Her voice was high-pitched and shaky.

I sat up quickly. "Let me guess, I'm all over the news now."

"What is going on there? How did they find you?"

"How bad is it?"

"I imagine if you sneak to the front room, you'll see how bad it is. You made the national lineup this morning."

"Shit," I cursed. Rumi looked at me from the doorway. "Mom, let me get up and I'll call you back in a couple minutes."

I got up, threw on a cotton robe, and tip-toed through the hallway into one of the spare bedrooms on the street side of the house. News trucks lined the street, with the reporters on the grass in our front yard. My stomach clenched.

"Fuck," I whispered. "Fuck, fuck, fuck, fuck." I sneaked downstairs, avoiding windows. They hadn't entered the beachside, and the back of the house seemed to be a safe zone. I turned on the TV in the kitchen and saw my mom's house in all its glory. The reporter was confirming the wife of Andrew Foster was also Julia Dunham's daughter. I stared, openmouthed, at the newscast.

I dialed my mom. "I am so sorry Mom," I said, voice cracking.

"Are they harassing you?"

I sat down on the floor in the kitchen, wanting to hide from the world. "Mom, I'm fine, but I'm not leaving the house any time soon, and they're not on the beachside yet."

"Well, just stay put for now. They can't stay there all day, and if they don't see you, maybe they'll leave."

"Yeah, not much of a story if I don't show my face, right?" I said. "How are you Mom? I'm sorry to drag your name through all of this. It's a PR nightmare for you."

She barked out a laugh. "*That's* what you're worried about? I couldn't care less! I only want to make sure you're okay. I'd come home, but I think that would make it worse. No one has found me here yet."

After everything she has been through, she was just worried about me. Tears pricked my eyes and I leaned my head back against the cupboard. "Okay," was all I could say.

"Oh honey, I wish I were there to help," she said. "Is Charlie with you?"

"No, he's home. I don't want to drag him into this mess either."

"Well, don't think for a minute he'd care about that either," she said. "Listen, go make some coffee and try to hang out for the day. Wait them out."

I took a deep breath. "Thanks, Mom," I said. "Are you sure you're okay?"

"Oh honey, I'm just worried about you. Check in with me later?"

"Sure thing," I agreed.

"We're in this together. Don't forget that."

I smiled through tears hearing her final words to me. We had overcome so much and somehow ended up on the same side.

I texted Charlie to warn him not to come over today. He called shortly after.

"You're up early," I said.

"I could say the same about you," he said, sounding sleepy.

"Oh, I woke you up," I said. "Go back to sleep. I'm sorry."

"Why can't I come over today? Are you going somewhere?"

"Hmmm, no, not going anywhere today," I said. "I have about thirty reporters outside my door. I'm hiding out, and you're staying put."

"You what? Like hell I'm staying away," he

insisted, suddenly sounding alert.

I sighed. "Please, listen to me," I said. "My mom and I agreed that if there is no activity, they'll get bored and leave. I have enough food here to last me three weeks."

"Where are you at?"

"Honestly. I'm perfectly fine," I lied. "They're not on the beachside yet, so I'm in the kitchen."

"So what am I supposed to do? I can't just not see you today," he said, pouting.

"I'm sure we will survive one day off. Don't you have to work?"

"I do, but I was still planning on a run this morning with you."

"Charlie, there are sidewalks all over town. And Sadie isn't going to care where you take her as long as you take her out." He didn't say anything.

"And I'm hoping that by tomorrow they'll be gone," I said calmly. "There are no cars outside, and the windows are all closed up from us last night."

"Ahh, last night," he sighed, remembering it. "That wasn't just a dream?"

I closed my eyes. "If that was a dream I'm going back to bed."

I heard him smile. "That would make two of us," he said. "Are you sure you don't want me to come over? I could sneak in the back."

"Hmmm, tempting, but we're not taking any chances right now." I peeked out the back window, and the beach was still empty. "You'll just have to live with the memories for today."

He sighed. "But you have to promise to call if anything weird is going on, all right? I can be there in ten minutes flat if needed."

"I know, and yes, of course I'd call you," I reassured him. "I need some coffee, so just call or text me later. You know where to find me."

"And you know where to find *me*. If I were you I wouldn't watch any news today."

"Netflix it is."

"Keep your chin up," he said. "And I'll talk to you soon."

"See ya," I said, hanging up.

The house was so quiet, and I didn't have a clue as to what to do with my time for the day. I started some coffee and went upstairs to change into something other than a robe. The thought of not having to go anywhere or see anyone appealed to me. I threw on yoga pants and a sweatshirt, pulling my hair up into a ponytail.

I carried a cup of coffee and my mom's laptop into the family room. The blinds were completely drawn so no one could see in or out. If they came around the back they might be able to spy on me, so I sat on the floor, resting the computer on my lap.

I typed in her password that Jeri told me. I knew it was snooping, but felt justified in saying it was business. I spent the next couple hours going over files, notes, and chapters from her new book. The working title was *Four Guideposts for a Happier Life,* and looked like it was going to be another bestseller.

My mom's books were treasured by people all over the world, who felt understood and validated after reading them. I never read any of her books before, but connecting with them now overwhelmed me. *Why did I resist this for so long?*

I picked up my phone and called Linny.

"Jesus, it's about time," she snapped. "I only called you twenty times last night."

I broke down at the sound of her voice.

"Oh my God! I'm just kidding, G," she yelled.

I sniffed, trying to calm down. "It's not you," I said. "I've just had a rough morning."

"Oh yeah, you have a crowd outside your house. Those fuckers... want me to come over? I'll curse so much they won't be able to televise it."

I laughed through the tears. "No, I'm in hiding right now, so stay away. I think they'll go away eventually."

"Is there anything I can do? Is Charlie at least there to keep you company?"

"Haha, you're funny. No, he's at work," I said. "But I have a question for you."

"Shoot," she said.

"Have I always been a dumbass or was it only after I left for college?"

"Hmmm, that's a tough one. By dumbass, what *exactly* are you referring to? Because there are some things that you've always been a dumbass about."

"Like?"

She sighed. "Gracie, this is a conversation to have over some drinks, preferably in the presence of two hot bartenders. Not when you're down and cooped up in your mom's house."

I sighed. "I just feel like I've lost so much because of the choices I've made," I said. "And yes, it's falling into place now, but look at all these years I've wasted."

"What happened to letting go of your past and looking towards your future?"

"Well, it seems my past doesn't want to let go. It's followed me here and is holding me hostage in my own house."

"You got me there," she conceded. "But still, you gotta look at how much you've changed for the better just in the time you've been here. Your mom always says *'this too shall pass,'* and it always does, even though it feels like we're going to be stuck in hell forever."

I sat there and thought about it. There was a knock at my door, and I dropped the phone. "Shit, they're knocking on my door," I whispered. "I'm gonna go."

"Okay," she whispered back. "Text me if you need anything."

I closed my eyes. "Thanks Linn, I owe you one."

"No you don't," she said. "You've been saving my ass since you got back in town. Sit tight, they'll be gone soon."

"Will do, chica," I said, and we both disconnected. The knocking stopped, and I crawled onto the couch and pulled the blanket up to my chin. I just lay there thinking about my mom's latest book and how closely the words hit home for me. I closed my eyes and drifted off.

After I woke up, I spent the rest of the day watching season one of *Lost* on Netflix and going through all of my mom's old books. At one point I grabbed a highlighter and started to mark up the passages and quotes that I wanted to remember. Getting hungry, I sneaked into the kitchen, pulled out the Tupperware of chicken salad, and ate it right out of the bowl on the floor in the kitchen.

The press still hadn't gotten to the beachside, but I wasn't going to take any chances. I peeked outside once and noticed about half of them still there. Charlie had called and said that Tim had been in again looking for me. He told him I had left town overnight knowing what Tim was up to.

I knew Tim would hang out for a while longer just to see if that was true, but eventually he would figure out that there was no story here. I would never give him the satisfaction of hearing my side of anything ever again.

There were so many things I was unsure of, and yet

all day long, I kept coming back to the things that made so much sense: Charlie, my mom and her work, and Linny. These were the things that mattered most.

I would have to let go of the fact that I may never understand what really happened on *Lost*.

Chapter Twenty-Four

The following day was pretty much the same. There were a few diehards who refused to believe I wasn't in my mom's house. I did what anyone else would do in my situation: I continued to take notes in all of my mom's books while making my way through season two of *Lost*. Out of all the choices on Netflix, I had picked the one that described me best.

Charlie and Linny continued to check in with me hourly, and I was grateful that the press had decided to stay away from the beach completely. It was the last day in April and the rain was making it difficult for them to hang out. They were the hawks of the news world, and I believed they could sense a mouse running across a floor if they sat still long enough.

Not being able to run was the most challenging part of this whole experience. I felt anxious and edgy, needing to move my body in some way. I missed seeing Charlie too. I wanted to hold him close again feeling his heartbeat on my skin, but I knew that we would have to wait it out another day.

I couldn't get a hold of my mom, so I texted Gordy. He replied quickly.

GORDY: *She's fine. Just talked to her on the*

landline.

ME: *Good. Let her know I'm fine too.*

GORDY: *You're quite the story these days Sis. They're all wondering where you're hiding!*

ME: *Well that's good I guess. Still have a few newsies left here. Waiting them out.*

GORDY: *I had a couple calls yesterday but I just said no comment and hung up. No one else has bothered me.*

ME: *Sorry about all this. Does Mom hate me?*

GORDY: *No one hates you. You didn't bring any of this on yourself. And Mom is in her happy place right now. You're fine.*

ME: *Thanks. Let me know if you hear from her again.*

GORDY: *Love you Gracie. You take care.*

I sat on the floor in the kitchen looking out the French sliding doors. The rain had started coming down harder making the lake grey and ripply. A rumble of thunder shook the house. The lightening pierced the sky, shooting across the lake, a sight both shocking and beautiful. I checked the weather channel app on my phone, smiling at a giant mass of red coming from the Chicago/Wisconsin region across

Lake Michigan towards us. Heavy rain and thunderstorms were on the radar till 10:00 tonight. *God was cutting me some slack today.*

Knowing no cameraman would ever go out in this unless they actually worked for The Weather Channel, I felt confident to stand up in the kitchen. The blinds in the front were all still closed, and the only way one could see me was if they were on the beach. I put my headphones on, listening to Jack Johnson, and pulled out a yellow bag of chocolate chips.

How hard can this be?

I read through the directions once and made sure she had all the ingredients. I followed the directions to the letter, and fifteen minutes later I was sliding my first tray of cookies into the oven. I took a picture of them and sent it to Linny. She sent back a thumbs up emoji.

Finding comfort in my hideout, I turned the oven light on and sat on the floor to watch them bake. Despite all the drama my life continued to produce daily, I was actually happy. I grabbed my notebook that was sitting on the bar and began to write. In step five my mom recommends at least fifteen minutes of daily mindless writing. Pen to paper, write whatever is going on in your head.

The endless loop of repetitive thinking will continue until you get it out of your head and on paper. Once you can see what you're thinking, you can choose better thoughts. Then, in a moment of clarity, you'll begin to see what matters most in your world, and you'll be able to let the other stuff go.

I wrote about Andrew and the girls. I wrote about Charlie and Linny in my life again and how comforting it was to have them. I wrote about my mom and how I couldn't believe I had pushed her away for so long. I wrote about Jeri. I wrote about hiding out. And I wrote about what I wanted in my future.

While writing I noticed an amazing smell coming from the oven. I peeked in and they had flattened slightly and looked golden brown. I took them out, sliding them on the cooling rack one at a time. They were the most perfect cookies I had ever seen, and I couldn't wait to taste one. I took a picture of the finished product for Charlie. He called one minute later.

I answered, laughing.

"Are you trying to kill me?"

"It might be unfair to tempt you with warm cookies, I guess."

"I've said all along that you don't play fair, but this is just plain mean," he teased, smiling.

"Not sure what to do with myself and all of these cookies…" I sighed.

He hung up. I laughed, trying to call him back, but he didn't answer. He worked until 4:00 today, and I knew he would try to sneak over tonight. I knew I didn't play fairly, but I was at the end of my rope.

After the next tray was in the oven, I began to write again. This time, it flowed freely and detailed until my hand was cramping. I hadn't written this much in freehand since my college days. I continued to write and bake till the last tray came out of the oven. It was 7:30, and I had convinced myself that milk and cookies would be an appropriate dinner. I heard a tapping on the back window, and Charlie stood, soaking wet, in a ball cap and a yellow Frankfort Park employee raincoat. I shook my head and giggled. He gave me a look, *open the door already*.

I unlocked the door and slid it open. He took me in his arms, kissing me hard, unconcerned about how cold and wet he was. Without breaking the kiss, he slid the door shut and turned the lock. He reached down and picked me up, carrying me up to my room only setting me down to pull my clothes off. He laid me on the bed and tore off his raincoat and jeans, then crawled on the bed himself.

We lay there afterwards, both panting and exhausted, when he finally spoke.

"My name is Charlie," he said, nuzzling my neck. "I didn't catch your name, though."

I kissed him back. "Nice to meet you, sailor."

"I missed you," he whispered, pushing my hair off my face.

"I didn't miss you at all," I joked, and kissed his shoulder and breathed in the scent of him. "Mmmm, you smell like soap."

"And you smell like cookies," he said. "You would be in serious trouble if you baked more often."

I laughed. "If this is trouble, I'll go work for Linny," I said. "I had no idea you had such a sweet tooth."

"One of my many weaknesses," he admitted. He turned on his side, propping himself up on his elbow, his other hand resting on my stomach. My stomach fluttered as he leaned in to kiss me again, then a serious look crossed over his face.

"Everything okay?" I asked.

He stared at me and shook his head lightly. His eyes were searching mine, his forehead creased. I sat up quickly, searching for my clothes.

"Hey," he said with alarm. "Where are you going so quickly?" He pulled me back down and covered me with the sheet. "What's going on?"

"You look like you're scared to tell me something."

"Well, I am," he said. "After not seeing you for two days and being here with you now, *like this*, I do have to tell you something."

My heart was beating out of my chest, afraid this was the end. I had found someone, opened up my entire heart to him, and he wasn't going to accept it. "Just say it. Get it over with," I demanded, turning away from him.

He pulled in closer to spoon me, his arm holding me tight around my waist. "What are you so afraid of?"

Scared, I shook my head. "I have lost so much in the past month and I don't want to lose you too."

I could feel him sigh, his breath warm on my shoulder. "Why on earth would you think you're losing me? I'm not going anywhere," he said. "And if you would just turn around so I could look into those eyes, I'd tell you that I think I'm falling in love... With you."

I turned to look at him, dazed. "You think you love me?" I asked.

He smiled. "I don't think it Gracie, I know it, and I knew it the night of the bonfire. It's fast and doesn't make any sense, but I don't want to go another minute without you knowing how I feel."

I blinked. "Is this really happening?" I whispered.

He nodded. "Yes, and I'll keep telling you until you get it through that stubborn skull of yours. Gracie Dunham, after the year I've had, I didn't think it would be possible to love anyone again, but I'm not even going to try and fight this. I'm falling in love with you, and I'm not going to push you, but at this point you're stuck with me. I can only hope you feel half of what I'm feeling."

"Pinch me," I said.

"Can I kiss you instead?"

"A month ago, I didn't think I'd ever be happy again," I said. "I thought my life was over, and I'd spend the rest of my time trying to forget what he did to me. Not only did I think I'd never find love again, I thought I was unlovable." I took his hand in mine. "I realize now that whatever I had before wasn't love. I didn't have this connection with him, and I am in awe of what you have so patiently given me."

His smile was lopsided. "Is that just your long-winded declaration of love for me?"

I cradled his face with my hands and nodded. "It is, and I knew it when you came over the night Jeri died. You saved me, and in that moment, I knew. I may have tried to fight it to protect you, but after that first kiss you had my heart." I leaned in and kissed him.

"Silly girl, trying to protect me," he said. "Don't you know that's my job?"

"You're good at your job," I said. "Speaking of jobs, where did you get that coat today?"

He laughed. "It was left at the bar a year ago and has just been hanging in the back. I walked right by the press and even stopped to see if they needed anything."

"You didn't! What did they say?"

"They politely declined and said they weren't going to be much longer."

"I love it," I said, laughing. "You're brilliant."

"And hungry," he said. "Are you hungry?"

"I'm always hungry," I replied, and he rolled his eyes.

"Someone as tiny as you can't possibly be hungry all the time," he said, getting up.

We dressed quickly and went downstairs in search

of food. He went for the cookies, finishing his second one before I could pour myself a glass of water.

"Oh. My. God," he said, his mouth full of cookie. "I have officially died and gone to heaven."

They were pretty good for my first time. "You know, those are virgin cookies," I said, wiggling my eyebrows.

"Well, I promise to go slower with this one then."

I giggled. "You are so bad."

"And you love it," he said. He grabbed the milk out of the fridge and reached above me for a glass.

I picked up my phone and noticed two calls from my mom. "Oh shit, what now?" I sighed.

I dialed my mom and she answered on the first ring. "Hi honey," she said.

"Hey Mom, is every okay?"

"Well, I just wanted to check in with you and see how things were going there," she said.

I watched Charlie dig into his fourth cookie after dunking it in his glass of milk. He wiggled his eyebrows as he bit into the cookie in slow motion.

I stifled a laugh. "I'm good Mom," I said. "Most of the press is gone, and a storm has come through, so the ones that stayed are stuck in their vans."

We made small talk for a few minutes, but the hesitation in her voice told me there was something else on her mind.

"Well, Mom, I'm going to get going," I said, hoping she would stop beating around the bush.

"Actually, honey, there is one other thing I wanted to talk to you about," she said, hesitantly.

Of course there is. "Okay, what's up? Need me to do some damage control online?"

"Oh no, I'm not too worried about that," she said, stalling. "I've just been doing a lot of thinking here. I probably have too much time on my hands, but it's so peaceful and the Gulf Coast is so therapeutic..."

"It is, I remember. I haven't been there in years, but we have the lake here too."

"I know," she said, agreeing with me.

"Hey Mom, I know you're trying to tell me something, and the best way to do it is to just spit it out. After everything we've gone through together, there's really nothing that would surprise me anymore."

I could hear her take a deep breath. "Well, I'm glad to hear you say that honey, because I'm not coming home."

And just like that, she said the one thing I never would have guessed.

Part Three

"And so rock bottom became a solid foundation on which I rebuilt my life."

J.K. Rowling

Chapter Twenty-Five

Step 6: The Art of Balance

It's been weeks since my mom broke the news that she wasn't coming home. At first I was hurt, but once she explained that she just needed to stay in Florida long enough to finish her book, I felt better.

On Sunday, Officer Marks called to tell me that Andrew accepted a deal with the DA to avoid the trial completely. He pleaded guilty for thirty years in a medium security prison in Jackson. Had he gone to trial, he could've been sentenced to sixty years without parole. With this development, he'll be out by the time he turned sixty.

Several news anchors called the house looking for a comment from me, but I didn't give them the satisfaction. A book publisher offered me an advance to write about my side of the story. It proved how cutthroat these people were and made me more grateful to be out of that industry.

"Penny for your thoughts," Charlie said, setting a chicken caesar salad in front of me. It was a Wednesday afternoon, and I was taking a break from working upstairs on the rooftop patio Lakeside opened up every Memorial Day. Country music was blaring, Jimmy always rigged the jukebox.

I sighed. "I was just thinking of Andrew and all the stupid reporters who want to hear my story."

"How many times do I have to tell you that name is not spoken in this fine establishment? He-who-shall-not-be-named is rotting in a cell until we are the ripe old age of sixty, and you just need to move on." He picked a crouton off the top of my salad and popped it in his mouth. "Diet Coke?"

I nodded. "It's kinda hard to forget when I get home every day and there are ten new messages from reporters or publishers. The story just won't die."

He set the soda down in front of me. "Well, I have had enough of Andrew Foster and won't hear it anymore. I give it a week, tops, and he'll be out of the news completely."

"Till the baby is born," Jimmy said, coming up behind me. He snuck a crouton off my salad too. "The story will pick up interest again after that."

"Can I get a side of croutons for both of you to eat?"

They smiled in unison. "Sorry," Jimmy said. "I'm just going to make myself a burger."

He walked back into the kitchen, singing the whole way. "*I can hear his voice when I put it to my shoulder, a gun's like a woman, son, it's all how you hold her.*" Charlie shook his head and rolled his eyes.

"You two making any progress up there?"

I nodded and took a sip of my soda. "I have most of

the trim painted, and once that's done I'm going to work on the bathrooms. They're disgusting."

"Are you sure you don't have to do more stuff for your mom? I feel like we're using you," he said.

I shook my head. "This is exactly where I want to be, and you need all the help you can get if you want that open by Memorial Day. Besides, my mom has been writing in Florida and is sending me the work each night for me to go over and edit. It has been the best part of all of this," I said. "I had no idea I would ever be able to work so closely with her on this new book."

He came around and sat down next to me. Between 2:00 and 5:00, the restaurant had few customers in the off-season. Once Memorial Weekend hit, they would be busy from open to close.

"I love to see your face light up when you talk about this book and working with your mom. I've never seen you this excited about anything."

I smiled. "Well, it's like nothing I've ever done before," I said. "I feel a little guilty, because I was so adamant about hating her work for so long. I feel like a hypocrite."

I had shorts on with tennis shoes, and he ran his hands along my legs. "Can you save a little of that for later? I have a job to do, and *that* can get distracting."

His grin widened. "Honey, you haven't even seen distracting yet," he said, snaking his fingers inside the hem of my shorts. I swatted his hand.

"Do I need to teach him some manners, Gracie?" Jimmy said, setting his plate on the bar beside me.

I giggled. "Thanks for the offer, but I think I can handle him," I said. His burger was the size of his plate, and he had several fried mushrooms on the side. "Jesus Jimmy, is that the heart attack special? Don't you want to live to see your thirtieth birthday?"

He filled a glass with ice water and sat down. "Mock me all you want, but don't think for a second I'm giving you a mushroom."

"She's cleaning the upstairs bathrooms next," Charlie said. "You'll give her whatever she asks for."

I smirked at Jimmy, and he set a mushroom on the side of my plate. The front door opened and a leggy brunette walked through with a barely-there mini skirt and a pale pink T-shirt on.

"This must be the three o'clock," Charlie mumbled. They had been doing interviews for summer help for the past week during the down times in the afternoons.

"Want me to sit in with this one?" Jimmy asked.

"It's all right, you can eat. I got this," he said, grabbing his legal pad from the other side of the bar. "First impression?" he whispered.

"She'll get lots of tips," Jimmy said, wide-eyed. Charlie shook his head and walked her over to the table.

She looked at us briefly, but then centered her focus on Charlie. It's a good thing I'm not the jealous type, because she was working any sex appeal she had to get this job.

"I don't think I need to tell you this, but it's incredible how happy he is now that you two are together," Jimmy said. "He's not even the same person he was a month ago."

"Maybe it's just fate's way of saying we both suffered enough. We definitely needed some breaks coming our way."

He shook his head. "That's the truth. And even though I was a little jealous at first, you two belong together. I can see that now."

I looked at him and those baby blue eyes. "I can't tell you how much that means to me. I never wanted to hurt you, Jimmy."

He brushed it off. "I'm fine Gracie-girl. Seeing you both this happy, while sickening at times, is still totally worth it."

I finished my salad and nibbled on the mushroom.

"You about ready to head back up for a little bit? I want to finish power washing the bar area."

"Yup, I'm going to finish the trim today so I can start the bathrooms tomorrow," I said. "I thought maybe adding some white lights along the trim of the whole upstairs might add some sparkle up there. Think Charlie would be okay with that?"

"I think he'd be okay if you wanted to make the upstairs a brothel," he said, dryly. "Check out the interview over there. She is really working it."

I glanced their way, and she had her V-neck pulled down further. She twirled her hair while she answered his questions, smiling the entire time.

Jimmy sighed. "Poor girl doesn't have a chance. Charlie hates girls who flirt," he said. "Me, on the other hand, would've hired her on the spot."

I snorted, refilled my Diet Coke, and we both headed back upstairs. It was a beautiful sunny Michigan day, and the music was blaring up here too. I took a note out of Jimmy's book and began to sing along with it, feeling happier than anyone had a right to feel.

—

The next couple weeks flew by, being as busy as we were. With the warm weather approaching, Linny started bringing the kids over for dinner or even just a sandy playdate. I couldn't get a handle on her and Gordy, but felt that she was growing increasingly unhappy.

One night after dinner, we settled on beach chairs while the kids built sand castles and chased each other.

"So," I said, taking a sip of wine. "Spill it. You look miserable tonight."

A single tear slid down her cheek. "I know you have your suspicions about me and Gordy. Nothing's ever happened, but we have been closer than we should be." She ran her hand through her hair, staring at the lake. "He called me last night to say they're going to try counseling. He said we can't text or call because he has to give it a fair shot, and if I'm involved it's not fair."

I grabbed her hand. "Oh Linn," I said.

She nodded, wiping her nose with the back of her hand. "I don't even know what I was hoping for, but this feels so final. And Barry is just not going to try with our marriage. At this point, I'm done."

I looked back out at the water, watching the waves come in. "Linny, you have to decide what you want without Gordy being a factor in any of this. If you want to divorce Barry, then do it. He doesn't make you happy, and from what I see, doesn't even care about any of you. That's not a marriage, it's an arrangement."

She nodded again. "I know, it's just scary though," she said. "I've been married since I was twenty-one and I don't know anything different. I don't know if I can be a single parent."

"You already are! He doesn't help you at all."

She took a deep breath, watching the kids pack the sand into tiny little cone-shaped houses. "But look at me," she said. "Who will ever get involved with me if I leave him. I've gained forty pounds since Trevor, I work too much, and it's not like I have a sparkling personality either."

My heart broke for her, because she didn't see herself the way everyone else saw her. "Now you listen to me," I said, kneeling down in front of her. "You are one of the best people I've ever known. You have a heart bigger than anyone else's, and you are the funniest person I know. No one gives a shit what you weigh. Leaving Barry isn't about finding someone else. It's about taking care of yourself."

"Ha," she said. "You're so full of shit your eyes are brown."

I tipped my head at her. "So you think Gordy was just leading you on for the fun of it?"

Now she really started to cry. "I know. I'm just feeling sorry for myself. To think that I can't even text or call him now is killing me."

"Well, call me crazy, but staying with Barry because you can't be with Gordy is a recipe for misery. You gotta get out of there, or at least kick him out."

"I'll think about it, but I can't do anything right now." she said.

Trevor took a shovel and destroyed the entire city Charlotte made. She stood up and kicked a healthy amount of sand in his face. He fell and clutched his face screaming, and Linny jumped out of her chair. She picked him up, scolded Charlotte, and started to walk back to the house. I helped Charlotte, who was also crying, pick up the sand toys. I kissed the top of her head and grabbed her hand as we walked back to the house. Whatever choice Linny made, one thing was for sure: nothing would be easy for her, and she would need our help either way.

Chapter Twenty-Six

Step 7: Live in the Moment

This weekend would be Memorial Weekend, and the official start of summer for our little beach town. We didn't need the Summer Solstice to get busy around here, and the whole town had been buzzing all week. Michigan Winters here were beautiful, but we were known as a quaint town with a lighthouse and beautiful sandy beaches.

After weeks of hard work, the rooftop finally looked complete. Charlie and Jimmy took turns working upstairs while the other made sure the restaurant was taken care of. They hired a dozen new waitresses and four new bartenders to work both up and downstairs. Charlie gave me full control of any rooftop decorations, including the twinkly lights. With the music and the lights, it felt like a romantic little hideaway, and I knew they would be packed every night. I would be lucky just to see Charlie, let alone have any time alone with him.

My mom had one section left in the book and was working on it every day. The heat had hit Florida, and she wanted to come home soon. Every day she highlighted sections she had written, and I would use her laptop to make any corrections or give ideas. She had relented weeks ago to go buy the latest MacBook and we used her iCloud to keep track of everything. I don't know how, but it seemed to be working, and I was enjoying every word of this book.

I was working on a section alone on the rooftop. I had brought a glass of wine up here after eating dinner with Charlie downstairs, and the sun had set an hour ago, so I turned the lights on and turned the music down a bit. Sitting by myself, I savored the moment of peace. Helping Charlie and Linny, the days seemed to pass too quickly.

I heard the door slam at the bottom of the stairs. Charlie walked up the stairs and stood there smiling. "If I didn't know any better, I'd say you created the perfect summer spot up here."

He had been up here every day, but hadn't seen the lights in action. "It's nice, isn't it?" I asked, closing the laptop.

He turned slowly and gave a low whistle. "Gracie, this is… amazing."

"Wait till you see when the lanterns are lit," I said. A tiny lantern sat on every table in the middle, and I had bought about a million citronella candles to put in them to keep bugs away up here.

He just shook his head, eyes dancing around the space. "I just can't get over it," he said. "C'mere."

He wrapped me into a hug, and we started to sway

to the music.

"Didn't think to make a dance floor," I said.

"Shhhh." He tipped my head up and kissed me, still swaying to the music. I had gotten so used to his easy affection, but with the lights and music, this felt different. Romantic. Attempting to live in the moment, I didn't stop him.

He pulled away and looked at me, eyebrows furrowed. "What's going on with you? Usually, you never let me kiss you in public, even when we're alone."

I shrugged and raised my eyebrows. "Step seven: live in the moment."

His eyes lit up, "So you're just going to learn how to go with the flow and savor the moment, after twenty-eight years of planning and festering?"

I smacked him on the butt. "The answer is yes, and next week it'll be twenty-nine years, thank you very much."

He scrunched his face. "May thirtieth?"

"The thirty-first," I confirmed. "Last day in May," I beamed. Growing up, birthdays were always special, but after I married Andrew it was just another day. If it hit on a weekend, we'd go out to celebrate, but more often than not, we both had to work.

"We're going to come up with something special for you. I hear the twenty-ninth birthday lasts for a while if you're a woman." He leaned in for another kiss. "You taste sweet," he said.

"It's the chard," I said. "I love my sweet wine."

"I'll have to come up and refill that glass in a while," he said. "But I'll let you get back to work, and I have to go down for a while longer. Jimmy is closing, so we can leave in about an hour. Would you mind staying at my place tonight? I can drop you off in the morning."

"Sounds like a plan," I said, pulling him in for one more kiss.

He pulled away, shaking his head. "I like step seven," he said, walking back towards the stairs. "And I love what you did up here. It's gonna be a hit this summer."

I stood where I was, surrounded by the lights, and just took in that moment.

Chapter Twenty-Seven

I needed to run and do some laundry before going into Lakeside today. We had to set up the bar on the roof and make sure everything was in working order for the weekend. Technically, the rooftop didn't open until Saturday morning, but they planned to have special guests tomorrow night as a test run.

I noticed a couple messages on my mom's machine as I was making coffee. The first one was from Terrence, my lawyer, stating that we were given a court date scheduled for October second. I couldn't wrap my brain around the fact that I had to wait so long, but he assured me he would get the earliest possible date when I first met with him. He also mentioned that Andrew would most likely be allowed out of jail for the hearing, but wasn't confirming if he would make the trip. I didn't want to face him at this point, but step seven wasn't going to let me ruin my day with something so far away.

And out of my control.

The second message was from a woman named Margaret Wilson from the New Life Summit asking my mom to call her. I remembered this name because my mom specifically said she would contact her to cancel her speaking engagement with them for next week. I never checked with my mom about this because I didn't think I needed to.

I dialed my mom's number.

"Good morning, honey," she said. I could hear seagulls in the background and knew she was having her coffee on her porch.

"Hi Mom," I said. "How are you doing?"

"Couldn't be better," she drawled. The longer she stayed, the more southern she sounded.

"Hey Mom, question for you," I said. "Did you ever call Margaret from the New Life Summit to cancel your talk?"

Silence.

"*Mom*? Did you cancel?"

She took a deep breath. "Um, I think that might have slipped my mind with all the writing I've been doing down here."

"Mo-om!" I said. "She is going to be so mad and you will never be asked to do one of these again."

"Oh, don't be so dramatic," she said. "Why don't you call her and explain the situation. I'm sure she'll understand."

I huffed. "Fine, whatever," I said. "I'll let you know what she says."

"Oh, please don't be mad at me," she said. "I spent your entire life with you mad at me, and I've gotten used to you actually liking me for a change. I'm sorry, I really am."

I ran my hand through my hair. She was right. "I'm

not mad, and yes, I'll take care of it. I'll call you later."

"How are things with Charlie?"

She knew how to soften me. "He's good, Mom. Really good," I said.

"Okay, honey, so glad you're happy," she said. "I'll talk to you later. Love you."

"Love you, Mom," and we hung up.

I poured a cup of coffee and took it to the patio, refusing to be annoyed right now.

There were several people walking the beach this morning, and I couldn't wait to get out there. I would call Margaret after my run, knowing it was not going to be pleasant canceling at this point. I checked the weather app and was relieved it would be clear all weekend. Possible showers on Monday, but that would be okay. Most of the business would be Saturday and Sunday, and the weather looked like it would be perfect for the beach and the rooftop.

I watched the waves come in, thinking that I might be the happiest I had been in what seemed like forever. I was doing work that I loved, my mom and I seemed to find a common ground after so many years of animosity, and I was surrounded, every day, by people who loved me. It just didn't seem real.

I slammed the phone down and screamed. After a moment I picked it back up and texted my mom, afraid of what I'd say if I had to talk to her.

ME: *Margaret is NOT letting you off the hook. You will have to find a flight home by Tuesday.*

My mom didn't answer right away, and I replayed bits of the conversation in my head...

"*I am terribly sorry for your mother's loss, and Jeri was a beautiful spirit, but at this point we cannot change our schedule,*" she had said. "*I have a signed contract here in front of me that says your mother will give one of her talks on* The Eight Steps to a Life You Love. *People come across the country to hear her.*" She didn't sound sorry at all.

There was nothing I could say to change her mind.

MOM: *Well that poses a problem.*

ME: *YES IT DOES! You have to come home.*

MOM: *I want you to calm down and call me later. Talking right now isn't going to fix anything.*

ME: *The only option is for you TO COME HOME. You can finish the book here.*

MOM: *Stop yelling in caps please. I'm turning my phone off and will talk to you later.*

And that was that. I was still sweating from my run

and couldn't cool down now. I was pacing the kitchen like a caged animal. I called Linny for back up.

She answered on the second ring. "I'm on my way over there," she said. "Bringing you treats."

"Good. I'm going to need them. How far away are you?"

"Uh-oh, what did that fucker do now?"

I shook my head. "I will talk to you when you get here," I said. "Just come on in, I'll leave the front door open."

I went upstairs and stripped down, throwing my things in the hamper my mom bought in hopes of wrangling my dirty clothes. I took a quick shower and threw on shorts and an oversized Lakeside T-shirt. I threw the laundry in before going down and finding Linny on the patio with a cup of coffee and one of her famous yellow boxes sitting on the table.

I refilled my mug and went out with her.

"Spill it. What happened?"

Anger was still bubbling in my chest. "My mom is expected to do one of her speaking engagements at a conference next week. She was supposed to cancel but never did," I said, looking in the box. I picked a Little Bird, hoping it would do its job. "I called the woman in charge this morning, who also happens to be a bitch, and she is not letting my mom off the hook. She has the contract. She didn't explicitly say this, but I think she'd sue if my mom broke the contract. After everything else, this is the last thing my mom needs."

Linny had sunglasses on and I couldn't read her expression. "Is she coming home?"

"She knows, but I don't think she has any intention of coming home. I don't know what I'm going to do."

"Well, you're not going to panic," she said, calmly. "I mean, this is your mom's career, and I guess if she doesn't want to do it, then that's it."

"Linny, this is self-help suicide! With this new book coming out at the end of the year, she needs everything to be in line. Canceling now is going to look really bad."

She smiled and looked out at the lake. "Okay, if I say something, will you promise not to hurt me?"

"If it's a way to fix this, I'll kiss you."

Her smile grew slowly. "Why don't *you* do the talk?"

I sat there blinking, not understanding. "What do you mean?"

"I mean, *you* take her place as the speaker. You've been following her book. Who better than you to give a testimony. Plus, after all the shit you've been through, you'd get a huge crowd."

My mouth dropped open. "Well that's not even funny, and not a possibility."

She shrugged one shoulder, "I imagine if you called this woman back, she would totally be up for it. You would draw in more people than your mom would."

"How could you be my best friend and think this

would even be an option?"

She pulled her glasses on top of her head. "Jump off the bridge, Dunham. Stop hiding and let go. You are so much like your mom, and you could totally do this. What better revenge than this to learn from what that asshole did to you? It's poetic."

"Oh. My. God. Do you think my mom did this on purpose?" My heart raced.

"What do you think? Maybe she did, or maybe Jeri is keeping you on your toes. What does it really matter?"

"I can't," I said. "I can't even think about this right now. I have to get over to Lakeside."

"Well, you're gonna have to deal with it at some point, and I would love to see you leap," she said. "You going to be there all day? I could come over for dinner with the kids if you want."

I smiled. "I would love that. And we can eat on the rooftop. They will be the first guests up there."

"Oh they would love that," she said. She took a final sip of her coffee, and stood up to hug me. "I know this seems like a giant monkey wrench, but think about what I said."

I nodded into her shoulder. "I don't think I can do it, but I will mull it over."

"That's my girl," she said. "I have to get back to the shop, and I will see you tonight. I'll text with the time."

"Sound's good. Thanks for the treats. My ass thanks

you too," I said, as she walked out.

After she left, I grabbed my phone and texted my mom.

ME: *I'm sorry for yelling in caps. Please call me when you want to talk about it.*

I knew she wouldn't respond till later. My mom was nothing if not predictable. I finished getting ready and headed over to Lakeside.

Step seven was beginning to suck.

Chapter Twenty-Eight

It shocked me how quickly I ditched step seven and worried all day about the speaking engagement. Damn Linny and her stupid idea. I wanted Mom to come home, and couldn't figure out why she chose now to challenge my stubbornness.

We worked all day stocking the bar upstairs. Countless trips with boxes of alcohol and glassware took hours, and by the time we were done, I was sweating and exhausted. At 4:30 Charlie poured me a Diet Coke and made me sit down at one of the tables.

"What is going on with you today? You are working yourself into a tizzy, and we have more than enough time to finish tomorrow."

I took a long drink, draining half the glass. "I just have a lot on my mind," I said.

He cocked an eyebrow. "Even during the almighty step seven?"

Tears welled up in my eyes, and I covered my face with my hands.

"Whoa, what is going through that head of yours?"

I shook my head and wiped the tears away. "My mom is supposed to have a speaking engagement at a national conference next week, and she never canceled. She said she isn't coming home, and the person in charge has a contract and will use it if she has to. I just don't know how to fix this one," I said.

He scratched at his stubble, a habit I loved. "What does your mom say?"

"To stop texting in all caps."

He laughed easily. "That's funny."

"It's not," I said. "Linny told me to take her place." I wasn't really taking it seriously, but wanted to see his reaction.

His eyes lit up, and he held my gaze. "I'm sure you told her how you felt about that."

"I didn't mince words."

"But is that even an option? I mean, did you talk with the person in charge to see if you could do that?"

I shook my head. "I can't wrap my brain around that. It's not an option to me." I drained the rest of my soda.

He took my hand in his. "Now I know you don't want to hear this, but it's not that bad of an idea," he said.

I closed my eyes. I had given it a second thought and even a third. I took a deep breath and blew it out. "Do you really think I could do something like that?"

"I think," he said slowly, "that you are very much your mother's daughter, even though you don't see it all the time. I know you still see yourself as daddy's girl, but lately you just seem to have your mom's attitude inside you."

He was looking at me so intently. "So now you

know why I have a lot on my mind," I said. "Even during step seven."

He smiled and nodded. "I do see, and it's okay. We're all gonna love you no matter what you choose to do," he said. "But before you fester any more about this, you need to talk to your mom and see what you're really dealing with."

He was right. I took another deep breath and blew it out.

"You sigh a lot when you're upset," he said, smiling. "That's a good piece of information for me."

"I hadn't noticed."

He chuckled and took my glass to refill it. "The bar looks great though. Everything seems to be set up here."

"Do you mind if I eat dinner up here with Linny and the kids?"

"Actually, that's a good idea. I'll let one of the new servers take your table tonight, and you can let me know how she does."

I stood up to hug him when he came back. "Thank you," I said.

He kissed the top of my head. "It'll all work out. It always does."

"I have a divorce date," I said. "Terrence called this morning and said October second, and Andrew may or may not be there." I sat back down and took another drink.

"That's good news."

I nodded, "It is. It's just weird to think I'm still married to begin with. Nothing could feel further from the truth."

"Yeah, that waiting period sucks. I remember just wanting it to be over," he said. "There should be a cheating clause in divorce to get out of it sooner." He looked at his watch and scowled. "I would love nothing more than to sit with you all night, but I do have to get back downstairs. I have a meeting with one of our suppliers. Are you okay?"

"I'm good, go ahead. You should have Annie come up though and make sure the bar is functioning," I said. "And I'll get the menus and silverware cart up here as well."

He shook his head, "You keep this up, and I'll have to start paying you."

"You can pay me in other ways," I said, smiling. I stood and kissed him on the cheek. "But not until later, sailor."

"Well, thank God for later," he said, walking away. "I know we're supposed to be in the moment, but later is looking pretty good right now."

I smiled, watching him walk down the stairs. I picked up my phone and called my mom.

"Are you calmer now?" she asked, answering.

"I am, but it hasn't made the problem go away."

She sighed. "Honey, do you think it would help if I called her? What was her demeanor?"

"Bitchy. She read directly from your contract, and

she's not going to budge. If you don't do this, I think she'll sue."

My mom sighed. "Well, that isn't an option."

"Mom," I said. "Linny seems to think I could do the talk," I blurted out. Silence for a beat.

"And what do you think about that?" she asked, cautiously.

I shook my head. "I can't take it seriously. I'm not exactly a public speaker."

"But you could be…" she said, thinking out loud.

"We don't even know if she would want me to do that. Remember it's your name on the contract."

"Text me her number again and I'll call her to see what we can do. Maybe she'll let me off the hook completely if I talk to her."

"Okay, but call me back and let me know how it goes," I said.

I hung up and texted her the contact information for Margaret. And then I waited. Ten minutes later she called me back.

"Honey, I have good news and bad news," she said.

"Oh jeez, good news first," I said.

"She's letting me off the hook."

"And bad news?" I closed my eyes and held my breath.

"She was downright giddy at the idea of you speaking," she said. "And before you freak out, I did have her change the time allotment in the contract from forty-five minutes to twenty-five."

I rested my head in my hands. *What the hell I was going to do?*

"Why does everyone think this is a logical idea? I don't think I can do it, Mom." The anger burned in my stomach.

"Oh honey," she said. "Once you get over the initial shock, you'll tackle this like you've done with everything in the past two months. I have never seen anyone handle adversity with so much courage as you."

"This was not listed in my job requirements," I said. "I can't talk right now. I need to get out of here."

"Call me later, please," she said before I disconnected.

Feeling trapped, I went downstairs, grabbed my purse behind the bar, and stomped out of Lakeside without looking at anyone.

Outside, I made a beeline for my car, but Jimmy stopped me before I got there.

"Hey, what's going on with you? You can't drive like this." He grabbed my keys and folded his arms.

"Jimmy, just let me go."

"Charlie would kill me if I let you leave this upset," he said. "Spill it."

I took a breath and looked him square in the eye. "Goddamn it Jimmy, give me my keys," I said, not wanting to be rescued. I wanted to rescue myself. "All I need is a break."

His eyes grew large, and he handed them over. I

thanked him, got in my car, and roared away. I knew he meant well, but having Charlie take care of me was enough. I didn't need to break down for anyone who came along, and I just wanted to stand on my own two feet.

When I got home, I walked right through the house and didn't stop until I was standing at the base of the lighthouse. The wind blew my hair off my face and the seagulls squawked overhead. I studied the landscape, noticing a few sailboats out in the distance and relished in the thought of summer.

It had been so long that I was here during an entire summer, and I smiled remembering Gordy and me hanging out all summer long when we were little. We loved when this sleepy little town would open up and become a tourist attraction. This lighthouse alone brought in thousands of people who went on lighthouse tours.

My phone rang.

"Are you okay?" Charlie asked quietly.

"I am now," I said, scanning the water. "Standing by the lighthouse and taking it all in."

He blew out a breath. "You scared the hell out of Jimmy, by the way," he said, smiling.

I smiled too. "Yeah, tell him I'm sorry. It was the only way to get through to him. It's a good thing *you* don't scare so easily."

"Okay, I'll let you be," he said. "I just wanted to make sure you were all right. Are you coming back?"

"Yes, I'm still meeting Linny and the kids there for dinner," I said. "I just needed some air."

"Okay, take all the time you need. I will see you in a while."

"Hey Charlie," I said, before he hung up.

"Yeah?"

"Thank you."

I took a deep breath of lake air and walked slowly back home. I didn't know how, but I had a feeling that everything would be okay.

—

When I got back to Lakeside, I walked around the bar and hugged Jimmy and apologized.

"You should have to sing tonight for that," he said. "Or at least take a shot of my choice."

"I will gladly do the latter, but you will never get me on that stage Jimmy, so stop trying."

"My mama always said never say never," he said, winking. "Someday, you are going to get up there and serenade us all."

Dinner on the rooftop helped calm my nerves. The kids wandered around, investigating the entire rooftop. Charlie showed them how to use the bar gun for fountain drinks, and Trevor especially liked getting everyone's sodas.

"Gee, thanks for that Charlie," Linny said, when

Trevor went for his third glass of soda.

"No problem Linn," he said, grinning. "I'll teach him how to pour the perfect draft as soon as he gets tall enough."

"Barry will love that," she said dryly. "Maybe Jimmy can teach him some of his martini recipes as well."

"Things better between you two?" I asked cautiously. She hadn't mentioned anything since we were on the beach last.

She frowned, eyes down. "No changes, other than I'm tired of waiting for Barry to decide what he wants," she said. She stirred her drink, studying it. "I'm thinking of filing."

Charlie stood with the kids by the bar. "Hey kids, why don't we go downstairs and see what Jimmy is up to. Maybe he can make us some cool drinks."

I smiled gratefully at Charlie who just winked at us. "He didn't need to do that," she said. "I'm not going to get into it, and I'm done caring about the men in my life. I just want to make some decisions based on what the kids and I need."

"That sounds like the smartest thing you could do right now. At some point you just have to save yourself."

"Speaking of saving yourself," she said, "what are you doing about next week?"

I shook my head again, peeling off the label from my Bud Light. "Well, my mom successfully got herself off the contract, but added my name in her place."

Her eyes bugged out of her head, and she threw her head back laughing. "You have *got* to be kidding me," she said, slapping the table. "I tell you what, Gracie, your mom has some balls."

"I don't see how that's going to help me at this point," I said, stubbornly. "I'm going to make an ass of myself in front of hundreds of people."

She grabbed my hand and squeezed. "You will do no such thing. It will be brilliant."

"I don't know, you and Charlie seem to think there is this other person inside of me that is capable of being like my mom, and I think you're both *loco*."

She stood up, going to the bar. "I know this is something you can do, and you won't realize it until it's done. Until then, you're going to fret and worry about it, and eventually come up with something that's perfect." She dumped her soda and rinsed the glass out, setting it on the dryer mat. "I hate to leave you like this, but I do need to get the kids home. Trev has been struggling lately, and I'm trying to maintain a more structured schedule for them."

I stood and hugged her tightly. "Thank God I have you," I said. "And thank you for believing in me."

"Where is this conference by the way?"

"I'm lucky, it's in Charlevoix so I won't have to travel far."

She shook her head. "In my next life I want to be

your mom. She is the bomb."

"Yeah… sure." I led her downstairs.

She hugged Charlie, who was sitting on a barstool with a kid on either side of him playing tic-tac-toe on napkins. My heart melted.

I sat down with him once they were gone, and he put his arm around me pulling me in close.

"How's my girl?" he asked.

"Mmmm, I'm better now," I said, leaning into his shoulder. "I could just stay here for the rest of the night."

"Well, I'd much rather set you up on this bar, and well… you can use your imagination," he whispered.

"And someday, when there is no one here, you can do that," I whispered back. Two can play this game. "In fact, I look forward to that, but until then your imagination will have to do."

He dropped his head. "Just when I think I can out-tease you, you do that to me."

I smiled sweetly and batted my eyelashes up at him. "I may look innocent, but you have shown me the dark side."

"No, innocent is not how I would describe you," he said, admitting defeat. "So, is Linn okay?"

"I think she is going to be just fine, once she figures out exactly what she wants."

"Probably true for most of us," he said. "What about you? Are you okay?"

I sighed. "I am probably going to mope and bitch

and complain for the next week, but eventually I will be fine," I said. "I figured I'd go home and try to wrap my brain around it."

He cocked an eyebrow. "I can come over later if you want a study break."

"Six words," I said. "How fast can you come over?"

"Six words," he said. "I wish this bar was empty."

Jimmy walked over. "You two are *sickening*. I can totally tell what you're talking about even without hearing anything." He wiped down the bar in front of us and walked away in a huff.

Charlie walked me out and wrapped me into a bear hug. I've never felt safer or more protected than I did when he was holding me. Like the possibilities were endless. I held on tight, not wanting this moment to end, and he stood with me patiently.

"Step seven is my favorite so far," he said, kissing the top of my head. "You're even slowing me down to find these moments."

I smiled, and reached up to kiss his cheek. "We'll practice more of this later."

"You bet your ass we will," he said, walking back toward the bar. "See you in a little bit."

Chapter Twenty-Nine

Step 8: All You Need is Love

I spent most of the weekend working on my speech. Not exactly how I planned to spend Memorial Weekend, but everyone else was busy with their restaurants, so it worked out for the best. I took a break on Friday night to have dinner on the rooftop with some of Lakeside's favorite customers, as well as Mrs. Darnell, who was so happy to sit with me. Jimmy filled her in about me and Charlie, and she appeared genuinely happy for both of us.

Other than that, I sat on the patio watching Ted Talks, YouTube videos, and reading my mom's books for help. After watching video after video of amazing speakers, I realized that the only difference between the ones on the stage and the ones in the audience is they had learned from something, usually tragic, and were brave enough to talk about it.

Bravery was the difference, and I wasn't sure I had that in me. Bravery and courage were not words I used to describe myself, but amidst all this researching I stumbled over a quote from Maya Angelou: *"when you learn, teach, when you get, give."* I knew that one quote would be the starting point of what I wanted to say. If I went with the intention of showing people that life goes on, my job would be complete.

I wanted to express that heartache and struggles are everyday occurrences in life, and it was our job to persist and find the joy. I knew how easy it was to allow depression and the drama of life to take over, but in the end, we're given no guarantees. We must all choose to live and love our lives each day, problems and all.

By Monday afternoon I felt comfortable enough to show Linny what I had come up with. I stood in her kitchen and gave my speech, with her employees coming in and out trying to keep up with the customers. Linny stopped what she was doing and sat on a barstool she had by a makeshift desk, but no one else paid attention to me. They acted as if they had public speakers in the kitchen on a daily basis and ignored me.

At the end, she clutched her hands to her chest and cried. "That's just perfect," she said, wiping away tears with her apron. "I don't know how you did it, but I can't imagine your mom coming up with anything better than that."

"Honestly Linn, I wasn't going for tears during my speech. I want to give them hope," I said.

"You do! And that's why I'm crying," she said. "From seeing you a few months ago to where you are now is just amazing." She got up and hugged me. "Is

Charlie going with you?"

I shook my head. "He offered, but I think I need to do this by myself," I said. "Having him there would make me more nervous."

"Probably, but still, you want to do this alone? I can find someone to cover that day if you want," she said.

"Not necessary. I don't want to make this a big deal."

"And miss step seven in all of this? Just promise me, when you're on that stage, and you're listening to the applause, take a moment and soak it all in. You have to at least do that."

I took a deep breath. "I'm just hoping there is applause."

"There will be Dunham, there will be."

I called Charlie from the hotel on Tuesday night. I was slated for 9:00 the next morning, and I couldn't calm my nerves down.

"I was wondering if you were going to call me," he said, quietly. "I even tried to find out your room number so I could send you a glass of wine, but they wouldn't give it to me."

"Oh, I'm in seven twenty-five," I said, curled up on the bed. "And I would've gratefully accepted that wine. But don't send it now. I'm too nervous to drink anything but water."

"Just think, in twenty-four hours it'll all be over," he said. "And then we can focus on your birthday."

I smiled at that. "My birthday? What's to focus on?"

"Oh I have plans for you, old lady." I could almost imagine the crinkles in the corners of his eyes when he smiled. "So keep your calendar open for this weekend."

"I suppose I could do that," I said, feeling the knots in my stomach release a bit. "For a tall sailor like you, that is."

"Anything I can do to take that edge out of your voice? I feel helpless right now."

"Honestly, I just need to suck it up. I'm going to take a Tylenol PM and go to bed," I said. "But I am glad I got to talk to you. I was worried you'd be behind the bar and not notice your phone."

"Nope, I was waiting for your call all night. In fact, I was so worried about you, Jimmy just told me to go."

"Oh, you're not working?"

There was a knock at my door.

"Sounds like you have a visitor," he said. "I hope you don't have your other boyfriend there. That would be awkward."

My heart started to race as I walked to the door. I opened it and there he was, phone still pressed up to his ear. I leapt into his arms wrapping my legs around his waist.

"A sailor could get used to that kind of greeting," he said, closing the door behind us.

"I didn't want to ask you to be here with me, but I am so glad you're here," I said, holding him tight and kissing his neck.

"Well, why on earth wouldn't you ask me?" He stole a kiss before I answered.

I didn't want to talk about the speech or being nervous, none of it was going to steal this moment away from me. I kissed him and started to unbutton his shirt. We fell on the bed, laughing, shedding clothes as quickly as possible.

After, he looked over at me, panting. "Glad I didn't send room service after all. He would've been shocked with that tip."

Everything felt so perfect and joy bubbled up from within. I pulled in close to him, resting my head on his shoulder and wrapped my leg between his.

"Uh, if you get any closer, we'll be doing it again," he said, sarcastically.

"Might be your lucky day," I said.

He raised his eyebrows. "Can I inquire what you would've done with this *pent-up energy* if I didn't show?"

"If you didn't show, I would still be here in fetal position like I was before you knocked on the door," I said.

"Well I got here just in time then," he said and

kissed the top of my nose.

We laid there for a few minutes listening to the sounds around us. Mostly I was listening to his heartbeat. I had grown fond of that.

"Are you hungry?" he asked me. "I didn't eat dinner, and I'm going to order room service."

"I was going to order food after you called, but somehow got preoccupied."

He smirked and reached for the menu from the nightstand. "What sounds good?" he asked.

"As silly as this sounds, I just want the grilled cheese," I said. "My nerves are still kicking in, and I don't want anything too heavy." I kissed his shoulder and headed to the bathroom. I grabbed my T-shirt and underwear on the way. He was just hanging up when I came back out.

He had already put his shorts back on. "So," he said, looking for his shirt. "I hate to bring it up, but are you ready for tomorrow morning?"

My stomach clenched. "No... yes," I said. "I don't know, in all honesty. There's not much I can do now except try and stay calm."

He pulled me into a tight hug. "And that's where I come in," he said. "I knew you'd be a bundle of nerves today, and when you didn't call me before you left, I had a feeling you'd need company."

"Mmm, I'm so glad you did," I said. "It's like I can feel my heart racing and have no control over slowing it down. And I've been nauseous for days just thinking about it. I honestly don't know how I'm going to get through it."

"Do you want to go over it now? Maybe saying it out loud would help you."

I shook my head. "I've said it so many times in the past two days, and I don't want to change anything. And you can be there tomorrow, but I don't want to be able to see you. That would make me too nervous."

"Whatever you need," he said. "I'll stand outside the room with a cup held against the door if you want."

We settled on the bed, leaning up against the headboard, and he turned on the TV. I made him stop on an old episode of *Criminal Minds*.

"Violent movies are out of the question, and yet you find the most twisted show on TV and that's *okay*?"

I giggled. "Well, yeah, it can get gruesome sometimes, but I really like the characters."

He shook his head as we watched the team try to find a killer who was kidnapping girls and kept them in a barn.

"So, I'm thinking that after tomorrow morning is over, we go out to breakfast because I'm not going to be able to eat in the morning," I said.

"Do you have to stay here another day for the conference, or do you plan on coming home?"

"I don't think I have to stay, and I can't wait to get back home and put this behind me."

He had a twinkle in his eye, looking at me. "Do you think, even for a second, that you might like what you're about to do in the morning?"

I shook my head before he finished. "The one thing I've learned is that I loved the writing aspect of it, but I am terrified to go up on that stage. If I could find a way to do the writing and use it somehow, I would. I'll have to play with that when I get home, but in my heart, I don't see myself as a speaker like my mom."

"Fair enough," he said. "I'm still so proud of how you tackled it, and I think that even though it's going to be tough, you'll come out just fine."

A knock at the door signaled our room service. They wheeled it in on a cart and set everything on the table by the window. Charlie tipped him and he left.

We ate our dinner and exhaustion took over. I gave him the remote, and snuggled into the crook of his arm. The only thing I kept saying to myself is the last thing he said before room service arrived… *"you'll come out just fine."* Over and over, those words consoled me.

The last thing I remember is he kissed my hair and whispered, "I love you."

I closed my eyes and smiled.

Chapter Thirty

9:00 a.m.
Main Hall

"To stand up here in front of all of you, knowing what you know about my story, is nothing short of a terrifying experience for me. I won't pretend that you know me as Julia Dunham's daughter, but rather, as Andrew Foster's wife. We all know *his* story, but my story, for the most part, has remained a mystery. And I am here today to tell you how one woman can reach the lowest of the lows, yet still find a way to create a new life out of all the rubble. It hasn't been easy — and yes, I've cried my bodyweight in tears — but standing here today is proof that every ending is always a beginning… sometimes we just don't know it at the time."

Once I got through that beginning, I breezed through and didn't stop until my twenty-five minute allotted time frame came to a screeching halt. I glanced at Margaret offstage, and she gave me a circling hand motion to wrap it up. I watched people nodding with me, crying with me, and even smiled at a few lame attempts at jokes. Somewhere in the middle of my speech I noticed my mom standing with

Charlie in the back of the room. Her hand covered her mouth and tears were streaming down her face. Charlie had one arm around her and was smiling at me. Instead of making me nervous, he calmed me down and I knew the rest would be downhill.

At the end, people stood and clapped for me, and I held my hand over my heart nodding at Charlie in the back of the room. Margaret came out to thank me, and then introduced my mother on stage. She crossed the stage, arms open, and hugged me like she never had before. If I hadn't been there myself I wouldn't have believed it. The moment was surreal, and the applause became deafening. I walked off stage with Margaret holding my hand. My mother took her remaining twenty minutes, something I realized they had been planned all along.

As soon as we were off stage Margaret turned and also hugged me. "That, my dear, is what we call a home run," she said.

My knees started to tremble. A chair appeared immediately, and I continued to shake and broke out into a cold sweat. She handed me a bottle of water, and I gulped half of it down in one drink.

"Nerves are just kicking in," she said. "This is normal for the first time. Some speakers have this reaction every time they give a talk."

"Well, thank God I'm never doing this again," I said.

She winked and turned her focus back to my mom.

—

My mom wanted to stay in Charlevoix for the remainder of the conference, so I rode home with Charlie and left her my car. Too exhausted to ask any questions, I concluded this was her plan from the beginning. Several news vans were outside the hotel when we left, but I held onto Charlie's arm and didn't let go until we were in the truck. I didn't know if any reporters were inside, and at this point I didn't care. I wasn't going to do any book deals or interviews, but I was also done hiding from my story.

"So, I talked to Linn and she'd like to treat you to dinner tonight," he said. "And no kids so you two can have a little fun. I'm giving Jimmy the night off, so naturally he'll be there too."

I closed my eyes and beamed. "That sounds like a plan," I said. "After I take a ten-hour nap."

"After this morning, you deserve one," he said. "I know you hated every second of it, but you were really good up there."

I smiled and looked out the window. "It's probably something everyone should have to do at least once in their lives, but I'm good being a one-hit wonder. I'm not as good at controlling my emotions as my mother is."

"Well, thankfully you don't have to make that decision any time soon," he said. "By the way, don't make any plans for Friday."

"My birthday? What have you got planned?"

He raised his eyebrows. "I could tell you," he said, "but then I'd have to kill you."

I laughed, "C'mon, you can't mention my birthday and not give me any hints."

"I can and I will," he teased. "Linny has something special planned for most of the day, and then we're going to have dinner on the beach. The restaurant might go up in flames that night, but all of us will be there to celebrate with you."

I didn't know how or when it happened, but life fell into place at the precise moment I rolled into step eight. I witnessed my mom's genius that everyone had always talked about. All the steps to get to this point prepare you to finally see and receive the love in your life.

I have never felt so openly happy in my entire life, and I finally understood how people could say Julia Dunham changed their lives. For the first time, I was excited to wake up every day and I couldn't wait to see where my path was going to lead me.

Falling in love with your own life doesn't happen overnight, but when it does happen, it's like waking up from a long nap and realizing every dream came true during that time. Every choice you make, every thought you think, creates your world. You can hide from what it is you really want, or you can embrace it and dive in. Sometimes we accept our lives the way they are, too afraid to take any chances, but taking chances is when the magic really happens.

Sometimes you just have to leap.

Epilogue

May 31

I stood on the bridge, the *outside* of the bridge, harnessed in and feet bound together. I had been shaking uncontrollably for the last twenty minutes as they geared me up. Linny and Charlie were behind me, safely on the side where you didn't have to jump off.

"Dunham, you got this," Linny said, quietly. "You have done nothing but leap since you got home, and now you just have to do it."

I turned to look her square in the eye. "This will go down in history as the worst birthday present *ever*."

Charlie smiled and remained calm. He put his hands on either side of my face and pulled me in for a kiss. "I'm with Linny… you got this," he whispered.

My jumper guide, Russell, called me back into position. My knees were shaking, and I grabbed the bridge with my hands behind me.

"Okay love," he said, with an endearing British accent. "Here we go, on my countdown. Just study that group of trees ahead of you, and pick out your favorite one. When I hit one, you are going to keep those arms open and jump towards that tree. Got it?"

I nodded, even though I couldn't breathe. I felt Charlie's hand squeeze mine, and heard Linny laugh nervously behind me. I wanted to say something, but my heart was beating so fast, I thought I might faint.

Russell held the back of my harness and put his other hand on my shoulder for a squeeze. "She's a quiet one," he said. "Usually they're screaming or crying by now."

I zeroed in on a beautiful oak tree ahead of me that had to be planted to calm people down in this situation. My hands started to shake as I tried to release my grip off the bridge.

"Jesus, can we just go already?" The edge in Linny's voice sent chills down my spine.

"Alrighty then," he said.

Everything went into slow motion. Memories flashed with every count, only this time I wanted to embrace them.

"Five…" Running on the beach.

"Four…" Charlie reaching for our first kiss.

"Three…" Reading Jeri's letter.

"Two…" My speech in Linny's kitchen.

"One…" Hugging my mom on stage.

And I jumped.

The End

About the Author

Mo Parisian lives in Lansing, Michigan along with her husband and two sons. She works full-time as a nanny (triplets!) and also writes for thenovelway.com, her website. Figure skating and hockey have been a part of her life for as long as she can remember, and if she's not writing, you can find her reading or searching for the perfect chocolate chip cookie recipe.

What We Know Now is Mo's first novel.

Acknowledgements

This book you hold in your hands has been a labor of love for so many years. Yes, *years*. And, as with any project, I got by with a little help from my friends.

First and foremost, I want to thank my current editor, Susan Anderson, with Poole Publishing. Editing, cover design, and formatting… she was a godsend! I never knew editing could be fun, but she made the process enjoyable. Her keen eye and constant support made me believe this was actually going to happen, and here it is!

I also want to thank the Shore Indie Contest and all the editors involved who so generously gave their time and knowledge. My editor, Katie McCoach helped me grow from someone who writes, into a writer, and I will be forever grateful for the #ShoreIndie experience.

More than anything, I want to send buckets of love to my family and friends who have supported me along the way. From Linda, who has literally read every word I've ever written, to my Hockey Moms who remind me what friendship means through daily texts. Amy, *over a cliff*, my gladiator friend. And Jenny, you answered all my uncomfortable legal questions Google couldn't, so I could have a lawyer read this without rolling their eyes. So many people read this and encouraged me to continue… thank you all!

My biggest fans, Evan and Blake, inspire me to be a better mom (and person) every day. And to Toby... your ability to make me laugh after 22 years of marriage is the reason I fell in love with you. I couldn't do this without you!

For those of you wondering, Frankfort, Michigan isn't fictional at all, but my version of it is. The town, especially a house along the beach, was my inspiration for this book and I thoroughly enjoyed escaping there every day to write this for you. Northern Michigan is considered God's country, and this little beach town holds true to that statement. Thank you, Frankfort!